DEADLY ANTHEM

DAVID HEALEY

INTRACOASTAL

DEADLY ANTHEM: A Novel

By David Healey

Intracoastal Media digital edition released January 2020. Print edition ISBN 978-0-9674162-3-6

Cover art by Juan Padron

BISAC Subject Headings:

FIC014000 FICTION/Historical

FIC032000 FICTION/War & Military

1

AUGUST 24, 1814

Rear Admiral George Cockburn watched another Royal
Marine collapse into a puddle of red wool on the dusty
road to Washington City. The August heat and humidity had
proven to be a far more fearsome opponent for the British
invaders than the American forces they had encountered.

Adhering to their strict discipline, the other marines did
not so much as pause, but marched right over the fallen man.

Beside the admiral, red-faced in the heat, rode Major
General Sir Robert Ross. The general hadn't failed to notice
that the summer sun had claimed another soldier.

"Get that man off the road and be quick about it!" Ross
shouted.

Several troops broke ranks and scrambled to obey the
general's direct order. They knew that Ross, a veteran of the
long years of war against Napoleon Bonaparte, was not a man
to be trifled with and that the heat had not improved his
patience.

Each British soldier wore leather brogues with iron
hobnails in the heel of the shoe, blue-gray cotton breeches the
thickness of sailcloth, a shirt buttoned to the neck, the distinc-

tive red woolen uniform coat, and a black campaign hat made of lacquered felt, complete with decorative cockade. Cockburn watched as the fallen marine's hat tumbled to the side of the road. The seven-inch tall hats resembled stubby top hats and were not much use against the mid-day sun.

Seeing the marine's motionless body being moved, Cockburn gathered that the man was stone dead.

"Brains must have baked inside his skull like a bread pudding," Ross muttered.

"That is quite a vivid description, Sir Robert," Cockburn said. "I do hope that bread pudding is not on the menu tonight."

Sir Robert grunted amiably. He and Cockburn understood each other perfectly as professional soldiers. Over the years, they had also become friends.

On this day, it was Ross who commanded the overland invasion force of Redcoats. Cockburn's fleet had long since subdued the Chesapeake Bay. He was along as an observer, and if truth be told, to satisfy his own desire to play a role in the sack of the American capital.

Cockburn removed his bicorn hat and mopped his brow. The admiral's hat, made of wool felt and heavily adorned with ribbon and feathers, was beastly hot to wear, but Cockburn was too correct to trade it for a sensible broad-brimmed hat. As an officer, he had the advantage of being on horseback, but there was no more breeze to be found in the saddle, and just as much dust.

As the younger son of a Scottish baronet, Cockburn had spent countless hours riding across his family's vast estate and was an excellent horseman. His father had sent him into service with the Royal Navy when he was nine, and Cockburn had risen quickly through the ranks. He was a highly capable officer. He was glad of this American war, now that the French were contained in Europe. War was everything to an officer. It was an opportunity for advancement and for enrichment through taking prizes of war. Peace meant half-pay and the sort of doldrums where an officer might go for years without advancing in rank. Lacking war and any chance to distinguish oneself, rank was based on seniority. Once peace arrived, Cockburn would quite literally have to wait for the officers ahead of him on the seniority list to die of old age.

Despite the August heat and the overall hardships of the campaign, he had welcomed every opportunity brought by this war. His conquest of the Chesapeake Bay had made him highly unpopular with Americans, who derided him as *Cock*-burn—because he was so cocky—while the rear admiral himself preferred the pronunciation, *Co'burn*. During his marauding across Maryland, he'd often had his men raid newspaper offices and seize all of the letter Cs from their type boxes so that his name could not be used in a derogatory fashion. The British officer was touchy about such things, even with a war on.

So far, the fighting had mostly been one-sided. The American forces had mounted a last-ditch defense of the city at Bladensburg. However, facing disciplined British ranks, the Maryland militia had quickly broken and run in order to save themselves. Already, the battle was becoming known as "The Bladensburg Races" for the fleet-footed actions of the militia. Somewhere in the American lines had been the United States president, James Madison. Apparently, he had run off with the rest.

The only Americans who had put up any real fight were the sailors under Commodore Joshua Barney. Barney's men had fought on land as an artillery unit. Cockburn had finally met his longtime adversary when the guns had been overrun. Cockburn had spent a few minutes talking with Barney, who was wounded in the fighting. Cockburn had seen to it that the American received the best care possible from the British surgeons. As a general rule, Cockburn did not think much of Americans, but the capable commodore was an exception.

Through the heat and haze, the American capital slowly came into sight.

"This is the capital?" Sir Robert sounded aghast. "No wonder the Americans did not bother to defend it."

"It is not much to look at," Cockburn agreed.

For two aristocrats who had seen some of the world's greatest cities—London, Paris, Naples, and Vienna—the American capital left them the opposite of awestruck. Weeds grew in the avenues leading into the city. Hogs rooted in midden heaps and chickens pecked at insects along the sides of the road. A few of the troops tucked chickens under their arms to make a handy dinner that night.

Adding to the atmosphere of desertion and disrepair was the fact that almost every American had fled the city, save for a few drunken bands of rapscallions intent on looting the vacant capital. The Redcoats ran them off with fixed bayonets.

The buildings of the capital were disappointingly modest. The capitol building itself, home to the Americans' new-fangled system of democracy, was nothing impressive. A few sheep and cattle grazed in the unkempt grounds.

At the opposite end of the overgrown and deeply rutted Pennsylvania Avenue was the White House, home to President James Madison.

It was toward this last building that Cockburn and General Ross rode. Modest did not begin to describe the president's so-called mansion. Cockburn's ancestral home was far grander.

Not so much as a guard was posted, nor was there a door locked. Cockburn entered with a retinue of Royal Marines, muskets and bayonets at the ready, but they found no need for the added security. The White House was utterly deserted.

"Jemmy's gone and run off," Sir Robert said with satisfaction, referring to President James Madison.

Officers and men alike wandered the presidential mansion. They were amazed to find that the White House dining room was set for a feast. Dishes of roast chicken sat covered on the sideboard, along with breads, cakes, and boiled garden vegetables. To Cockburn's relief, there was no bread pudding.

Several bottles of wine had been set out as well. Clearly, the Americans had planned a victory feast but had found at the last minute that it was necessary to abandon the capital. Their spies informed them that the Americans had set up a government in exile in the town of Brookeville, some miles to the north of Washington.

Cockburn looked with curiosity at a large, empty frame. Whatever portrait it had contained had been cut out by the fleeing Americans.

The Royal Marines set about searching the White House for anything of value. Cockburn was reminded of a pack of terriers set loose. But the men were quickly disappointed. There was more pewter than silver. Not so much as a gilt-framed mirror. The president lived with few trappings of wealth.

Cockburn picked up an embroidered cushion off a chair at the far end of the table, where the first lady would likely sit. "I believe that I should like nothing better than to help myself to Dolly Madison's seat," he said, making a crude allusion.

He glanced at the head of the table, where a document lay rolled up near what would be the president's chair. The document was tied elaborately with ribbon. Curious, Cockburn picked it up and read the document. His eyes widened at the words on the page, as well as the signature at the bottom of the letter.

Cockburn rolled the document back up, and hurriedly slipped it into a pocket of his heavy naval coat.

"What did you find there?" Sir Robert asked.

"A menu, of all things," Cockburn lied smoothly. "I shall keep it as a souvenir."

"What a fine meal they have prepared. We can't let it go to waste."

They sat down at the table, joined by some of the younger officers, and helped themselves to the food and drink. Several bottles of white wine sat in buckets of ice cut months ago from the nearby Potomac River, and the cold wine was consumed quickly. The fact that they were enjoying what was intended to be the American victory feast made a wonderful sauce.

A sweaty captain of Royal Marines appeared in the doorway. Outside, a summer dusk was finally beginning to fall, although it did not offer much relief from the heat. Thunder grumbled on the horizon. Some of the Royal Marines beyond the window carried torches.

"What are your orders, sir?" the captain asked Sir Robert, who was busy with a chicken leg.

"Burn it," Cockburn suggested to the general. "Burn it all."

Sir Robert nodded his consent, and the Redcoats set to work with their torches. The summer night soon glowed for miles around as the flames claimed the United States Capitol, the White House, and the Navy Yard. The British even burned the Library of Congress with all the leather-bound works of law and literature still on the shelves. The flames could be seen far out into the Chesapeake Bay and down the Potomac River as well. It was a sign to all that war had truly come to the quiet Maryland countryside on this August night.

Cockburn nodded with satisfaction as he watched the city burn and patted the document in his pocket, pleased that the war would not end anytime soon.

2

Franklin Scott Keane, distant descendant of the man who had written *The Star-Spangled Banner*, gripped the edges of the podium like it was a ship's wheel in a storm. Keane could be forgiven for being nervous, considering that this was going to be his first public talk in more than two years.

Although he felt anxious, his movements were measured and graceful, not at all the gawky gestures of a quirky academic. A magazine profile had once described him as a tidewater gentleman, and he looked the part. Tall and lean, he had dark eyes and hair, which tended to become wavy when he went too long between haircuts. That had been happening a lot lately without Amanda there to remind him. He had discovered that it was just one of the many ways that he had come to miss his wife. More than one person had noted that with his curling dark hair and fine-featured face, that he bore an uncanny resemblance to his famous ancestor.

He was about to deliver a paper entitled, "Renovation Under Fire: The Impact of the British Amphibious Raids of 1813 on Tidewater Architecture." The National War of 1812 Symposium was in the town of Easton this year, which made it an easy drive from Keane's home on Maryland's Eastern Shore.

The room was crowded to the point that every seat was taken and several people stood along the back wall. The audience was a mix of scholars, preservationists, and graduate students. Tweed jackets, argyle sweaters, and a myriad of eyeglasses were on full display.

It was almost unheard of for a concurrent session to be full at the symposium, which had been held now up and down the East Coast and even in Canada, for more than twenty years. He knew, because he had attended several of them. Keane also knew that the people in the meeting room had not turned out to hear the topic of his paper.

Although he held a Ph.D. in history, Keane was not a professor like many in the room, but was a senior field officer for the Great American Preservation Society. Commonly known as GAPS, it was a heavily endowed organization that advocated for preserving America's endangered historic places, from buildings to battlefields.

Unfortunately, to Keane's chagrin, GAPS had taken on a more political tone of late, standing firm in the wave of political correctness that wanted to rub out the uglier aspects of American history. Their new director, Charlene Dearborn, had shown by her resolve for preserving the past, scars and all, that she wasn't one to back away from a fight. There had been some controversial news coverage as a result, some of it unfavorable. Keane was all in favor of standing up for history, but he worried that their stance could undermine other projects.

Dearborn didn't see it that way. She liked to invoke Churchill in defense of GAPS, "You have enemies? Good. That means you've stood up for something, sometime in your life." Keane didn't always agree lately with his boss about what GAPS should be defending.

However, the controversy involving GAPS did not explain this packed meeting room at the stylish Easton Hotel and Conference Center.

No, the people in this room hadn't come to hear his talk, but to catch a glimpse of a man that many thought of as a murderer.

"There are still two seats in the front row," Keane said into the microphone. "If anyone is brave."

A couple of people moved forward, although there now seemed to be even more people squeezing in through the door at the last minute before it closed. If his talk was this crowded, it must surely mean that the other concurrent sessions were not. That wasn't going to win him any new friends.

The session chair, Walter Howell, glanced at his watch, then cleared his throat. As Walter stood and introduced the session, Keane looked out at the audience, seeming to take them in one by one. He recognized more than a few faces—the community of historians was a small one.

He spotted Ted Shelmire, chief ranger at Fort McHenry National Monument and Historic Shrine, sitting with his arms crossed and a sour expression on his face. It was a little strange to see him wearing a navy blazer and gray slacks, rather than his usual U.S. Park Service uniform. At the back of the room stood a few older men and women, one of whom actually used a cane, but Chief Ranger Shelmire wasn't about to offer up his seat.

He noticed an attractive, platinum-blonde woman watching him frankly, a coy smile playing across her lips. Keane's gaze flicked away, embarrassed. A young woman in a rather frumpy, pilled skirt got up and went to the woman with the cane, then pointed at the chair she had just vacated. The older woman accepted with a grateful smile.

"Contrary to the rumors, we won't be handing out free drink

tickets after the talk," he began, taking a weak stab at humor. He heard a few polite chuckles, but he noticed several pairs of eyes boring into him with a range of emotions, from curiosity to skepticism to even flat-out dislike. Keane moved his gaze above their heads to a blank space on the back wall, took a deep breath, and began: "In May 1813, with the Chesapeake Bay firmly in the control of Royal Navy forces commanded by Rear Admiral Cockburn ..."

The crux of the talk was that the destruction wrought by marauding British forces had prompted a new wave of building across several waterfront towns and plantations. The knowledge was useful for dating buildings and identifying building styles.

Forty minutes later, Keane wrapped up and took a few questions. The session broke up quietly. Keane sensed an air of disappointment in the room, as if the attendees had been expecting something more exciting than a presentation on early nineteenth-century home remodeling. Keane was at a loss as to what fireworks they might have expected.

What he did know was that he was relieved the talk was over. He was looking forward to a glass of wine in the exquisite hotel bar. He turned to the session chair and said, "Walter, thank you again for hosting this lecture. Let me buy you a drink. I know I could use one!"

The session chair stammered, "Thank you, but I have other plans."

Walter put his head down and hurried away. Keane was somewhat put off by what was obviously an effort to avoid his company. He had hoped that delivering this public lecture would begin a new chapter and help him put the past behind him. Perhaps he'd been wrong about that.

He heard a voice at his elbow. "Did someone mention a drink?"

He turned to find himself face to face with the attractive

blonde woman who had been eyeing him so intently throughout the lecture.

Keane forced a polite smile. He'd been more interested in a little collegial conversation with Walter, but he didn't see any way of avoiding this woman without seeming rude. "Shall we?" he said.

3

A few minutes later, Liz Graham entered the hotel bar feeling worn thin. She found conferences physically exhausting. It wasn't the information itself, which was exciting and energizing, but the endless swirl of people that necessitated small talk. This was no easy task for an introvert.

She felt the need to be "on," considering that she was eager to start making a name for herself. The result was that each exchange felt like a potential job interview or networking opportunity. She had recently landed a part-time job, but would be needing something better down the road to put a dent in her student loans.

Although she would gladly retreat to her room to curl up with a good book on her Kindle—or better yet, an hour or two of HGTV—she had some unfinished business first. She had one or two contacts whom she needed to sidle up to. She hoped that she could hold out for another half hour or so. And then ... HGTV bliss.

She was passing one of the elegant raised tables with high stools rather than chairs, when she happened to notice the previous speaker there, Franklin Keane, apparently deep in conversation with an elegant blonde woman a little older than him. Liz found Keane attractive and interesting, but the fact that he was talking to this stylish woman—a cougar with makeup if truth be told—underscored the fact that he was out of her league.

At that instant, Keane happened to look up and catch her eye. Liz forced a smile. As if by reflex, Keane reached out and touched her elbow. Liz had no choice but to stop.

"That was very kind of you to offer your seat to Doctor Hough."

"Doctor Hough?"

"Doctor Hough is the older woman to whom you gave your seat."

"It was my pleasure."

"Won't you join us?"

Ordinarily, Liz would have created some excuse to decline. A pressing dinner engagement with an old friend. A sick cat at home. But Keane's kind eyes gave her pause. She had heard the rumors, but could this man really be a murderer? Across the table, the blonde woman pursed her lips sourly, not very eager to have Liz join their table. Some perverse emotion gripped Liz.

"Why, thank you."

Keane stood politely as she took the empty stool, and waited until she was seating before sitting down again.

"You have me at a disadvantage, I'm afraid," he said.

"Oh? How's that?"

"You attended the lecture, so you know who I am."

"Oh! I'm Liz Graham."

"It's a pleasure to meet you, Elizabeth."

"Just Liz."

"If you say so, but I would say that you are selling yourself short. Don't forget that there was once an Elizabeth who was the greatest woman of her age."

Keane smiled. Somehow, he also smiled with his eyes. She

saw nothing lascivious in the look, but only warmth. Liz had scoffed at friends who claimed how a single look from the right man could make their hearts melt. She'd thought the description was outlandish—until that moment.

Keane introduced the blonde as Helena Montague, and explained that she was on the board at the Belmont Mansion in Philadelphia. Still dazzled, Liz had a hard time keeping up.

When the waitress came by, Liz was about to order when Keane turned to her and asked, "What would you like?"

Ordering for her was a bit old school, like standing when she came to the table, but she found that she liked the attention. His manners were impeccable. How old was this guy? She noted the beginnings of crow's feet showing at the corners of his eyes. He also had a scar resembling a cursive letter r along one cheek that gave yet more character to his face. But Franklin Keane was hardly careworn. Liz decided that he was just a few years older than she was.

She decided on a tonic and lime. She had found that she just didn't sleep right after so much as a drop of alcohol. This hadn't exactly done wonders for her social life in graduate school.

Turning back to her new companions, she was horrified to hear herself blurt out to Keane, "I've heard so much about you!"

Keane winced. "I'm sure it all has to do with my work for GAPS," he said with just a hint of sarcasm. He sipped from a glass of wine.

Helena was also drinking red wine, with a glass that was rather close to the edge of the table. "What brings you to the conference, *Liz*?" she asked.

"Well, I've just recently taken a job as interim director of the Cannonball House in St. Michaels."

Keane jumped in. "Ah, so you're the new director! Congratulations. You know, that's one of the properties that GAPS has been consulting on."

"So I've heard."

From across the table, Helena looked Liz up and down with the sort of appraising eye that a cheetah uses on a gazelle. Liz had seen that look before, in the disdainful eyes of cheerleaders, popular girls, and more recently, HR directors. Liz could see that this chick was intending to shake her like a shih tzu with a chew toy. Helena asked, "Where did you work before?"

"I was finishing up my master's degree," she said. She did not add, *at Towson State University*, which had about as much panache as reproduction furniture made out of particle board. But a degree was a degree, and it had been enough to land her a job in the field, at a time when paying jobs in history were scarce as hen's teeth, as the expression went. Liz could explain that the idiomatic expression came from the mid-1800s and reflected the fact that chicken don't have teeth, so something as scarce as hen's teeth would be rare, indeed. Such knowledge wasn't much in demand in the job market.

"You seem a little old for a graduate student," Helena remarked.

Ouch. Was this chick for real?

Keane cleared his throat uncomfortably. "I thought that the talk this morning on Commodore Barney's flotilla was fascinating," he said in an effort to change the subject.

"I'll have another glass of merlot," Helena announced. She looked at Keane. "What about you?"

"I'm fine," Keane said

"Please, Franklin, don't make me drink alone," she said. Not waiting for Keane to do his thing and order for her, she caught the attention of the server, and raised two fingers like a victory sign. Refilling Liz's tonic water did not seem to be a priority.

The wine came. These were not stingy pours and the glasses were large. Helena drank and absently set her glass down even closer to the edge of the table.

"So, you're on the board of an historic property? Belmont

Mansion?" Liz prompted the blonde woman. She admitted, "I'm not familiar with the Belmont."

"Well, it is a lovely example of Palladian architecture in Fairmount Park, just outside Philadelphia city limits," Helena said, sounding suspiciously as if she was repeating a visitor's brochure by rote. "The Belmont played an important role in the Underground Railroad."

Keane and Liz waited expectantly, but Helena did not elaborate.

"It sounds like a wonderful place," Liz said politely.

In her limited experience, what Liz had learned about board members of historic properties was that they were seldom real historians, although that did not mean they were uninterested in history. Instead, most board members were boosters for historical properties, lending their community connections and either donating time or money to the cause. Boards were vital to historic preservation, although, oddly enough, they sometimes got in the way of the real work of historians. Many board members seemed to prefer schmoozing, or simply being associated with a well-known property.

"Before you came along, Franklin and I were just discussing his work on the Star-Spangled Banner House in Baltimore. It's simply marvelous." She reached across the table and touched Keane's hand.

Wow, Liz thought, impressed in spite of herself. This woman knew how to get a man's motor running.

Liz knew that Keane was famous for three things. One was being a descendant of Francis Scott Key, who had so famously written the poem that became the National Anthem, after witnessing the bombardment of Fort McHenry in Baltimore Harbor. He was also supposed to be rich, which might explain why Helena had latched onto him. The third item of fame—or perhaps infamy— was that Keane was widely believed to have murdered his wife.

Liz felt sidelined by Helena's conversation. Every time that Keane politely tried to include her, the blonde chick ignored Liz and kept her eyes on Keane. She kept touching his hand, and letting it linger. She could see Keane being drawn in by her attention, and who could blame him? Helena was an attractive and sophisticated woman. She was also an extraordinary flirt. Liz could see that Helena was all wrong for someone like Franklin Scott Keane. However, another glass of wine, another barrage of flattery, and he wouldn't have a prayer. Then, Helena was going to devour him whole just like a female praying mantis eats her mate.

It was time for action.

Her eyes fell upon Helena's wine glass, which was still quite close to the edge of the table. Quickly, a plan took shape.

Was she really going to do this? It was so unlike her.

"I really should be going soon," Liz announced. "Let me give you my card."

She'd had them made especially for the conference, in hopes of making new connections, and with not a little pride in the newly minted "MA" after her name. She flipped one down in front of Keane with a little snap learned from her poker-playing days in grad school, then reached across with a card for Helena.

The back of her hand hit the wine glass and knocked it into Helena's lap.

Helena gave a shriek, but somehow managed to catch the glass before it shattered on the floor.

Cougar-like reflexes, Liz thought.

The liquid, however, sloshed from the glass. The lovely dress was immediately drenched in red wine.

For a split second, Helena Montague glared at Liz as if she might attack with her claws.

Then Keane was rushing over, offering a handful of cocktail napkins. Helena was busy dabbing at the dress with the napkins, which came away soaked in red. Keane stood by help-lessly because he couldn't exactly help blot the front of the woman's dress.

"I am so sorry!" Liz cried. "That was so clumsy of me!"

"Accidents happen," Helena said icily.

"You have my card. Please send me the cleaning bill, or I can replace the dress."

"However would you make your student loan payments if you did that?"

Keane cleared his throat. "Here, take my coat," he said. "Use it as a cover-up."

"Thank you, Franklin, that's very kind. I will see you tomor-row." At that, Helena left abruptly. She did not bid Liz a good evening.

Keane watched her go, then turned to Liz and said, "That had to be one of the clumsiest fake mishaps that I've ever seen."

Liz felt her face turn redder than the spilled wine. "Oh!"

Keane was studying her. "You are an interesting person, *Elizabeth* Graham."

"You must think I'm a horrible person."

"No, you are a study in contradictions. You went from giving up your seat for someone who needed it, to spilling wine on a socialite. I would not say that one action entirely negates the other, although ruining what was probably an expensive dress was a bit extreme. Kate Spade, if I'm not mistaken."

"I don't know what to say for myself."

"This just proves that historians are more daring than people give them credit for," he said. He put some bills on the table to cover the tab. "Have a good evening, Miss Graham."

4

J ust ten miles to the west, Bob Lindermann squinted into the dark interior of the Cannonball House in St. Michaels. The house had gone through some rocky management at the hands of the tiny nonprofit that owned it and was temporarily closed to the public. He knew that the Great American Preservation Society had recently stepped in with some funding and guidance, and that the house was awaiting a new part-time director to take the reins.

He clicked the light switch, but nothing happened. The electricity appeared to have been turned off. The historic house definitely needed some new management.

The Cannonball House's claim to fame dated back to the War of 1812, when during the British bombardment of the town, a cannonball plunged through the roof, rolled across the attic floor, and then came bounding down the staircase to the first floor, terrifying the young mother downstairs. Fortunately, the cannonball had been solid shot rather than an exploding shell. Her husband was off with the local militia, defying the British. The story of the cannonball had been repeated so many times, and in so many versions, that it had simply become part of town lore.

Displayed on the mantle of the house was a six-pound cannonball, somewhat larger than a baseball. It was hard to say if this was the actual cannonball fired by the British. Lindermann paused for a moment to admire the burnished iron sphere. Some claimed that he despised history, but quite the opposite was true. He had made an avocation out of debunking historical legends and myths because he found the research delightful. Most of the fondest legends were built on a house of cards, teetering, and did not withstand the slightest breath of truth. Wrecking those beloved houses of cards had not won him many fans, and more than a few enemies.

What had brought him to the Cannonball House was a rather mysterious email promising him information about the truth behind the St. Michaels legend. Intrigued, he had skipped the evening sessions at the nearby War of 1812 symposium he was attending to drive down to the Cannonball House. But no one, it appeared, was there.

His limp ponytail was gathered from strands of gray, thinning hair, making it more of an homage to youth than a going concern. It had been cool back in the seventies and eighties, but now it seemed a little sad, like those people who insisted on wearing cowboy boots when they lived in New Jersey. Lindermann had added one of those dating apps to his phone since his divorce, but he wasn't getting many swipes. In fact, he wasn't getting any—in all senses of the word.

He sighed. No matter. He had his history to keep him company. He had managed to anger a few town councils and tourism directors, but seldom had he felt any sense of physical danger. Still, this empty house spooked him. The whole business of meeting his source in this eerie old house was all starting to seem a bit too cloak and dagger for him. Lindermann decided that it was time to go.

He passed the stairs that the famous British cannonball had come bounding down on August 10, 1813. It was easy enough to imagine the terrified young mother that summer night more than two centuries ago.

A voice from the darkness caused him to jump, and snapped him back to the present.

"Oh! You're here," Lindermann said.

"I didn't think you'd show," said the man. He had a deep voice, at once both gruff and cultured. Something about the voice sounded familiar. In the dim light, his source seemed to be wearing a navy blue suit, which put Lindermann more at ease. He doubted that someone who meant him harm would have worn a suit.

"When you said you had some information for me, I couldn't resist," Lindermann said.

"You have made quite a reputation for yourself," the man said. "What historical bubble are you looking to burst this time?"

"Well, we're in St. Michaels, aren't we? 'The town that fooled the British.' At least that's what the sign says on the outskirts of town. But did the townspeople really fool the British? Ha! We'll see about that."

"That won't make you very popular here," the man said.

"I'm not interested in popularity," Lindermann said. "I'm interested in truth."

"Good. In that case, you and I have some shared interests," the man said. "You see, I am looking into some rumors about the Star-Spangled Banner."

"Oh?" Lindermann's mind raced. This was far beyond what he had expected. Anything to do with the Star-Spangled Banner was far bigger than the legend of St. Michaels. The Star-Spangled Banner was also of current interest to him, considering the project that he was working on. How could this man possibly have known that?

The man stepped closer. Lindermann noted that the man was smaller than him, but looked far more fit. There was something vaguely familiar about his face.

"Wait a minute," Lindermann said. "Aren't you that guy on TV? Is that you?"

"Never mind that," the man snapped. "Recently, you had a meeting with a colleague of mine. Esteban Galarza from the Smithsonian. You two were discussing the Star-Spangled Banner. What did you two talk about?"

"Wait, I don't understand. I thought we were going to discuss the attack on St. Michaels?"

"I think we just did. And now we're moving on. What I'm really curious about is the conversation you had with my friend Esteban about the Star-Spangled Banner."

How on earth did this man know about that? Galarza had been a fabrics historian at the Smithsonian, and he had been helping Lindermann with some research. Some very big research. So big, in fact, that Lindermann hadn't even shared all of the details with Galarza.

Lindermann thought of Galarza in the past tense, because, rather shockingly, he had been killed in a mugging just two weeks ago.

"Hold on. I thought that you had information for me, but it seems that's not the case," Lindermann said. "In fact, it seems like you are looking for information from *me*. I don't appreciate being lured here on false pretenses."

He turned to go.

"Lock the door," the man said.

Confused, Lindermann wondered just who this idiot thought he was ordering around. Then he heard the floor creak behind him and a large man emerged from the shadows where he had somehow managed to go unseen. He went to the door and there soon followed the sound of a lock clicking.

Up until that moment, Lindermann had felt intrigued, then annoyed; now, he felt frightened. "What's going on?"

"That is what we are here to ask you," the man in the suit said. "Tell me again what you met with my colleague about."

Just a few questions, he thought, and then these guys will let me go. "Nothing in particular. He just shared some facts about the flag."

This wasn't exactly true, but the last thing that Lindermann planned to tell this man was anything about what he had found, or what Esteban had been helping him with.

"Did Esteban say anything about Anacreon?"

"Anacreon?" Lindermann's mind raced, looking for some connection. What in the world? He knew that *The Star-Spangled Banner*—the National Anthem—was set to the tune of *To Anacreon in Heaven*, an old English drinking song. It was a rather ignominious origin of the National Anthem; it seemed ludicrous that this is what the man wanted to know about.

"Anacreon," the man repeated.

Lindermann barked out a laugh. "You mean, the *song*?"

"Did Esteban say anything about the Star-Spangled Banner being in any danger?"

"No." Lindermann took a step back and bumped right into the man behind him.

"Hold him, Blister."

Lindermann felt his arms being pinned by the big man. What kind of a nickname was Blister, anyhow? *Not a good one.*

He struggled, but it was useless. The big guy had one hell of a grip. He watched the other man go over to the mantle and pick up the iron cannonball.

"Look, if you're from the St. Michaels Chamber of Commerce or something, I'll drop this whole 'Town that Fooled the British' business! You can hang onto your local legend. Just let me go!"

"You're not going anywhere, Mister Lindermann, at least not

until you tell me what I want to know. I really don't care about the St. Michaels legend, but this other question is very important to me. What else did you and Esteban discuss about the Star-Spangled Banner?"

"I've told you already! Nothing important. I swear!"

"Put his hand on the table."

He struggled, but the man behind him had a grip like a vise. This wasn't like in the movies, where you gave the guy an elbow in the ribs and broke free. Lindermann found himself looking down at his fingers, splayed across the tabletop. The wood itself was old and scarred, somehow making his own fingers seem that much frailer.

"Last chance, Mister Lindermann. Anacreon?"

His interrogator raised the cannonball.

"I told you—"

The cannonball smashed down on his hand. Lindermann howled in pain and struggled even harder, but it was no use. His interrogator smashed the cannonball down again. And again. Lindermann writhed in agony.

Through tear-filled eyes, he looked down at his broken hand. One of the fingers skewed away from the others at an unnatural angle. The pain was awful. He whimpered.

"Anacreon, Lindermann." No more *mister* now.

"I've told you all that I know!"

"I need to make sure of that. It's very important to me." The man nodded at Blister, who pinned his hand to the table once more.

"Please!"

This time, quite unexpectedly, the cannonball smashed down on his right knee. He actually felt something crack. The pain was excruciating. He struggled, but those strong arms held him.

"Remarkable, isn't it, to think about this thing coming through the roof," his interrogator said, tossing the cannonball in his hand to test its heft. "It's no wonder that the lady of the house was terrified."

Lindermann whimpered. He was having trouble standing up straight. "Don't do this—"

"You have another hand, Lindermann. Think about that for a moment, before you answer my next question."

He sobbed and his body convulsed with pain.

"Stop, please stop."

"Have you had enough? I wonder. Now, what did Esteban tell you about Anacreon? Why did he meet with you, anyway?"

"We talked about the flag!" Lindermann was babbling now, but even the pain wasn't enough for him to reveal the true nature of his discovery. So far, the man hadn't asked about that, which meant it was likely that he didn't know. "The fabric. The density of the weave. That's all! Nothing about goddamned Anacreon! Are you crazy?"

His interrogator raised the cannonball and held it poised over Lindermann's broken hand. The man sighed. "I believe you."

He lowered the cannonball.

"Thank God. Look what you've done to me! I need a doctor."

The man returned the cannonball to the mantle.

When he turned around to face Lindermann again, he held a gun. It seemed to have a long barrel, which Lindermann's muddled brain recognized as a silencer.

"Don't do this! I'll tell you anything you want to know!"

"The Q&A is over," Lindermann's interrogator said. He nodded at the big man holding Lindermann. "You'd better step away, Blister."

Finally, the grip on him relented as the big man let go.

The gun came up and shot Lindermann through the heart.

5

Francis Scott Key stood at the rail of *HMS Tonnant* and breathed deeply of the night air. Haze obscured the sky and the September night was warm and sticky. The Royal Navy officers complained about the Chesapeake Bay humidity so much that Key found himself taking umbrage at their comments. If they hated it so much, he wanted to say, why didn't they sail for England and leave good Marylanders alone?

Key sighed and shook his head to clear it. He'd had rather more wine tonight than he was used to drinking. The officers of the Royal Navy drank copiously, told ribald stories, and peppered their conversation with enough obscenities to make a Georgetown lawyer blush.

"A fine night, isn't it, Mister Key?" asked a voice at his elbow. "I wanted to tell you that there is coffee in the wardroom."

Startled, Key turned. "Oh, it's you, Doctor Brown," Key said, seeing that it was the ship's surgeon. Doctor Brown was the only civilian aboard, and occupied a strange position on the ship in that he was seen more as a gentleman than an officer. "It is a fine night, although I would have thought you would say that it was too warm."

Brown chuckled at the note of chagrin in the lawyer's voice. "Mister Key, I have sailed around the globe and can tell you that Baltimore harbor is hardly the worst place I have visited."

Key, who even as a successful young lawyer had never been more than forty miles from the farm where he'd been born in Frederick County, was impressed. "*Hardly* the worst place? I suppose that is reassuring."

Brown nodded toward the star fort in the distance. "I would imagine that the weather is going to be the least of anyone's worries, soon enough. I daresay that between *Tonnant*'s eighty guns and those of the fort, it shall be plenty hot for everyone before long. Have a good evening, Mister Key."

"You as well, Doctor Brown. Thank you for the offer of the coffee."

Brown moved off, leaving Key alone at the rail again.

It had become clear that the British intended to attack Baltimore. Key had found himself nominally a prisoner aboard the ship, in order to prevent him from warning American forces of the impending attack or provide any intelligence about British forces.

He had come to be aboard *HMS Tonnant* in a rather roundabout way. Just two weeks before, when the British had invaded and burned Washington, a local physician named Doctor William Beanes, after hosting General Sir Robert Ross at his home, had helped to arrest some British deserters plundering the area.

When the general got wind of the fact that the sixty-something physician was interfering with British troops, deserters or not, he had been incensed enough to have Beanes arrested and brought aboard the British flagship. It didn't help that Beanes spoke with a Scottish accent—in British eyes, he was a traitor. Key and Colonel Jonathan Skinner had been asked to intercede and negotiate for the release of Doctor Beanes. They had done so successfully thanks to letters that Skinner had obtained from grateful British troops who had been treated by Doctor Beanes.

Key and the two other Americans had been informed that they would not be going anywhere for the time being.

Although technically they were prisoners, they were certainly not treated as such. They dined with Admiral Cockburn and General Ross, along with the other officers. However, it was these very dinners that had left Key appalled.

Cockburn and the other officers were supposed to be gentlemen, but Key found their company obnoxious. If these were English aristocrats, then Key was not terribly impressed by what was supposed to be the cream of British society. It did not help that Cockburn, in particular, made no real attempt to hide his disdain for all things American.

"I found your capital to be rather provincial," he had stated. "Hogs and chickens rooted about on the grounds of your president's mansion. Your democracy holds itself in esteemed company, indeed!"

Cockburn and the others had laughed heartily at the stories about shooing chickens out of the way. They seemed to have delighted in putting it all to the torch to teach the Americans a lesson—and planned to do the same to Baltimore.

Key gazed at the night-shrouded fort, trying to make out the ramparts in the late summer haze. *Oh, say can you see ... see what?* He wasn't sure yet, but he knew that he had the makings of an opening line for a poem. What he needed now was some inspiration. The random phrase hung there, but Key knew that the rest would follow in time. He was forever writing poetry, and he loved wordplay, which made him a good lawyer.

He went below, in search of that coffee that the surgeon had mentioned. With the British blockade, tea and coffee had become scarce commodities across the United States. Key had to admit that it gave him a bit of satisfaction to be enjoying the coffee at British expense, although he knew it was a petty emotion.

The ship was busy with officers scrambling to and fro, preparing for the battle that was sure to come. Even if he did not particularly like Cockburn and his compatriots, Key had to admit that the Royal Navy was a formidable opponent. Given the lack of success that the Americans had experienced in the Chesapeake Bay, he shuddered to think of what might happen to Baltimore, even with the defenses under the capable command of Sam Smith in the city and Major Armistead at Fort McHenry.

Cockburn had apparently ordered coffee to be served in his quarters. A bottle of port stood on the table as well. Key smelled the coffee and ducked inside. The busy officers scarcely paid him any attention. Except for Cockburn.

"Ah, Mister Key. I hear that you are something of a versifier."

"That is true, sir."

"You might think of a good limerick to mark the fall of Baltimore."

"A limerick?" Key knew that limericks had originated years ago, but they were hardly the stuff of literature.

"I daresay the fall of Baltimore can't be worth much more than a limerick. Certainly not an ode. And don't ask our Lord Byron to write it. You did just kill his cousin in that abominable action on the Eastern Shore."

He was referring to the death of Captain Sir Peter Parker, a 28-year-old baronet killed in August while leading a diversion raid on the other side of the Chesapeake Bay. Parker had led a substantial force of Royal Marines and sailors ashore with plans to wreak havoc on the local militia. The plans depended on the militia being caught unawares in the dead of night. However, the local defenders were far from incompetent and turned the tables on the British by ambushing them at a place

known as Caulk's Field. Several British troops died, along with
Parker.

Now, Cockburn had an audience. He grinned around the
room. "Let me share one of my favorite limericks to inspire you,
perhaps."

Key tensed. "Please don't trouble yourself, sir."

"Oh, I insist." Cockburn cleared his throat elaborately and
launched into the limerick: *"There was a young lady from Kent ..."*

Once Cockburn had finished, the officers laughed heartily.
Some slapped the table merrily, causing the coffee cups and
port glasses to rattle. This sort of bawdy poem was typical fare
for them. Just last night, one of the officers had shared an
obscene story about a young lady who kept a pet eel. Key felt
his face grow red. Cockburn knew that his American prisoners
were more prudish about such things. He was having fun at
American expense, yet again.

"You show remarkable wit, sir," Key said, controlling his
voice with an effort.

"That goes without saying, Mister Key. Do have some coffee.
My men and I are going to inspect the guns that will pound
your fort into submission."

At that, Cockburn and his retinue of officers went out,
leaving Key alone. Cockburn's servant did not lift a finger to
serve Key, so Key poured his own coffee.

He approached the table that served as Cockburn's desk.
The surface was covered with reports and maps. Hoping to
glean some information that might be useful to the American
cause if he was ever allowed to leave Royal Navy custody, Key
perused the documents. Frankly, there was nothing that he
could make sense of—perhaps a military man might, but Key
was a lawyer, after all. He did notice one document still rolled
up, as if to keep it out of sight. Perhaps this document had some
real value.

Key took a sip of coffee, using it as an opportunity to see if anyone was paying attention to him. The servant had gone out, and the Royal Marine sentry outside the door stared ahead as if carved from wood.

He put down the coffee and unrolled the document.

He saw that this was a letter, dated August 24th—the day that British forces had burned Washington.

The letter was signed by President James Madison.

Key's curiosity grew. He read the document carefully, with all the skill of a lawyer and wordsmith. What he saw made his eyes widen in wonder.

My God, he thought. *What is the meaning of this?*

If he was reading this letter correctly, the battle about to take place was pointless and unnecessary. The war should have ended more than two weeks before. He thought of the losses at the battle of Caulk's Field on the Eastern Shore, as well as the battlefield deaths likely here in Baltimore. Many lives would have been saved, both British and American, had hostilities ceased last month. But he also knew that the moment of opportunity had come and gone.

Key suddenly felt outraged that this letter should be left on Cockburn's desk as if the contents had no meaning or value. Apparently, Cockburn's disdain of Americans extended to letters written by the president. President Madison had extended an olive branch to bring the war to an end, and the British had ignored it.

After another glance at the door to make certain that he was still alone, Key moved quickly. He rolled up the letter and slid it down the front of his coat. If Cockburn caught him with the document, there was no doubt what the consequences would be. He was here as a guest, but Cockburn surely would not hesitate to hang a spy.

Sweating now in the September heat inside the admiral's quarters, Key forced himself to walk nonchalantly out of the room and past the sentry. He was not sure if President Madison was being wise and prescient by writing such a letter, or if he had succumbed to some urge for treachery or even to some momentary weakness of character. But Key did know that once he was off this ship, this letter could cause enormous repercussions. Perhaps what mattered now was not bringing the letter to anyone's attention, but just the opposite. Key felt that under the circumstances, such a letter would be better off in his possession, than in Rear Admiral Cockburn's.

6

L iz awoke feeling parched by the stale air of the hotel room. It took her a moment to realize that it had been the chime of her phone that woke her up. A text message? Who was texting her so early?

Alarmed by the thought of ailing relatives and sick pets, she grabbed for the phone.

There's a problem at the Cannonball House.

She thought it must be a random text, sent in mistake, until a second text arrived.

This is Franklin Keane, by the way. Want to ride over there with me?

Keane? That was unexpected. She had enjoyed meeting him in the hotel bar last night. It had been an intriguing conversation—*God, those eyes*—but also a bit disconcerting. After all, this was the man who was rumored to have bumped off his wife. Liz realized that she didn't believe any of that for a minute. She hadn't gotten any kind of creepy vibe from him. Keane just seemed, well, too *nice* to kill anyone.

But what was he thinking by texting her so early? It wasn't even eight o'clock in the morning. They hardly knew one another. She started to feel miffed. Of all the nerve! She regretted giving him her business card with her phone number on it the night before. Even if he worked for GAPS, that did not make Keane her boss. She hadn't even officially started her new job at the Cannonball House.

In spite of all that, she found herself texting back, *Sure.*

Lobby twenty minutes.

That was a bit off putting. What kind of woman did he think she was? Just to go jaunting off—

But as she thought it, she realized that she was already in the bathroom, running the shower.

* * *

KEANE WAITED IN THE LOBBY, indulging himself in one of his favorite pastimes, which was people-watching. The hotel lobby was a good place to do so, not only because of the interesting clientele—for example, who *was* that mysterious woman, dressed all in black, right down to her fur coat—but because of the elegant surroundings.

The architecture and decor was pure tidewater colonial, with arched doorways, painted woodwork, a fireplace with touches of green Connemara marble, and what appeared to be silk wallpaper with a pineapple motif. Shiny as opal, the polished stone floor was covered here and there with rich oriental carpets, all presided over by a grand, sweeping staircase.

Large windows overlooked Washington Street, busy with pedestrians on their way to work. More people to watch.

The mysterious woman in black caught him looking the second time he glanced her way, and although he quickly averted his eyes, he felt her gaze lingering on him with interest until the bellhop appeared with her cart of luggage and they disappeared out the lobby doors. Keane felt relieved; the last thing he wanted were any female entanglements. He still felt too loyal to Amanda.

He glanced at his watch, a well-worn Timex Marlin given to him by his grandfather, and looked at the elevator. He wasn't quite sure why he had texted Elizabeth, who had not even started her job at the Cannonball House, other than being prompted by some sense of intuition. It was a kind of gift he had inherited from the Irish side of his family. His grandfather had used that gift to make a great deal of money. Keane had chosen to develop his own gift in other ways.

Still, if he left now, there would be no real harm done. He could text an apology later. It wasn't like she wouldn't be able to find her way to St. Michaels.

He glanced at the door, then looked at his watch again.

Exactly twenty minutes after he had sent Elizabeth Graham his text message, she emerged from the polished brass doors of the elevator.

His first thought was that Elizabeth was not like the stylish mystery woman he had spotted earlier in the hotel lobby. She clumped off the elevator in boots she had pulled on against the fall morning chill, wearing dark blue tights, a brown leather jacket, and a cream scarf. Her brownish-blonde hair hung limp, still damp from the shower, and she didn't have on one bit of makeup.

Keane felt a stirring of interest. He shoved the feeling away, regretting that he hadn't just gone on to St. Michaels alone.

"Good morning," he said.

"What's happened?" she asked.

"I'm afraid there's an emergency at the Cannonball House. As the interim director, I thought that you should be notified."

"What's the emergency?"

"I don't know. The GAPS director is going to text me as soon as she hears anything. In the meantime, we may as well head down there."

"I haven't even worked there one day yet!"

"Well, you don't have to go—"

"Are you serious?" At the same time, the doubt that he had felt earlier seemed mirrored in her own face. "I don't normally do this, just so you know."

"Do what?"

"Go for rides with strangers."

Keane didn't know what to say to that. Instead, he walked out to give his slip to the valet, who had just driven up in Keane's car, a vintage Corvette Stingray. Surrounded by blocky SUVs and standard-issue sedans, the car's swooping lines made it a stallion among carriage horses.

Elizabeth said, "You've got to be kidding me. This is your car?"

"It's a 1979 Corvette," Keane said. "Great year."

"Really?"

"Sure. *This Old House* premiered on PBS. *Alien* came out. *My Sharona* was on the radio. Oh, and did I mention that it was one of the last years for this model? There's not a Corvette since then that even comes close to having as much style."

Elizabeth pointed at the license plate. It was one of Maryland's beautifully designed Chesapeake Bay plates, but what really stood out was that instead of the usual anonymous mix of letters and numbers, Keane had opted for a vanity tag that read, OSAY.

"Gee, could that be a Star-Spangled Banner reference?"

He gave her a lopsided grin. "Hop in."

He pulled out onto Washington Street, passing between shops and stately offices and brick-lined sidewalks. They also passed the Talbot County courthouse where a statue of Frederick Douglass stood opposite a statue of a Confederate soldier. It would be challenging to find two monuments to such opposite causes, facing each other as if ready to fight a duel, anywhere else in the country. It was also ironic that Maryland technically had not been part of the Confederacy, but a so-called border state. The fact that Maryland had remained in the Union was thanks in no small part to President Lincoln's willingness to lock Southern sympathizers away in places like Fort McHenry until they took an oath of loyalty to the Union.

A couple of young protesters stood on the lawn, holding signs urging that the Confederate monument should be removed. Keane frowned at the sight. He and GAPS director Charlene Dearborn had been having a feud over the Confederate statue issue. Not this particular statue, which was so far off the beaten path here on the Eastern Shore that it was all but forgotten, but the many similar monuments that decorated courthouse lawns and public parks in larger cities and towns across the South. Keane thought they should be removed if there was a community consensus to do so, while Dearborn had very publicly defended the monuments. The disagreement had resulted in a chilly silence between them, broken only by the text message about something going on at the Cannonball House.

"What kind of incident are we looking at here? I would have said burst water pipes, but it's not cold enough for that."

At that moment, as the Corvette idled at a traffic light, Keane received another text message from the GAPS director. He was so surprised that he didn't put down the phone even when the light turned green, until a vehicle behind him gave an almost apologetic beep. In DC, every car behind him would have laid on the horn the instant that the light changed.

"I'm afraid it's a little more serious than that," Keane said, finally shifting into gear.

"Oh no, did someone vandalize the house?"

"Much worse," he said. "Apparently, there has been a murder."

7

─────────

The news that there had been a murder at the Cannonball House left Keane and Elizabeth stunned, but they didn't have a single detail to speculate about. Instead, they discussed the town's history.

"How much truth do you think there is to the legend of St. Michaels?" Keane asked.

"I haven't studied it," Elizabeth admitted. "I thought there would be plenty of time for that once I settled into the Cannonball House."

Keane nodded. The Cannonball House was just part of the town's association with the War of 1812. St. Michaels had become known as "The Town that Fooled the British" for a clever ruse. It was said that the British fleet had sailed up the Miles River in the dark, intending to catch the town by surprise. Having been warned, the townspeople had a surprise for the British. Lanterns were hung in a copse of trees near town on the riverfront. All lights in town were extinguished. When the British arrived, their ships bombarded the empty woods, mistaking the lanterns for the lights of the town. The Royal

Navy sailed away thinking that they had taught those former colonials a lesson. Meanwhile, the town was spared.

It was just the sort of amusing story that suited a charming tourist town—a dust-up with the British, but nothing too bloody or gory. As far as Keane knew, a young boy and a couple of militia soldiers had been killed in the bombardment, which was tragic enough for their families, but it had been no bloodbath.

"I've always thought that it was a delightful story," Elizabeth said. She laughed. "There may even be a nugget of truth somewhere in there."

Keane smiled. "Why do you historians always have to ruin a perfectly good legend by asking questions about what really happened?"

Elizabeth laughed. "Speak for yourself!"

"I have found that legends are as true as people want them to be. Why let actual historical facts get in the way? Quite a tourist draw has built up around this War of 1812 story. One of the more popular events would be the ghost walks through town."

"Ghost walks?"

"I understand that several people have seen a boy with a lantern," Keane said. "Apparently, he was killed by a stray cannonball and his spirit now haunts the town."

"That poor boy. I wonder if that much of the story is true? The ghost tour sounds like fun, even if I don't believe in ghosts." When Keane did not comment, she added, "Don't tell me that you of all people believe in ghosts!"

"Let's just say that there are a lot of things in this world that can't be explained away by the historical record."

"You're a historian who believes in ghosts? Last night you called me a study in contradictions. I might say the same about you, Doctor Keane."

"Where knowledge and understanding end, legends begin. We can look down our noses at local legends, but our livelihood doesn't depend on the tourism aspect of those legends, ghosts and all."

Keane received another text from Dearborn and took his eyes off the road long enough to read it.

"Anything new?" Elizabeth asked.

"I'm afraid that the murder victim was someone like us, who liked to get at the truth of things. My director just texted me that the victim was Bob Lindermann. He attended at least part of the War of 1812 symposium yesterday."

"That guy? Oh, I've heard all about him!"

Keane nodded. "He had a reputation for busting myths, which didn't make him popular with a lot of people. Was he in town to disprove a cherished legend that St. Michaels tricked the British? I wonder. In any case, his body was found at the Cannonball House."

"You think someone killed him to save the legend?"

"That is for the police to find out, but I would say it's a theory."

They crossed the Miles River bridge and rolled past an impressive sign made of carved wood that announced, *Welcome to St. Michaels. The Town that Fooled the British.*

"Here we are," Keane said.

* * *

KEANE PULLED up in front of the house on St. Mary's Square. A lone unmarked state police car was parked out front, and the house itself was surrounded by yellow crime scene tape.

No crowd of curious onlookers surrounded the old brick house. By the front door was a brass plaque, green with verdigris, placed years ago by the Daughters of 1812 to commemorate the home's history. Preservationists had differing opinions about such plaques.

Keane nodded at the plaque. "Notice that the word plague and plaque differ by one letter," he said.

"You think it has to go?"

Keane smiled. "That's a decision for the new director to make."

Such plaques were a minor headache for preservationists. It wasn't unusual for these plaques to be inaccurate, but words cast in metal had an authority about them. It wasn't so easy to update the information. Removing the plaque altogether wasn't always an option. In fact, some felt that such plaques were simply part of the history of historic properties. That was how Keane felt about them. Without the intervention of the Daughters of 1812, it was entirely possible that the house would have been covered in vinyl siding, or God forbid, bulldozed to make way for another structure.

A detective in an off-the-rack JC Penney suit appeared in the doorway. He crossed his arms and watched them come up the brick path.

"Keane," he said.

"Detective Crawford."

"What are you doing here?"

Elizabeth glanced anxiously from Keane to the state police detective. It was plain from their tone of voice and their stony glares that the two men didn't like each other.

"GAPS is consulting on this property. I am here to help protect the historical integrity of the property and answer any questions you may have."

"Integrity? That's an interesting word choice, coming from you."

"I'm just here to help, Detective."

"Well, I do have lots of questions. Just not about the Cannonball House."

Keane said nothing.

Detective Crawford seemed to notice Liz for the first time. "Who's this?"

"Allow me to introduce Elizabeth Graham. She is the new executive director here at the Cannonball House."

The detective did not offer to shake hands with Elizabeth, but gave her a vague nod of acknowledgement. His gaze remained fastened on Keane. Finally, he said, "I'm not letting you inside yet."

"Isn't the crime lab finished?"

"Huh. I almost forgot that you're extremely familiar with homicide investigations, Keane. Yes, the techs are done. They didn't interfere with the *integrity* of the house. I can't say the same for the bloodstains, but you're gonna have to take that up with the perp." He paused. "By the way, where were you last night?"

"Really?"

"Just curious."

"I was at a symposium in Easton."

The detective finally turned his attention to Elizabeth and looked her up and down. "Symposium, huh?"

"Look, if the lab techs are done, then why won't you let us inside?"

"Because I don't want to."

The detective shut the door in his face.

Out on the doorstep, Elizabeth was staring at Keane. "Wow, that was ... hostile. What was that all about between you two?"

"History," Keane said. "Come on, let's go get something to eat. Detective Crawford will leave eventually."

* * *

THEY RETURNED to the Corvette and drove a couple of blocks away to park near a restaurant.

"We could have walked," Elizabeth said.

"I'm fairly certain that Detective Crawford would have given me a parking ticket, at the very least. At the very worst, he might have shot out my tires."

"You said that you two have some history?"

Liz had been struggling to keep up with Keane as he strode down the sidewalk on long legs, apparently eager to get even farther away from Detective Crawford. He came to a stop so suddenly that Liz walked past him and had to turn around. "I'm sure by now that you've heard that my wife drowned two years ago while we were on a sailing trip. It happened not too far from here."

"I heard," Liz admitted.

"The detective back there is convinced that I killed her and he's not the only one with that opinion. There are people around here who think that I got away with murder."

Liz didn't admit that she had heard those rumors. She hadn't known Keane for more than a few hours, but he did not strike her as a man who would murder his wife. "I'll just be sure not to go sailing with you," she said.

Keane gave her a sideways glance. They walked on in silence until they reached the restaurant.

"*The Dancing Crab*," Elizabeth said, noting the sign above the door. The wooden sign included a picture of a crab with top hat and cane, apparently tap dancing, an interpretation of Fred Astaire as seafood. "Sounds promising. I have to admit that I'm not all that familiar with St. Michaels yet."

"When in St. Michaels, one needs to have a crab cake. Or crab soup, or crab bisque, or crab imperial—"

Elizabeth laughed. "I think I get the idea."

Yet when the server arrived, despite the many menu offerings featuring seafood, Keane ordered a cob salad with grilled chicken. Elizabeth went with the crab cake sandwich.

"No seafood for you?" she asked, raising an eyebrow. "Allergies?

Keane sighed. "Memories. When I was a kid, I spent summers working for a waterman. Nothing puts you off seafood as much as remembering how a bucket of bait smells after several hours in the summer sun."

"What a lovely picture. I wonder if it's too late to change my order."

"Forgive me, Elizabeth. That was rude of me. I know that's not exactly lunchtime conversation."

"Actually, I'm more taken by the fact that the great Franklin Keane worked on a crab boat. Ha! I thought a rich kid like you would be off at sailing camp for the summer."

"It was my grandfather's idea. He thought it would build character."

"Did it?"

"No more than any summer job. We're just lucky there wasn't a tannery nearby, or maybe a quarry, or we would have ended up scraping hides and breaking rocks." Keane was surprised at the note of bitterness in his voice. Just thinking about Jack Keane tended to do that to him at times. He forced a smile. "It wasn't all bad, I suppose. My cousin, Beau, loved it. He's the outdoor type and works as a fishing guide and hunting guide. Sad to say, all that those summers on the water did for me was to permanently put me off crab cakes and make me fluent in Delmarvese."

"Delmarvese?"

"Let's just say that you may need a translator the first time that you talk to a real Chesapeake Bay waterman."

The waitress came with their food. She had been friendly enough when taking their orders, but either she had recognized him in the interim, or someone in the kitchen had pointed him out.

"I thought you looked familiar. You're pretty brave to show

your face around here," she said, then turned to Elizabeth. "Honey, I hope you know what you're in for."

She cracked the plates down harder than necessary and walked off without bothering to ask if they needed anything.

"Wow. You get that a lot?" Elizabeth asked.

"Like I said, a lot of people think I did it. People on the Eastern Shore have strong opinions and long memories."

"You could move away. With your job, you could live almost anywhere on the East Coast."

"Where would I go? I'm a Marylander. My family has lived here for more than two centuries."

Elizabeth glanced at her crab cake. "Should I be worried? Maybe she spat on it back in the kitchen."

"I think you're safe. If she was out to get anybody, it was me."

It was clear to Keane from the way that Elizabeth attacked the crab cake, that she wasn't too worried about the food having been sabotaged.

"What should I do?" Elizabeth asked, once she had made a dent in the sandwich. "The Cannonball House may be closed for a while."

"The police will keep it shut down for a week or so at most. Until then, you could explore the area. Have you been to the Maritime Museum here in town? What about the Harriet Tubman park? They're both quite fascinating."

"What are you going to do?"

"Me?"

"About the murder at the Cannonball House."

"I'm going to let the police do their job. Detective Crawford is very capable, believe me. And I'll be going ahead with my job, which is to preserve historic properties."

"Just to be clear here, Franklin, but technically, you're not my boss or anything like that, right?"

Keane shook his head. "No, not at all. You report to the

Cannonball House board of directors. GAPS is just consulting on the house."

"Good to know."

"Oh?"

Elizabeth nibbled a French fry and smiled. "It's just that I wouldn't want any conflicts of interest."

8

Later that night, Keane returned to the Cannonball House alone. The crime scene tape was still up, but there were no police around. It was a clear fall night filled with stars, with a New Moon that cast little light. Keane stood for a while, letting his eyes adjust to the darkness and getting his bearings.

He had thought about bringing Elizabeth along, but this was something that he needed to do alone. He was glad that he'd had a chance to discuss Amanda's death with her. It wasn't an easy subject but he felt better that they had gotten that out in the open and cleared the air. Elizabeth seemed to have given him the benefit of the doubt, which was more than he could say for a lot of other people.

Not so much as a single light was on within the house, so that the dwelling seemed to be brooding there in the dark. That was just fine with Keane. For what he had in mind, he had found that the presence of electric lights dispelled the aura he was seeking.

He tried the front door. Locked. The back door was locked as well. Keane wasn't entirely deterred. This was an historic property, but it wasn't Fort Knox in terms of security. He checked under the planters on the brick patio for a hidden key. Nothing. He paused, looking around the patio and the back of the house. Nodding to himself, he reached up and felt around the top of the bracket that held the faux lantern to the brick wall. His fingertips touched a slim metallic object. Here was the key.

Inside, he locked the door behind him.

The house was very still. It did not take him long to discover that part of the reason was a lack of electricity. He mused that one of Elizabeth's first tasks as executive director of the Cannonball House would be paying the electric bill. The lack of power meant that not so much as the whir of a refrigerator or the hum of a desktop computer disrupted the silence. The thick brick walls occluded any sound from the neighboring town.

It was subtle, but most people did not consider the impact of noise pollution. It was very rare these days not to overhear the sounds of traffic, or of a jetliner high overhead. The silence inside the house was in itself transportive to another era.

Keane made a slow circuit of the interior, moving quietly, trying to absorb some of the atmosphere of the old house. He wanted to feel the bones of the place. The air smelled of old wood, beeswax, and the charred interior of a brick fireplace.

He passed a dark stain on the floor in front of the fireplace. His nose wrinkled; from a boyhood spent hunting, he knew the odor of drying blood. So, this was where Bob Lindermann had been murdered. Keane studied the spot out of sheer curiosity.

He had brought along a Maglite that he kept in the Corvette for peering into attics and exploring cellars of old houses. He used the flashlight sparingly, flicking it on just long enough to get his bearings. He did not want the neighbors to call the police to report seeing lights in the house. Technically, he was sure that the house was no longer a crime scene, no matter what Detective Crawford claimed.

Small towns and rural counties generally called in the

Maryland State Police Crime Lab to investigate homicides. Keane was sure that by now that the forensic experts had dusted for fingerprints and searched for other clues. The body had been taken away, and the evidence collected. That would be about it; he knew from recent experience that the crime lab did not work the miracles one saw on television shows.

He had some right to be here, considering that he was the GAPS senior field officer who oversaw the integrity of the Cannonball House. He certainly was not trespassing. Still, that did not mean that someone like Detective Crawford would not welcome putting him in jail overnight if he found him here, just to be malicious.

Keane pushed such thoughts from his mind. He needed to be calm. Now was the time to get in touch with the particular aura of the house.

Having done this before, he had come prepared. He took a plain white, drip-free candle from his pocket and lit it with a vintage lighter. A bit of non-electric light helped to bring the interior of the old house alive. Shadows played over the corners and across the plaster walls. The dark stain across the wooden floorboards seemed to absorb the light. The soft glow would not be very noticeable from outside.

With any luck, he might run into Lindermann here tonight in order to understand who had killed him, and why. With retrocognition, however, one never knew how the past would present itself. In Keane's experience, some people and events had a more powerful hold over a place, no matter how distant. Events involving trauma and violence, people's emotions ranging from love to hate to grief—he had found that these all cast a long shadow across decades and centuries.

It was best to get comfortable. He sat down at a table and studied the play of flickering candlelight. Nothing spooky or threatening here. Keane felt at home. This was a good sign.

Keane was a professional historian. He never would have

shared with anyone how he had begun to involve himself in practices that other historians would have ridiculed. What he was about to do now was something that he called retrocognition.

Premonition was seeing into the future. Retrocognition was seeing into the past.

This window into the past was not something that Keane had invented. But it had become a skill that he groomed in himself. For the past two years, he had worked to channel this ability. He had spent a two-week vacation working with Native American shamans in New Mexico. Not so long ago, he had spent another period studying with traditional folk seers in Appalachia. Keane had been careful to tell people he knew only that he was on sightseeing trips.

Desperate after Amanda's disappearance to understand what had taken place that night, he had studied under others to learn how to better open his mind to the reflections cast by the past, and by the people and events that had come before. He compared it to the endless images in a funhouse mirror, or even to the way that the hum of a tuning fork vibrated long after it had been struck.

The causal energy tended to be focused around places— which tied in perfectly with Keane's interest in the past. There was history, of course, the sort found in records and archives, and there were stories and legends. Lately, Keane had been drawn into the more otherworldly local legends and lore asso-ciated with historical places. To call these "ghost stories" was much too simple. More than a few occurrences that had taken place in the old houses, ancient forests, and mournful marshes across the Eastern Shore encompassed far more than ghosts. In his mind, he had even given these supernatural legends and phenomenon a name, cryptofolklore.

Again, for fear of his professional reputation, he kept his

interest in retrocognition and crytofolklore very much to himself.

No one agreed, not even the mystics whom Keane had spent time studying under, but there were theories that time repeated itself in loops or that our reality was just one of many running parallel like the lanes of an interstate.

Keane had found it was possible to let one's mind drift into another lane, where time ran differently.

It probably helped that his mind was receptive to it, thanks to his family roots. Not the distinguished Key family, who were rather proper, but the nefarious Irish Keane family.

It was Keane's grandfather who had shared the more twisted roots of the family tree with his grandsons. Born in County Kerry, Jack Keane was proud of the fact that some in his clan had been chieftains and even cattle thieves. He had also spoken darkly and with some awe of what he called the "fey" ancestors from the Emerald Isle. Fey was a Celtic word that meant that one was open to the spirit world or that one possessed a kind of sixth sense. In Keane's case, he had worked to develop this inherited ability into retrocognition—seeing with his own eyes what had already taken place.

He knew that most would call it claptrap.

Except that he *had* seen, quite clearly, events from the past. It was enormously frustrating to him that he still had not seen what happened to Amanda. However, he had seen so much else.

Sitting in the Cannonball House, Keane kept his thoughts carefully blank. He held an image in his mind of a stone pool filled with water, with not so much as a ripple upon it. The dark water was still, cool, and inviting.

The shadows grew longer as the candle flame burned brighter. The silence inside the old house deepened.

Slowly, he became aware of a figure standing in the doorway. He tried not to look at the figure directly, not until he was sure that it had fully materialized.

The figure became less shadowy, but it was clear that he was seeing someone small and slight, yet full of energy. A boy. He looked to be about twelve years old. As the figure came more fully into focus, Keane looked directly at the boy, who seemed to be looking right at him. The boy wore knee-breeches, his shins bare and tanned, no shoes on his feet. He wore a white shirt and a homespun vest of linsey-woolsy with bone buttons. In one hand he held a lantern, which he raised. There was no flame within that Keane could see, and yet the lantern glowed with a strange blue light.

Keane was puzzled. If anything, he had thought that he might see Bob Lindermann here tonight. But if he had learned anything in his studies with shamans and seers, it was that the past gives what it gives, but not always what we expect of it.

The boy walked into the room and paused in front of the mantel. He seemed to be gazing at the dark hearth. He walked right across the bloodstain without seeming to notice it. If the floorboards were still damp with blood, the footprints left no mark. The boy crossed the room to the front door, then paused and looked back over his shoulder, as if inviting Keane to follow him. Then the boy's figure disappeared into shadow as he passed through the oak front door.

Keane rose from the chair.

He had never interacted with any of his retrocognitive visions before, and the idea excited him.

Quickly, he moved to the front door and opened it, hoping that the boy had not disappeared.

No, the boy stood there on the front lawn, waiting for him, still holding the glowing lantern high. Keane approached. As he did so, the boy lowered the lantern and raised his other hand. He was pointing at the sky.

Keane looked up. What was the boy trying to show him?

Was he pointing at the new moon? Darkness? The void of the universe itself?

Keane stared skyward. The pinpricks of stars began to organize themselves. When he and Beau were young boys, his grandfather had sometimes taken them on midnight rambles across the fields after the harvest was in. He had been surprised that his grandfather knew the constellations from long boyhood nights spent on watch as a shepherd back in Ireland. He had taught these same stars to his grandsons.

The autumn sky held Cassiopeia, Pegasus, and Andromeda.

Keane picked out Polaris, the North Star, in the Ursa Minor constellation. He realized with excitement that the boy wasn't pointing vaguely at the night sky. Nor was he pointing at all the stars. He was pointing toward Polaris. He had singled out a single star. What could it mean?

Keane lowered his eyes, hoping to learn more, but the boy had vanished.

9

Nearly 100 miles away, at eleven o'clock on a Sunday morning in early September, the Smithsonian's American History Museum was already busy.

Colonel Charles Montgomery, USA, Retired, stood just inside the museum entrance. If anyone had looked closely at the fit, fifty-something man with the close-cropped graying hair, they might have noticed the earpiece with its coiled wire in his right ear, just like an undercover Secret Service agent might wear.

He watched a heavyset mother waddle across the floor of the museum, followed by three small children that trailed her like ducklings. They passed below a sculpture, made of reflective metallic rectangles, that depicted the Star-Spangled Banner flag. It took no particular observation skills to determine that the mama and her duckling were tourists, considering that all three children wore bright green T-shirts that announced, "Proudly made in Tennessee."

The sight made Colonel Montgomery smile. He was doing this for them. He was doing this for every American's future.

He glanced up at the sculpture and frowned. He found it

far too garish and modernistic for his tastes. The metallic rectangles reminded him of one of those arts and crafts projects made from the shiny bits of beer cans. To label this as a sculpture was a stretch of the imagination. In fact, without the words beneath it engraved in marble that stated, "The Star-Spangled Banner: The flag that inspired the National Anthem," it would have been impossible to tell that it was a flag at all. What would have been wrong with a simple mural showing the flag in all its red, white, and blue glory? Contained behind the soaring sculpture was the exhibit area for the actual Star-Spangled Banner that had flown over Fort McHenry during the Battle of Baltimore on September 14, 1814.

While there were plenty of tourists, no museum administrators were working on a Sunday morning. Montgomery had counted on their absence to add to the confusion. As an experienced military officer, he knew that the best time to strike the enemy was when no one was in charge. Since the museum's opening that morning, none of the museum's security cameras had been recording, thanks to Montgomery's crack team of hackers. If anyone had been paying attention, they might have noticed that the security monitors displayed a looped image of the museum, taken on a Sunday morning last month.

He glanced at his watch, a Rolex submariner. At precisely eleven hundred hours, the fire began.

"I smell smoke," the mother with the ducklings announced. She wrinkled her nose and looked around. "Does anyone smell smoke?"

Smoke had, in fact, begun drifting from the American Democracy exhibit hall. His chief operative, a big man who went by the nickname Blister, had entered a few minutes before and planted a small incendiary device. Blister had lobbied for a bomb to create more confusion, but Montgomery had quickly nixed that idea. He wanted disruption, not a full-on antiterrorism response. Also, he was not interested in seeing any tourists harmed.

"We have smoke," said Blister's voice in his ear.

"Roger that," Montgomery replied. "What's your status, Red Team?"

"Rolling onto Madison Drive now," a voice responded.

That's when the fire alarm went off. The shrill, intermittent klaxon created instant pandemonium. The Tennessee mama gathered her ducklings and scrambled for the exit doors onto the National Mall, elbowing an Asian couple out of the way when they took a little too long. Security guards tried to keep order, although it was clear that they were just as confused as the tourists. This was the Sunday morning B team, just as Montgomery had planned.

Blister crossed the lobby and headed for the Star-Spangled Banner exhibit hall. Montgomery waited just a moment, then followed.

Several years before, the Star-Spangled Banner had been removed from the museum lobby. The flag had once occupied roughly the space now taken up by the garish sculpture. The Star-Spangled Banner had been elaborately restored stitch by stitch, and then relocated to a stunning new exhibit hall of its very own. The conservators liked to say that the iconic flag would be good for another two hundred years.

Montgomery entered the exhibit area, which was closeted from the rest of the museum. He slipped on a knit cap that pulled down to hide his entire face, with the exception of holes for his mouth and eyes, and Blister did the same.

He glanced at the interpretive exhibits, which included a "please touch" chunk of shrapnel from a British bomb. The dim lighting and seclusion gave the flag hall a hushed atmosphere that was more like a religious sanctuary than a museum exhibit. Even the shrill tones of the fire alarm seemed muted in here. Ionized and cleansed, the museum-quality air inside the hall seemed richer as Montgomery breathed it in.

The flag itself held court in a space large enough to accommodate its original size of thirty feet by forty-two feet. It was true that the flag appeared somewhat foreshortened, having lost several feet over the years to requests for souvenirs. A background image blended so well with the existing flag that it gave the illusion of being complete.

Montgomery couldn't help but notice that the fifteenth star was missing. The lost star nagged at him; for what he had in mind, it was best that no scrap of the flag existed elsewhere. He hoped that idiot Lindermann had been telling the truth about the lost star.

A glass wall separated the flag from the exhibit hall. Conservators had taken the added step of eliminating any electrical devices in the room itself in order to reduce the risk of fire. Dimly lighted from above, the broad stripes and bright stars—each two feet across—were bathed in a kind of reverential glow.

It was not unusual for groups of schoolchildren, and even adults, to be so moved by the sight of the flag and its surroundings that they actually broke into song, singing snatches of the National Anthem or even the entire song, *O, say does that star-spangled banner yet wave/oe'r the land of the free, and the home of the brave?*

You had to hand it to Francis Scott Key, he thought. Key had woven that eternal question into his poem, so that generations of Americans now took the measure of democracy each time that song was sung.

Montgomery's musings were interrupted by the approach of a museum security guard. The man must have spotted them going into the exhibit, against the flow of outgoing people.

"You need to evacuate right now, sir," the guard said. "Didn't you hear the fire alarm? You can't be in here. Let me escort you out of the hall."

Montgomery touched the stun gun in his suit pocket, wondering if he would need to use it. The guard was around six-foot-two, bigger than Montgomery, but soft through the middle and going gray. Still, he seemed to be taking his job seriously. He might be trouble.

Blister glided up behind the guard. For a big man, he could move silently. In half a second, he had his arms around the guard in a choke hold. The guard struggled, but he was no match for somebody like Blister, who choked him out expertly. The guard's body went slack.

"That's enough. Don't kill him."

"If you say so, sir."

The guard slumped to the floor.

Montgomery looked out from the Star-Spangled Banner exhibit entrance, just in time to see a crew of firefighters swarm through the museum doors, wearing face masks and breathing apparatus. A fire engine sat idling in the street between the museum entrance and the National Mall. Even considering the fact that this was the Smithsonian Institution, it seemed to be a remarkable response time.

The firefighters did not enter the Hall of Democracy, where the smoke had originated. There was no real danger of the fire spreading; Blister had made certain of that at Montgomery's insistence. However, the fire had created just enough smoke to cause a diversion.

The firefighters did not enter the Star-Spangled Banner exhibit hall, either, but went through an unmarked service door that gave entry to the museum's backstage area. They continued down a short hallway to a secure door with a keypad set into the wall beside it. One of the firefighters punched in a code, and a light on the keypad flashed from red to green.

They entered the same room as the Star-Spangled Banner

itself. The flag was mounted in such a way to give support to the fabric while making minimal contact with the cloth. The assistant curator who had provided the access code had explained everything. It was a simple matter to disconnect the support system and then roll up the flag. The firefighters had practiced this step, and as Montgomery watched through the glass, they completed it efficiently. Rolled up, the flag was surprisingly heavy at nearly two hundred pounds. It would have taken quite a breeze to set the flag snapping gallantly in the wind. The firefighters covered it with a long sleeve of white cotton made for this very purpose. Next, they hoisted the sausaged flag onto their shoulders and retraced their steps out of the backstage area, across the museum lobby, and out the museum doors to the fire engine idling in the street. A few curious bystanders may have noticed a man in a charcoal suit and a big man in a nylon windbreaker climb into the cab of the fire engine before it drove off.

Inside the cab, Montgomery glanced at his Rolex again. The entire operation, from starting the fire to exiting with the flag, had taken exactly six minutes. They were right on schedule.

Less than eight minutes later, the actual fire department arrived, along with several DC police officers to help with crowd control. But by then, the flag that had flown above Fort McHenry two hundred years before, the flag that had inspired the National Anthem and that had been part of the Smithsonian for more than a century, had vanished.

10

From aboard the ship in Baltimore harbor, Francis Scott Key watched fire and fury rain down on Fort McHenry. Already, the bombardment had been going on for hours. Key's ears—in fact, his entire body—felt concussed from the shelling. Like some murderous fireworks show, the bursting shells and rockets could be seen for miles out into Chesapeake Bay and even far inland. He could not imagine what it must be like to be one of the defenders trapped within the star fort's walls.

"This is a sight that is terrible to behold," he muttered to Jonathan Skinner beside him at the ship's rail. "And yet I cannot look away."

"I have never seen anything like it," Skinner agreed. Skinner was the official United States prisoner exchange agent whom Key had accompanied on the mission to free the hapless Doctor Beanes from the British after they had accused him of being a traitor and threatened to hang him. Beanes appeared at the rail from time to time, but mostly stayed below. He was an older man, and his ordeal at the hands of the British had left him weak and frail.

Although Beanes had been successfully released and was no longer in danger of being hanged by the British, all three men remained in the custody of the Royal Navy. Technically, they were not prisoners, but the British had refused to let them go ashore for fear that they would warn American forces of the impending attack. Key thought that was a little foolish; anyone sighting the fleet in plain view of the city would know that an attack was imminent.

It was possible that the British might release them now, but rowing out into the iron storm would be suicidal. No, for better or for worse, they were now committed to waiting out the bombardment. They would be spectators to what promised to be the destruction of Baltimore's protective fort.

Key might have been tempted to take the risk. Some dangers were closer at hand than the bombardment.

On impulse, Key reached inside his coat and touched the letter hidden there, to reassure himself that he had not lost it. He had only recently stolen it from Rear Admiral Cockburn's quarters. With the attack underway, Cockburn had likely been too busy to notice that the letter was missing. But if he discovered that it was gone, Key could be in deep trouble. Cockburn might order the Americans to be searched. If the letter was found in his possession, there could be no hope of diplomatic intervention on Key's behalf. He would be hanged as a spy. And yet, he felt that taking the letter was worth the risk. The question would be, what was he going to do with the letter? Tucked deep in his coat pocket, the letter felt hot as a burning chunk of shrapnel from the British bombshells.

Key had overhead the British officers aboard express their dismay that the land attack under General Sir Robert Ross had failed. The general was now dead, killed by American sharpshooters. Ross had been a popular officer and a hero of Napoleon's defeat in Europe. His death at the hands of the Baltimore militia had left the British angry and bitter. The attack had pressed on under the leadership of Colonel Arthur Brooke. However, the colonel's force of five thousand Redcoats had been surprised to encounter twice that number of American defenders. The American defenses were strong and bristled with artillery. Unlike the laughable American behavior at the "Bladensburg Races," where the troops had run away, these troops seemed determined to defend their port city.

The fighting had been sharp and savage at what the Americans had come to call the battle of North Point. Having run out of actual grapeshot and cannonballs, the American defenders had resorted to loading their cannons with scrap metal—anything from nails to horseshoes—and even with stones. At close range, the makeshift ammunition was more than effective. British losses had been heavy. Combined with the heat, isolated downpours that soaked their musket powder, and the loss of General Ross, morale had been low.

With the land attack seen as a failure, the British had now turned all their attention—and all their guns—on Fort McHenry. The British firepower arrayed against the fort was considerable. The embattled fort was all that stood between Baltimore and the invading British. Angry at the death of Ross and their defeat at North Point, the British had made it clear that they would sack and burn the city.

This knowledge made the guns firing on the fort seemed less like tools of war and more like an extension of British anger. At first, the Royal Navy had brought its prized warships within range of the fort and opened fire. With the tide out, though, the Patapsco River proved too shallow for the largest ships. The last thing that the Royal Navy wanted was for one of its ships of the line to run aground and become a sitting duck for the guns of the fort.

However, the vessels had been within reach of the fort's massive guns. One lucky shot by the Americans, and a valuable war ship might be reduced to splinters. It was not a risk that the

Royal Navy was willing to take, and the ships had been withdrawn farther out into Chesapeake Bay.

Instead, mortar ships had been brought up. These were more like sailing barges—not nearly so valuable as a man o' war. The sturdy barges were akin to floating fortresses. Their heavy mortars fired explosive shells that arced high into the air, and then plunged down toward the fort.

Each explosive sphere measured a foot across and was made of iron an inch thick. The shell exploded with such force that the iron shattered like glass, scattering burning-hot shards at the defenders below. It was this shrapnel, Key would learn, that had been responsible for the killed and wounded at Fort McHenry.

"A few of these shells fell short," Major Armistead would explain later. "A large proportion burst over us, throwing their fragments among us and threatening destruction."

A flag with fifteen stars and fifteen stripes flew above the fort, illuminated by the bursting shells. This was known as a storm flag, much smaller than the huge, ceremonial Star-Spangled Banner that the city's defenders had commissioned seamstress Mary Pickersgill to make. A delegation of defenders that included Armistead, Commodore Joshua Barney, and the overall commander of Baltimore's defenses, General Sam Smith, had gone to see Pickersgill at her home and workshop on Pratt Street.

There, Pickersgill had agreed to make them a flag. The sheer size of the flag meant that this was an epic task. The work soon outgrew Pickersgill's narrow town house and had to be moved to the vacant space in a nearby brewery. The flag required more than a million individual stitches. While Pickersgill had a small group working with her that included her daughter and an indentured African-American girl, it was often Pickersgill who did the actual sewing on the flag. She tended to work on it at night, after her better-paying flag-making work was done, sometimes sewing until midnight. Consequently, much of the sewing was done by the dim light of a lantern. She would be up again in the morning by five o'clock to start the new day.

Talk of the flag could be heard around the city, and the citizens of Baltimore took a great deal of pride in the banner, but Key himself had yet to see the massive flag.

And so far tonight, it seemed more likely that there would soon be a British flag flying above Fort McHenry.

Rocket ships had also been brought into play. These ships were outfitted with Congreve rockets that made a spectacular show, trailing red fire through the night sky before bursting above the fort. The sights and sounds were terrifying.

Under this barrage, what choice would any man have but to cower in fear? And yet, somehow, the defenders of Fort McHenry managed to marshal their courage and fire back at the British attackers.

Key heard raised voices and the sound of feet tramping purposefully across the deck. Remembering the stolen letter in his coat, he felt a pang of fear. Turning, he saw that Rear Admiral Cockburn was headed his way. As he usually was, Cockburn was surrounded by a retinue of officers. To Key's relief, it appeared that Cockburn was mainly concerned with the rate of fire of the ship's guns. He moved in close amidst a gun crew that was laboring in the September humidity, their shirts off and sweat cutting rivulets in their black powder-stained faces and backs. He bent low over the gun to check its aim, then nodded his approval and stepped away. The gun crew made its final preparations and then the gun leaped, sending another projectile toward the beleaguered American fort.

Cockburn noticed Key at the rail and moved in his direction.

"Ah, Mister Key. There you are. How are you enjoying the show?"

"I fear my ears shall never be the same."

"It won't be long now," Cockburn assured Key and Skinner. "Perhaps we could share a poem to pass the time?"

The other officers appeared amused. Since learning that Key was an amateur poet, Cockburn had enjoyed rankling him with his own bawdy limericks. Cockburn had a voice for command, and he began in a booming tone that carried well above the din:

THERE WAS *a young lad named Buck*
  Whose sister taught him to—

THANKFULLY, Cockburn was interrupted by the screeching whistle of an incoming shell. The missile plunged into the harbor just a few feet short of the flagship.

The limerick forgotten, Cockburn hurried to the rail. Key stepped aside to make room for him.

"How do they have such range?" Cockburn demanded. He turned to shout at the closest gun crew, his voice carrying clearly across the deck. "It's that star point closest to us. Fire upon it, damn you!"

Cockburn hurried away to oversee the guns, leaving Key alone.

Key felt a raindrop. They had been having a spell of hot, humid weather with pockets of downpours. It had been this weather that added to British difficulties during the battle of North Point. Now, it began to rain in earnest. Skinner ran for shelter, but Key found himself unable to leave the spectacle of the bombardment. Through curtains of rain, shells and Congreve rockets continued to fall upon the fort. Key adjusted his hat and tugged his coat more tightly at the neck to keep the rain out.

He continued to watch through the night, mesmerized by the bursting bombs. Some part of him understood that he was witnessing the event of a lifetime—how often did someone like him get to watch such a spectacular battle? He tried to guess how many shells filled the night. Hundreds? Perhaps thousands.

Finally, the night began to fade as the light grew to the east behind the British fleet. But there would be no bright sunrise this morning. Light rain continued to fall, mixing with the powder residue filling the air, to create a smoky mist. Key strained to see the battered fort through the mist. He fully expected to see that the fort had struck its colors in surrender. How could anyone have survived that bombardment?

Beside him, both Skinner and Doctor Beanes had reappeared now that daylight approached. A handful of British officers also crowded the rail. Cockburn, thankfully, had transferred to another ship during the night.

"They have struck the colors!" one of the officers said, watching through a brass telescope. The mood among the British grew merry, although they were exhausted from a long night of lobbing shells at the Americans.

Key felt his heart sink. He tried to see through the mist, but the fort was little more than a blur in the gloom.

"That's it then," Beanes said in his Scottish burr. He sounded as tired as Key now felt. "Baltimore has fallen."

As the early light grew, the outline of the fort became more distinct. The breeze increased and dispelled some of the mist. Key thought he could make out the flagpole, empty above the ramparts. But then he caught a glimpse of movement. A flag was being raised, but it was too far away for him to make out.

He turned to a British officer nearby. "If you please, may I borrow your glass?"

The officer handed Key his telescope, its smooth brass still warm to the touch from the officer's hands. Key put the glass to his eye and focused on the fort. He gasped.

The fort's defenders had raised an enormous flag above the smoking ruins. The breeze off the harbor caught the flag and it suddenly rippled above the smoking ruins, its bright colors standing out against the gray sky.

"Look!" Key cried. This must be the flag that seamstress Mary Pickersgill had made. "They have raised the flag!"

Key returned the telescope to the British officers, who were none too happy at the sight of the United States flag waving defiantly above the fort. But the bombardment had ended; already, preparations were being made for the fleet to leave these waters.

Key reached inside his coat for a pencil and a piece of paper. The only thing at hand was a letter, but thankfully the back page was blank.

Hands shaking with emotion, he began to jot words down on the page. It was a sketch in words more than a poem, an outpouring of feeling about what he was seeing and thinking at that moment. Key wished that he had some ability as a sketch artist, in order to capture this moment. But he had no talent as an artist. Instead, he would have to make his sketch using words. With the page spread on the damp rail of the ship, the pencil pressed deep into the paper, almost engraving the lines that came to mind.

The paper grew damp in the morning air, the pencil dulled, but Key could not stop. Key had written poems before, mainly for his own amusement. After all, any lawyer worth his salt was something of a wordsmith at heart. But this time was different. It was as if the words were simply pouring out of him.

AND THE ROCKET'S *red glare, the bombs bursting in air*
Gave proof thru the night that our flag was still there

.   .   .

THE RESULT WAS A MESSY SCRAWL, with words crossed out and others jotted in, smudged here and there with the smeared pencil or possibly by gunpowder. He wanted to perfect it, but there was no time—

"Ready to go ashore, sir?" asked a sailor.

The battle for Baltimore was finally over.

Later that night, Key worked to revise the rough draft of the poem in his room at the Indian Queen Hotel. By all rights, he should have been exhausted after being up all night watching the bombardment. His coat and his shoes were still soaked through, refusing to dry completely in the humid air.

The letter that Key had taken from Cockburn's quarters had survived unscathed. The president's words of capitulation now seemed bleak and hollow in the face of this victory. He could not quite decide what to do with the letter, so he did nothing. He tucked it back into his coat pocket. Instead, he focused on the words that he had written early that morning while still aboard the ship in Baltimore harbor.

Key felt exhausted—in truth, no one in the entire city had slept through the night—but the words of the poem itself seemed to energize him.

As he worked, a tune came almost unbidden to his mind. "O-oh, hmm, hmm, hmm, hmmmm," he hummed to the tune in his head. He had heard it before in the waterfront taverns of Baltimore and even being sung by British sailors deep in their cups aboard the Royal Navy ship. The song was known as *To Anacreon in Heaven.* He would give the tune new words, and new meaning.

In the morning, he showed the poem to his brother in law, Judge Nicholson.

"Remarkable," Nicholson said. He had long been a fan of Key's amateurish poetry, somewhat out of family obligation, but read this poem with genuine enthusiasm. As a Baltimore resident, Nicholson shared in the pride that the entire city felt toward having withstood the British attack. "This is just what every person in Baltimore felt in their hearts. In a few lines, you have told the story of what happened here!"

"I had a tune for it in mind," Key explained. He had a fair voice, and he sang it gently now. Looking over his shoulder at the words on the page, his brother in law joined him. When they had finished, both men felt a glow in their hearts. Having both witnessed the battle, they understood that Key had captured the moment perfectly.

"You must have this printed, Francis," Nicholson said. "This is just what the city needs now to mourn those who perished, and to celebrate our victory."

"Are you sure?" Key had written the poem more for himself; it had never really occurred to him to share these words with an audience beyond a few friends and family. He was nothing if not modest.

"Yes, I am sure!" Judge Nicholson said. He held out his hand. "Here, give it to me."

A printer was found and the poem was typeset. His brother-in-law had insisted that the author's name be on the broadsheet, and Key had reluctantly agreed. Besides, he felt too tired now to argue with his brother in law.

Within hours of the battle, the press whirred and clanked, creating broadsheet copies of Key's poem. Nicholson was too much of a gentleman to go about to taverns and other gathering places, handing out the sheets. Instead, he paid boys a few pennies to make the deliveries. More copies were sent to the fort, to be shared around to the defenders.

Within hours, *The Defence of Fort McHenry* was on everyone's lips.

11

K eane was still in St. Michaels when he got the call from
Dearborn. He had been deliberately putting off a
phone conversation in favor of texting. His boss seemed just
fine with that, which was worrisome. Their impasse over the
fate of Confederate monuments seemed to be continuing.

"Have the police arrested anyone yet?" she asked without
preamble, which was Charlene's usual approach.

"Short of someone standing there with a smoking gun, this
could take a while," Keane answered. "You know how these
things go."

"Do I?" Charlene let that response hang there a moment, as
if she wanted to make sure that while Keane might know about
these things from recent experience, she did not. "In any case,
we have other issues, Franklin."

"Well, there is that house in New Jersey that—"

"No, no, no," Charlene interrupted. "Bigger things. This
morning, I got a call from the director of the Smithsonian
Museum of American History. He requested a consultant. In
fact, he specifically requested you."

"Oh?" Keane and the Smithsonian director knew each other

professionally, but GAPS and the Smithsonian had never worked together before.

"Something to do with your area of expertise," she said.

"Of course. The War of 1812."

"Actually, he mentioned the murder in St. Michaels," she said.

"What in the world does that have to do with the Smithsonian?"

"That's for you to find out," Charlene said. "I've told you everything I know. He did say it was urgent, as in, drop everything and see him today."

"OK." Keane started to say more, but realized that Charlene was already gone. That in itself wasn't surprising. It was the nature of the GAPS director to be abrupt.

Keane sighed. Once again, they had managed to have a conversation without talking about the elephant in the room, or rather, the monument in the room.

Resolving that particular issue would have to wait. Apparently, he was needed at the Smithsonian. He was still puzzling out what it could mean when his iPhone chimed with an email.

Franklin, thank you for agreeing to meet me today regarding this urgent matter. This matter is best discussed in person. Best regards, Roger.

The email was over the signature line of Roger Biesty, director of the Smithsonian Museum of American History.

Now, Keane was truly curious. When it came to history, which was essentially dealing with matters that had taken place decades or even centuries before, there was seldom anything urgent. Keane was passionate about preserving history, but *urgent* was not a word that one heard often in historical preservation circles. There were a few exceptions, of course, usually involving bulldozers and real estate developers, or fires and hurricanes. What could an institution as esteemed as the Smithsonian possibly have gotten itself into that was *urgent*?

He was just going to have to drive to DC to find out.

* * *

KEANE BOUGHT coffee and headed out, hoping to beat the rush hour traffic into Washington, which was probably overly optimistic. When it came to Washington traffic, rush hour was almost all of the time.

Elizabeth Graham, the new Cannonball House director, had already caught a ride back to the War of 1812 Symposium in Easton. With the historic property still buttoned up by police, she had nothing to do. Keane had enjoyed meeting her and hoped that their paths would cross again soon. He sensed a spark of something there that went beyond mere professionalism, but it made Keane feel more guilty than excited. Maybe it would be best if they didn't meet again anytime soon. The thought of a woman in his life other than Amanda felt like betrayal.

He crossed the Chesapeake Bay Bridge, admiring the fantastic view of the broad blue water, and was soon navigating traffic on the Western Shore. He got on I-295 into the city because that route avoided all of the traffic lights on Route 50.

The Corvette looked fast and had loads of style, not to mention a robust V-8 engine, but it lacked most of the comforts drivers now took for granted, such as functioning air conditioning, heated seats, and a Bluetooth connection.

Keane stuck to the slow lane and drove near the speed limit, letting the modern road warriors in their high-tech Mercedes, Acuras, and even Buicks, zip past him. He preferred his other vehicle on trips such as this, but there hadn't been time to switch, so his Lincoln SUV was sitting in the garage at World's End.

He listened to classic rock on the FM radio. The news came on at the top of the hour and he heard a brief mention of the St.

Michaels murder, mainly for the novelty of having taken place in the Cannonball House, and the fact that the murder victim, Bob Lindermann, had been a librarian at the Enoch Pratt Library in Baltimore. He could hear the amusement in the announcer's voice. *A murdered librarian. What was the world coming to? Did someone have to pay one too many overdue fines?*

Most of the news was about the president speaking that day at the Conservatives For America conference. That was going to cause some traffic headaches as well, but fortunately for Keane, the conference was at National Harbor, just to the south of downtown. It wouldn't be a problem for Keane. He changed the channel until he found more music.

The busy highway seemed worlds and even dimensions away from what he had experienced the previous night at the Cannonball House. Some might say that he had seen a ghost, but Keane preferred the term *apparition*. Who had the boy been? Why had he pointed to the stars? What was that all about?

He was still wondering about that when he turned onto Constitution Avenue.

The grandeur of Washington never failed to impress him. He passed the soaring white dome of the Capitol, finally completed in 1866. There in the distance stood the Washington Monument. Just to the right of the monument was the new Smithsonian Museum of African-American history. To Keane's eye, the dark brown structure resembled the brooding hulk of a slave ship, a stark reminder of America's darker past.

On his right, he drove past the Smithsonian Museum of American History. Nearly four million people visited there each year. That was roughly the population of Oregon, Oklahoma, or Connecticut. Take your pick. Seen another way, it was the combined population of Delaware, Rhode Island, and Montana. One of the great benefits of the Smithsonian was that there was no entrance fee. In recent years, the Smithsonian had worked to bring traveling exhibits to those who could not make the trip to Washington to see its treasures. Keane had seen one such exhibit, focused on George Washington and colonial medicine, not long ago at his county library and found it wonderful.

He turned right, and then right again onto Pennsylvania Avenue. The Smithsonian administrative staff had their own parking area, accessed by a narrow, unmarked entrance. Fortunately, Keane had visited once or twice before. He pulled the Corvette into a visitor parking slot.

No sooner had he entered the building, then he was whisked into the director's office.

Biesty came around from behind his desk to greet Keane. There was no smile, however, on the former astronaut's face. Biesty had flown on a couple of Space Shuttle missions, and after leaving the Air Force had gone into museum administration to pursue his second love, which was history. For a dozen years, he had directed the Indiana State Museum in Indianapolis. He had only occupied the Smithsonian post for a couple of years. Each of the Smithsonian's museums had its own director, with an overall director of the individual museum leaders. Clearly, it was no small task to oversee a museum that hosted so many visitors each year and safeguarded the crown jewels of American history.

It was no wonder that Biesty appeared careworn today. However, the former astronaut still looked trim and fit, despite his white hair. His grip on Keane's hand was quite strong, and he did not immediately let go.

"I'm so glad that you could be here on short notice, Franklin," Biesty said. "I hope that you can help us."

"If I can, I certainly shall."

Biesty finally smiled, and then released his grip on Keane's hand. He gestured at a sitting area with a love seat and two compact leather chairs in a modern style. Keane was familiar enough with expensive furniture to suspect that each chair had cost several thousand dollars. It was a reminder that the Smithsonian had very deep pockets.

An assistant poked her head through the door, which prompted Biesty to ask, "Franklin, can we get you anything? Coffee? Tea?"

"No, thank you."

The assistant receded and shut the door firmly behind her. Keane had not expected a one-on-one meeting.

"I hope you don't mind that I went through Charlene to see if we could officially borrow you from GAPS," Biesty began.

"Proper channels," Keane said.

"I understand that you have been busy over on the Eastern Shore."

"We had an incident at an historic property that GAPS is consulting on," Keane said. "Actually, incident isn't the right word, I'm afraid. Someone was murdered."

"Bob Lindermann. So I heard. That's why I got in touch with you. Unfortunately, our problems may be related."

"Oh?" Keane did not see the connection. He waited for Biesty to explain.

Biesty tugged at the creases in his trousers. He seemed very agitated for a man who had once piloted the space shuttle two hundred miles above the planet. "The thing of it is, one of our assistant curators was killed in a mugging last week in Rock Creek Park."

Keane raised an eyebrow. The park on the outskirts of Washington had become infamous for several high profile murders and disappearances. He had not heard anything about the death of an assistant curator at the Smithsonian, which likely meant that the curator was a low man on the totem pole. The Smithsonian had a handful of curators and legions of assistant curators. Being an assistant curator was a bit like being vice president of a bank. The title sounded impressive, but you didn't have the keys to the bank vault.

Keane filled in the blanks. "Let me guess. Lindermann and your assistant curator had been working on a project together."

Biesty nodded. "Exactly. It's important to keep in mind that this project was on their own time and that it had nothing to do with the Smithsonian. Everyone in historical circles knew who Lindermann was, and consequently, most people steered clear of him. He was a professional librarian, but he wasn't seen as a professional historian. He was seen more like an author of one those historical picture books that are sold in tourist shops. Nonetheless, he had quite a reputation as a myth buster, a bubble burster. I think he delighted in the power it gave him in certain circles, actually, even if it made him unpopular."

"Do you think that was enough for someone to kill him? And kill your assistant curator as well?" Keane shook his head. "It's doubtful. In any case, you should be telling all this to the police."

"Oh, I have," Biesty said. "I've shared everything we know with the FBI."

"The FBI? How did the FBI get involved?"

"They are involved as of this morning," Biesty said.

Keane wondered why Charlene hadn't filled him in on that much. He worried that the rift between them was even wider than he had thought.

"Well, I will help in any way possible. GAPS will help in any way. But I have to say, Roger, that if the FBI is involved then I don't see how I can be of much help."

"What I want—what the Smithsonian wants—is for you to conduct a parallel investigation. The FBI is good at criminal investigations, but what we also need is an outside person who can see things from a historian's perspective. Details that the FBI might miss."

Keane was taken aback. The death of the assistant curator,

the murder of Bob Lindermann—it all seemed suddenly far over Keane's head. In his experience, law enforcement officials did not appreciate outsiders second-guessing them. They saw it as stepping on their toes.

Keane stood up. He was starting to think that this trip to Washington had been a waste of his time. Still, there might be an hour or two left in the day to take a stroll through the museum itself, something he had not done in the last couple of years.

"I appreciate your faith in me, Roger. Really I do. But if the FBI is involved, I would say that all of your bases are covered here. I'm sure that in the end, the people responsible for these homicides will be brought to justice."

Biesty remained seated. He looked up at Keane with an almost pleading look on his face. The former astronaut now looked positively ashen. Depleted. "There's more."

12

"What I am telling you now is absolutely confidential. The FBI knows, and that's about it right now, except for a few trusted staff members." Biesty looked at Keane intently. "Do I have your absolute confidence?"

"I wouldn't be here otherwise."

"Of course, I know that you had security clearance up until—"

Keane stirred uncomfortably on the expensive leather chair. He had quietly received Secret clearance a few years back for a GAPS project at the vice president's home at Number One Observatory Circle, located on the grounds of the United States Naval Observatory. Biesty had been checking up on him. Or perhaps Charlene had volunteered that information when she volunteered *him*.

The Secret clearance wasn't as impressive as it sounded; thousands of government employees and contractors in the DC area had at least that level of security clearance. Biesty himself surely once had Secret clearance as an astronaut.

Top Secret clearance was much rarer. Although he had

never been charged in Amanda's death, the investigation had disqualified him from renewal of Secret clearance at the time.

"I was demoted to a Public Trust Designee," Keane said wryly. "Basically, that means I can review documents in the National Archives without an archivist being present. Anyhow, for both our sakes, I hope that there aren't any state secrets involved."

Biesty nodded blankly, as if Keane's attempt at humor was not registering. "That's fine," Biesty said. "I just need to be able to tell the FBI that you have been vetted."

Keane leaned forward. "Roger, what is going on here?"

The former astronaut sighed, seeming to have come to some resolution. "Yesterday, we had a small incident here. What we *thought* was a small incident. Two incidents, as it turns out."

"Go on."

"First, there was a small fire in the American Democracy exhibit. It was deliberately set, although we weren't aware of that at the time. Our security people responded immediately. The fire alarm sounded, obviously, and the museum was evacuated as a precaution."

"This sounds like some kind of diversion."

"Well, that seems obvious in hindsight," Biesty snapped. It took him a moment to regain his composure before going on. "Suddenly, our security team was overwhelmed, which is where things got sloppy, as we used to say in the astronaut business. At any given time, several hundred people are visiting this museum, if not several thousand. You can imagine that things quickly became chaotic."

Keane nodded.

"A fire truck pulled up almost immediately, literally out front of the entrance doors. A team of firefighters rushed in, wearing equipment, breathing apparatus, the whole nine yards. So much was going on that no one paid them any attention. I mean, they *looked* like firefighters."

"Let me guess. They weren't actually firefighters."

"They made their way to the Star-Spangled Banner exhibit hall."

Keane stared. "But surely, the flag itself was sealed off."

Keane knew that the flag, as one of America's most precious symbols, inhabited a hermetically sealed room where it would be safe from anything other than a raging fire, or perhaps a bomb explosion.

"They had the access codes."

"The assistant curator's codes," Keane guessed. "The one who died in the mugging at Rock Creek State Park."

"I know they should have been changed. It was an oversight. Simply put, no one made the connection between a seemingly random mugging and a security risk at the Smithsonian."

"Once they had access to the flag, what did they do?"

Biesty sighed. "The firefighters were seen carrying out a large canvas bag. It appeared to be some sort of firefighting gear. I don't know, maybe spare hoses or something. The next thing anyone knew, the fire truck was gone."

"Roger, are you saying what I think you are?"

Biesty nodded, looking grave. "The Star-Spangled Banner has been stolen."

* * *

FOR THE SECOND TIME, Keane stood. His head was spinning. It was all too much to fathom. Mentally, he cycled through what he knew. The Star-Spangled Banner had been stolen. Lindermann and an assistant curator were dead. The FBI was investigating.

"Why hasn't this been all over the news, for God's sake?"

"We're trying to keep this quiet for now. At least, for as long as we can. That's the advice we received from the FBI."

Keane shook his head. "This is way out of my league, Roger. I would say that it is in capable hands with the FBI."

"There is no one who knows more about this subject than you do. Not to mention that you have a family connection with the flag and the National Anthem."

"I'm sorry. I just can't proceed with this."

"Sit down," Biesty snapped, suddenly in the pilot's seat once again. "There's something else you need to know."

Keane remained standing. He did not much appreciate Biesty's tone, or the fact that this was Biesty's problem, and now he was drawing Keane into it.

"Haven't you told me enough?" Keane demanded. "I can't imagine that there could possibly be anything more."

But Keane sat. He would at least hear Biesty out.

"As I said before, our assistant curator and Lindermann were working together on a project that concerned the Star-Spangled Banner."

Keane's mind raced ahead. "It seems likely that they were either part of this plot, or that they somehow got wind of it. They found themselves in the wrong place at the wrong time, so to speak."

"I've read some of the emails they exchanged. Lindermann and Galarza thought that they had found the missing star."

Keane snorted in disbelief. For more than 175 years, even long before the flag had come into the care of the Smithsonian, one of the Star-Spangled Banner's fifteen stars had been missing. The two-foot-wide star appeared to have been ripped or cut away at some point, leaving a gaping hole in the blue field that extended into the stripes themselves. Who had taken the star, and where it had gone, remained one of American history's great mysteries. For some, the legend of the star had even become a kind of holy grail leading to all sorts of archival quests.

Theories abounded about the fate of the lost star. Most of

these were based on legend and rumor. But an assistant curator at the Smithsonian and a research librarian for the Enoch Pratt had not been crackpots. People hadn't liked Lindermann, but his research was always solid. Had these two historians stumbled onto the truth?

Keane wasn't so sure. "Whatever Lindermann and Galarza thought that they had found, that star is long gone," Keane said.

"Look, you're right that the FBI is good at criminal investigations. Hell, they can probably look at some satellite surveillance video and figure out where the fire truck went. But they don't have any expertise with this topic. That's where you come in."

Keane sighed. He was preparing to leave Biesty's office again, this time for good. The story of the missing star was intriguing, but he really wasn't qualified to unravel a mystery in the present.

That's when he happened to notice a large framed photograph behind Biesty's desk. Given the museum director's background as an astronaut, it was no surprise that he had a photograph taken from what must have been a window of the space shuttle, with the rim of the earth visible, and beyond it loomed the star-flecked blackness of space.

Stars. Keane thought again of his strange experience the night before. The apparition of the boy had led him outside and pointed at the night sky. But not just at the sky or the stars, but at a single star.

A chill ran through Keane.

"All right," he heard himself say. "I'll do it."

13

Inside the mirrored elevator carrying him to the ballroom level of the hotel, Charles Montgomery did not bother to study his reflection. He felt confident in his appearance. Instead, his thoughts focused on the key points he intended to make during his speech at the Conservatives For America conference downstairs.

He was having some trouble concentrating, however, because he was still buzzing from the mission that he and his men had pulled off at the Smithsonian the previous day. They had done the impossible.

Incredibly, seizing the Star-Spangled Banner had been far easier than he expected. Keeping it to themselves was turning out to be the hard part. In a few days—on the 14th of September, the anniversary of the Battle of Baltimore that used to be known as Defender's Day—the entire nation was going to know what he and his team had done. Until then, they would have to keep quiet. Much to his surprise, there had been nothing in the news so far, which made their task easier.

Some might call what Montgomery had planned an act of brazen domestic terrorism. The colonel preferred to see it as an act of patriotism. It would be a wakeup call for America. As far as he could tell, most Americans had been sleepwalking through the past decade as the nation, and the Western world, degraded around them. He wanted to remind them of what was important.

Lost in thought, Montgomery stared at his reflection without really seeing it. He had silver hair cut short and blue eyes. His good looks were somewhat marred, or perhaps made more interesting, due to a slight ptosis of the right eye, likely brought on by firing heavy caliber weapons in his Army days. At five foot ten, he was neither short nor tall, but he was what used to be called "well made," with a perfectly proportioned body. He kept fit with daily workouts. His compound on Maryland's Eastern Shore had a state-of-the-art gym.

He had left the room impeccably dressed in a Pierre Cardin suit with a United States flag pin in the lapel and a two-hundred-dollar silk tie by Hermes that nicely complemented the color of his eyes. On his left hand, he wore a simple gold wedding band and a Hamilton watch. His twelve-hundred-dollar shoes shined. While he owned several such suits and ties and shoes—along with custom-tailored shirts—he did not vary much from that particular style. He joked that it was his modern-day suit of armor.

He might have been happier wearing an actual suit of armor if this had been, say, the court of Edward I and not the CFA conference. Deep down, he was disappointed to live in an age in which men did not wear swords, or revolvers on their hip, at the very least. Keeping one's weapons at hand prompted more gentlemanly conduct. Being armed with a smartphone was not quite the same.

At heart he was an outdoorsy, military man, having served long years in the Army, although he had spent most of his career shining a chair. He would have been perfectly at home getting off the elevator in fatigues or work boots and jeans.

However, the well-dressed man who stepped off the elevator looked as if he was ready for his thirty-second sound bite. Which he was.

He emerged into an elegant marble hallway. Soldiers with machine guns stood on guard, owing to the fact that the president of the United States was slated to speak later that day. Montgomery was unarmed, and he was no longer an active-duty Army officer; he was not sure if the presence of the soldiers made him feel safer, or more vulnerable. There was a fine line these days between security and oppression.

Several people approached him. By the time he had walked 20 feet, half a dozen people were walking alongside, struggling to keep up with his fast pace. When Montgomery went anywhere, he went there in a hurry. Five men were clearly ex-military, younger than Montgomery. They were the sort of young men eager to look good in his eyes. The sixth man was Blister, who was a bit older and much bigger than any of the others. These six were his closest men, and they had participated in the mission at the Smithsonian. Completing the group was a blonde woman with a stern expression, carrying a tablet device with an air of authority.

"Are we ready, or what?" he asked them.

"Yes, sir!" several responded, as if they'd been on the drill field instead of this fancy hotel hallway.

The woman waited until the *hooah* died down and said, "Fifteen minutes. Cutting it close. Remember, stick to your talking points."

Montgomery picked up the pace.

They made their way not through the main entrance, but through the speaker's entrance that required passing through several utility areas and stepping over thick electrical cables taped to the floor. Security people along the way stopped others to see their credentials, but only nodded at him; Montgomery was a recognizable figure.

Still, Montgomery had no illusions about his role. He was on the periphery of national politics. With any luck, his role would change soon and he could seize the spotlight.

In so many words today, for those who bothered to listen instead of networking, he would make it clear that his goal was to get back to American values circa 1820, when Andrew Jackson was president, or maybe the 1950s or the 1980s. Golden eras for America that should inspire the future.

There were low points as well that he would touch upon. The seventies. The eight lost years under Obama, or roughly three percent of the entire timeline of the United States. He was ambivalent about Kennedy. A Democrat and a Catholic, it was true, but a man with vision and American values. The colonel was willing to agree to disagree with a good man.

Montgomery understood that his allotted time on stage was just filling up another slot before the main event today, which would be the president's speech. Nobody was going to pay much attention to what he said. That was OK, at least for now. In the next few days, he would be doing something far more important than making a speech on the conference floor. He would be getting America's attention. Waking Americans out of their slumber.

His people had been doing some polls ... it wasn't even out of the question that Montgomery might run for office. *Senator* Montgomery had a nice ring to it. But first, he needed to stand out by being a voice of reason during a national crisis of conscience.

A crisis that he would create. A discussion that he would lead.

He was about to change America's future.

By destroying a symbol of its past.

14

K eane left Biesty's office, his head reeling. Through the administrative offices, he was able to access the floor of the museum itself. He popped out through an unmarked door onto the museum floor.

Even though it was a weekday, the museum was quite crowded. Some of the visitors spoke in foreign languages, while others were clearly Americans, right down to their flannel shirts and blue jeans. The very young mingled with the very old, and yet a sense of wonder and discovery was evident in the faces of every generation and nationality. The Smithsonian exhibits created a wondrous melting pot by appealing to a shared sense of curiosity. *Sumus omnibus hominibus,* Keane thought. *We are all human.*

Keane descended to the first floor, which housed the Star-Spangled Banner in its own wing. He could still remember, as a boy, coming to visit the flag when it hung in the museum entrance. For a few minutes each hour, the flag was revealed as the National Anthem played over tinny loudspeakers. Unfortunately, that practice had, for decades, exposed the flag to humidity and pollutants. In the early 2000s, a project had begun to stabilize the flag for future generations. The flag was taken down and moved to its current home.

Keane had to admit that the new exhibit was quite moving. The low lighting created a sense of mystery. The National Anthem playing gently in the background added to the sense of awe and history. It honored the Star-Spangled Banner in a way that the old display in the museum entrance never could. Many visitors now found the sight of the Star-Spangled Banner to be an almost religious experience.

Keane approached the Star-Spangled Banner exhibit hall, but saw that it had been closed off. A small sign announced that this area was undergoing repairs. There was definitely nothing that shouted, "The flag has been stolen!"

Biesty had stated that the Smithsonian planned to keep the theft quiet for as long as possible, perhaps even until the Star-Spangled Banner was back in its hallowed hall. Keane wasn't so sure—it was hard to keep a tight lid on a secret that large.

As Keane watched, a couple approached the sign, read it, and moved on, though their body language indicated that they were disappointed. For those who had traveled all the way from Montana or Nevada or Louisiana, a trip to the Smithsonian and a glimpse of the Star-Spangled Banner was a once-in-a-lifetime experience.

Until he saw for himself that the exhibit was closed, he might almost have thought that this was some elaborate practical joke, despite the fact that Biesty had been so genuinely distraught. Unfortunately, the theft of one of America's greatest symbols was all too real. Keane realized that he felt deeply affected by the loss of the flag. He supposed that the legend and lore of the Star-Spangled Banner were inherent to every American, but for Keane it went even deeper. Considering that Francis Scott Key had been his ancestor, you might say that the Star-Spangled Banner was somehow part of Keane's DNA.

The Star-Spangled Banner was a powerful symbol. It was

truly an American icon. Now it was missing. And it was his job to help find it.

* * *

KEANE CHECKED into the Willard Hotel on what he hoped would be the Smithsonian's dime. He would certainly submit it as an expense later. As one of Washington's most historic and deluxe hotels, the price of a night's stay in the Willard was enough to give even a rich man pause.

As opulent as the Willard might be, he nonetheless thought wistfully of World's End, his home on the Sassafras River on Maryland's Eastern Shore. Between the War of 1812 Symposium in Easton and now this stay in Washington, he already felt that he had been away from home too long.

His job with GAPS required a fair amount of travel, to the point that he was beginning to think that hell might involve being relegated for eternity to a never-ending series of chain hotel rooms.

Fortunately, the Willard was no chain hotel, and the thought of the long drive home, mostly in rush hour traffic, was not appealing. He would only have had to return in the morning to begin his shadow investigation.

Keane had been on the receiving end of a criminal investigation after Amanda's death, so he had too-recent knowledge of how the police did their work. Still, he had no illusions about being a police officer, and certainly was not an FBI agent. He had no official standing, other than Biesty's request. He did know just a thing or two about research, thanks to his role as a senior field officer for GAPS.

He opted for dinner at the Willard's elegant bar, enjoying the seared scallops with red bliss potatoes and a glass of Domaine Huet's 2009 Le Haut-Lieu Demi-Sec Vouvray in almost the exact spot where the likes of Abraham Lincoln and

Ulysses S. Grant had once dined. He could not detect any real aura of the past here, however. The bar was too noisy and modern, not at all like the haunting atmosphere of the darkened Cannonball House in St. Michaels.

Back in his room, he took out his MacBook and began his background research. He had found that almost everything useful about a police investigation was already online. He used his own secure hotspot to do the research.

He spent the evening learning what he could about the deceased Smithsonian assistant curator. Very quickly, he determined that other than the staff listing and a few brief articles about the fatal mugging, there wasn't much online about Galarza. He had no social media presence. No papers or professional presentations. Galarza had apparently been content to work quietly, in the background, as a capable technician. Nothing suggested that he had been working on a project with Lindermann as sensational as discovering the lost star from the Star-Spangled Banner. Had Galarza been a partner in Lindermann's brand of historical myth busting? From what Keane had read so far, it seemed unlikely. Like as not, Lindermann had needed a fabrics expert to analyze the material, and Galarza had fit the bill.

Even the news article about the mugging lacked details. News organizations tended to include every little detail, so he suspected that in this case, there hadn't been any in the police report.

Galarza had gone for a walk in Rock Creek Park, which he did each Saturday. His body had been found in a secluded wooded area. Galarza had been shot in the chest. His wallet was gone, and the news article had included the prurient detail that his pants were down around his knees. Between the lines, this seemed to infer that the murder was some sort of tryst gone wrong, perhaps involving a male prostitute, considering that Galarza's wallet was missing.

Now that Keane knew Galarza had somehow been involved in the theft of the Star-Spangled Banner, he wasn't so sure that the shooting was all that it appeared to be.

He found a brief obituary online. Parents deceased. No ex-wives or significant others. Galarza had a brother in California and a sister in Ohio. A handful of nieces and nephews. The lack of family in the area wasn't all that surprising. DC tended to be a place where people ended up, but weren't really from. Keane found the obituary depressing; surely Galarza had been more than the sum of these brief paragraphs.

Around midnight, Keane undressed and tumbled into bed, not much wiser for his research. On the face of it, Esteban Galarza had died in a random mugging, or possibly in a sordid tryst. And yet, as he fell asleep, Keane had a nagging suspicion that this assistant curator had somehow gotten mixed up in something else entirely that had gotten him killed.

15

I n the morning, Keane returned to the Smithsonian for a meeting with the chief curator of the Star-Spangled Banner restoration project, Lillian S. Fournier, who had been Esteban Galarza's supervisor. Director Biesty had already cleared the way for the meeting, so Keane was expected.

Fournier's office was not as grand as the director's and it was an actual workspace overflowing with projects, spread out like the offerings at a garage sale. Plastic tubs balanced precariously on various worktables, and Keane spotted a microscope surrounded by teetering piles of three-ring binders. She was a working curator, after all, right down to a white lab coat and no-nonsense eyeglasses with heavy, black plastic frames.

"Doctor Keane," she said formally, but with a smile. "How nice to meet you, even if it's not under the best of circumstances."

"Do you mean—"

Fournier got up and walked over to shut the door to ensure privacy, before returning to her desk. Once she was seated again, she said, "I know all about the flag. How could I not? I *am* the chief curator for the Star-Spangled Banner project." She had a direct way of speaking that made Keane like her immediately. "You should also know that I don't agree with Biesty that we should keep this quiet long enough to give the FBI a head start. This is a case where publicity would be good. Someone, somewhere, may know something. What I want to know is, what does Director Biesty think you can do?"

Keane smiled wryly. "I asked him the same thing. But he was insistent."

"I told him this morning that I would give him seventy-two hours," she said, a dead-serious expression on her face. "That's it. At that time, I am alerting the news agencies."

"What did he say to that? Surely, there would be some repercussions if you went against his wishes."

"There's nothing he can do about it. Once this gets out, he's the one who had better be worried about keeping his job. Not me."

Keane didn't want to be drawn into a bureaucratic power struggle. He shifted gears. "Why would anyone take the flag?" he asked.

"Maybe they plan to sell it on eBay. Did you know that one of Einstein's letters recently brought more than three million dollars?"

"I saw something about that. But wouldn't the flag have been damaged in the process of stealing it?"

Fournier shook her head emphatically. "You might think that the flag is fragile, but she's actually made from quite resilient fabric, keeping in mind that she is two hundred years old. Don't forget that the Star-Spangled Banner used to hang outside on the original Smithsonian castle, here on the National Mall. She flew in battle, for goodness sake. She's no Fourth of July throwaway, like what people wave at parades. Short of her being set on fire, I'm not that worried about the flag being damaged."

Keane noticed that as Doctor Fournier grew more

passionate about describing the flag, she had given the Star-Spangled Banner a feminine pronoun. He smiled. "Just like an old house; she's sturdier than she looks."

"Exactly."

"I suppose Director Biesty told you that I would be by to ask about Esteban?"

"He was our leading expert in his field of nineteenth-century fabrics." She sighed. "Poor Esteban. He deserved better. What was on the news about his pants being down around his ankles or whatever ... ugh, that was awful. It was more than anyone needed to know. Think of his poor family. Besides, I don't believe it."

Keane raised an eyebrow. "Oh?"

"Do I honestly think that Esteban met someone in the woods for sex?" She shook her head. "Maybe he was forced at gunpoint to do it, and then killed. Raped, in a sense, if you can call it that. Who knows? It's a crazy world."

"It is, indeed," Keane agreed. "But why do you think your assistant curator wasn't involved in some kind of tryst gone wrong?"

"Let me just make it clear that I could care less about some-one's sexual preferences," she said primly. "This is simply an observation, but I would have said that Esteban was not attracted to men ... or to women. He was kind of, well, sexless, actually. There are people like that, you know. Esteban wanted to be alone with his fabrics and his research. If you were to imagine a celibate monk working diligently in his tower, that's the picture I would paint of Esteban."

Keane knew the type from his own work. Many researchers were so good at their work precisely because they were so with-drawn from the kind of daily distractions that occupied the rest of us. It was the history field's equivalent of a policy wonk.

"Would you mind if I had a look at his work area?"

"That seems to be as good of a starting point as any," Doctor

Fournier agreed. "I should tell you, however, that the FBI has already been through his things."

"Of course," Keane said. "But I think it would be a good idea for me to at least see his desk, to get more of a feel for who he was and how he worked."

They left her office and entered the hallway, which was wide enough that it had been pressed into service for more storage. Cheap plastic shelves and cardboard boxes lined the sides. Somewhere among the clutter, Keane was sure, lurked a fire code violation. Doorways off this corridor led to various departments. Galarza had worked in a large room with several other researchers.

As an assistant curator, Galarza had been assigned a cramped space that was basically a cubicle created by fabric-covered panels. A desk, chair, and a section of particle-board bookcases filled the space. There was no door; the cubicle was open to those surrounding it, and Galarza had positioned his chair so that his back would be to the opening.

Except for a couple of succulents and a souvenir mug from Niagara Falls filled with pencils and pens, the desk itself was mostly bare. A wall calendar featured historic flags. The flag for September coincided with the green-and-cream banner emblazoned with a harp, flown by the Irish Brigade at the bloody Battle of Antietam.

"I've been watering the plants," she said. "I'll probably move them to my office."

The bookcase contained mostly reference works, although the top row held some popular titles, such as a guidebook to hiking trails in the Washington, DC, region. Maybe it had not been out of character at all for Galarza to have gone for a walk at Rock Creek Park that fateful day. Someone else could have known that he'd be there.

"What about his emails?" Keane asked.

"The FBI went through those as well. Just to be clear, there was no invasion of privacy. This was a Smithsonian computer and our email account, so all employees know that there's no expectation of privacy." She hesitated. "I probably shouldn't admit this, but I took a look before the FBI got here. I would recognize some anomaly right away. Zilch. Nada. All work-related stuff."

Keane noticed a few books by talking heads from Fox News and other conservative media outlets. The most recent addition appeared to be a copy of *Proudly We Hail*, the new book by Charles Montgomery, one of those talking heads. Keane remembered that he had seen the title on the *New York Times* bestseller list, albeit briefly.

Keane pulled the book off the shelf and opened it. To his surprise, the flyleaf was inscribed, *To Steve, A true adherent of Anacreon! Keep up the good fight for history.* Montgomery's signature was quite elegant, like something out of the nineteenth century.

"To Steve?" he wondered aloud. He knew this was the anglicized version of Esteban. "Did anyone here ever call him that?"

"No, he was always Esteban to us."

Keane held up the book. "Do you mind if I keep this?"

Fournier glanced at the title and considered his request. "The FBI has already been through here, and the family emailed me back that we can donate Esteban's things. Although I have to say, Doctor Keane, that Charles Montgomery doesn't seem like your kind of author."

"The funny thing is, I wouldn't have thought he was Esteban's kind of author, either."

16

K eane's next stop was Rock Creek National Park, where Esteban Galarza had been murdered. After his visit to the Smithsonian, Keane was even more curious about Galarza. He had gotten some sense of the man from his office cubicle, mostly from his small collection of books, but Keane wanted to know more.

Fortunately, the park was just a fifteen-minute drive away, right up 12th Street. It would even be possible to take the Metro Red Line to the park, but Keane opted against that because D.C.'s mass transit system had been notoriously unreliable lately.

He pulled up a map on his phone, surprised at the sheer size of the sprawling park in the heart of the metropolitan area. Keane was curious; he had never actually been to the park. With school back in session and it being a weekday, the parking lot was mostly deserted. Surrounded by the dense woods, the vibe that he got from the place was nearly spooky. He picked up a brochure on half-day hikes at the Rock Creek Park Nature Center.

"Perhaps you can help me," he said to the man behind the

desk, and held up the brochure. Judging by his white hair, this was one of the retirees that the National Park Service favored hiring. They were generally quite helpful and knowledgeable, and they worked cheap—mainly to get out of the house.

"You're looking to take a hike?" the man asked, looking Keane up and down doubtfully. Keane wore dove gray trousers, a blue blazer, and shiny brown shoes. It was an outfit more appropriate to the halls of the Smithsonian than the woods.

"More of a walk, just to stretch my legs," Keane said. "Actually, I was hoping to visit the spot where a man was murdered here two weeks ago. Do you know anything about that?"

The elderly staffer seemed to find this amusing. "A murder. Ha! Which one?"

"You make it sound like a common occurrence."

"The park is surrounded by the DC metropolitan area, sir. We get a lot of muggings, things like that, and unfortunately, more than a few murders—or else the bodies get dumped here."

"This particular murder victim was named Esteban Galarza."

The National Park Service employee shook his head. "Doesn't ring a bell."

"If I were to pick a trail, which one do you think I would be most likely to be mugged on?"

The old man looked at him and waited a beat before answering. "You're serious, aren't you? Mister, I would say— take your pick!"

Keane thanked him and moved on. Looking over the park brochure, he opted for the Boulder Bridge Loop Hike, just because it sounded interesting. The trailhead was just a short drive away.

No sooner had he parked the Corvette, then he received a text from Biesty.

Anything?

Met with your curator. She was very helpful.
What's your plan?
I'm at Rock Creek Park now, where Galarza was killed.
Pretty sure the SSB isn't there.

Keane didn't bother to text back. Director Biesty seemed to think that Keane was wasting his time, but he had his own methods. Some answers might be found in dusty archives, and other answers might be bound among these oppressive woods. The jury was still out on whether or not this was a waste of time.

Before he put his phone away, Keane debated texting Elizabeth Graham. He had some professional pretext to do that, just to see how she was getting along at the 1812 Cannonball House in St. Michaels. However, the truth of the matter was that he simply wanted to get in touch with her again. Keane had his thumb on the phone, but he hesitated. Should he hold off until he had something legitimate to text about? He didn't want to seem annoying, or God forbid, stalkerish, and Keane wasn't entirely sure of the etiquette here. Between dating Amanda, their engagement, and their marriage, he had entirely missed the era of relationships via texting. He put the phone away.

He started up the trail, which was wide and heavily mulched where it led away from the parking area. He was looking for where the murder had taken place, but of course, he had no real idea where that had been.

Keane didn't know exactly what he was looking for, but he trusted his heightened senses to give him some clue that he was close. He was surprised to find that the entire woods emitted a sort of sinister aura. There was little air movement under the trees, and the thick vegetation filtered out the light, making the atmosphere gloomy and humid. Gnats swarmed his face and buzzed in his ears. He waved them away, but even more returned.

He had been a little surprised at Galarza's choice of a hiking spot, thinking that a real hiker would want to get out into the countryside. However, no sooner had the parking lot disappeared behind him than he was transported. The park seemed world's away from the congested city surrounding it. He could hear muted car horns in the distance and the muffled rush of traffic, but here on the wooded path he was isolated and alone. Truth be told, it was the perfect place for a mugging.

He walked on until the groomed trail became a dirt path. His shoes were less than ideal, but they were comfortable enough. At one point, the trail climbed high above the narrow park road barely visible through the trees below. At another spot, the tree roots stood out across the ground like varicose veins. He did not find it particularly scenic.

He would have enjoyed reading what Thoreau might have written about the place. Although he was revered as a naturalist and the author of *Walden*, Thoreau had a less well-known career as an entertaining travel writer who mixed thought-provoking insights with a modern vein of snark. The closest equivalent that he could think of was the late Anthony Bourdain.

Visited the woods at Rock Creek Park, Keane could imagine Thoreau writing. *There were some fine sights, I am sure, but I could not see them through the gnats.*

Half an hour later, Keane was no closer to figuring out where the murder had taken place.

His luck changed when he emerged from the thickest part of the woods—leaving the gnats behind—and arrived at the Boulder Bridge that spanned Rock Creek, a lively tributary of the Potomac River. The bridge appeared to have been pieced together out of river rock. The brochure stated that the bridge had been built in 1902 and was now on the National Register of Historic Places. It seemed that it was also popular as a lovers' arch, where couples had their pictures taken. After the dismal woods, Keane found it to be a peaceful and attractive setting.

Just beyond the Boulder Bridge, Keane spotted a man in the middle of taking photographs of something in the woods beyond, using a long-lensed camera on a tripod.

"Hello," Keane said, once the man looked up from the camera.

The man held up a hand. "Shh," he whispered. "Do you see it?"

Keane strained to see into the trees.

"Ten o'clock, about two feet off the ground in that mulberry bush."

He saw a flicker of movement, and then the bird was gone. "Oh no. I hope I didn't scare him off for you."

"Oh, you're fine. I got a nice shot of him. Besides, Connecticut Warblers are common enough in these woods."

Keane smiled. "A birdwatcher, I take it."

"Among other things. I write the birdwatching column for the Washington Post. If you look on their website, you just might happen to see a photo of that warbler."

"I will have to read your column so that I can learn something about birds. I'm afraid my bird identification abilities are limited to what's a robin and what's not. I certainly couldn't tell a thrush from a warbler," Keane said. "Do you come to this park often?"

"Almost every day. It's the closest place where I can find real birds that aren't pigeons. I've probably taken thousands of photographs here of birds, bridges, wildflowers. Whatever I can shoot basically.

"Then you must know these woods well," Keane said. "Maybe you can help me. I know this may sound strange, but I'm looking for where a man was found murdered two weeks ago."

"Are you a reporter? Maybe I should recognize you from the Post, but the birdwatching columnist doesn't exactly spend a lot of time in the newsroom."

"No, I'm not a reporter." Keane hesitated, wondering how to explain his odd request. He realized that he hadn't thought this through. "He was a colleague of mine, and he was killed here in a mugging."

"A colleague?"

"From the Smithsonian."

The photographer snapped his fingers. "Ah! I remember that one. I saw the yellow tape up and all that, so I was curious. I looked it up in the Post and saw that it was some poor fellow from the Smithsonian."

"Can you point me toward where that was?"

"I can do better than that," the photographer said, closing up his tripod. "I can take you there."

They started down the trail and the woods quickly closed in again.

"Gloomy," Keane said.

"You might get a thrush back in here, but the best bird-watching is actually around the bridge and the maintenance yard."

"The maintenance yard?"

"Lots of forage for visitors."

It took Keane a moment to realize the man meant birds, not human visitors.

The photograph pointed out the spot. "This is definitely it. I remember this sort of forked tree in particular. The crime scene tape went down this hill, deeper into the woods. I don't think it made it into the article, but it was somebody's dog that found the body."

Keane thanked the photographer, who moved on in pursuit of more birds. Left alone, he studied the surrounding trees. In this particular spot, the undergrowth grew thick. Keane went down the hill, forcing his way through the brush. He reached a slightly more open area where the leaves seemed disturbed. A scrap of yellow tape was still tied to a sapling.

His first impression was that this wouldn't have been the first choice for any sort of liaison. Nothing was inviting about this spot. No, this was where you would bring someone to kill them. It was a wonder that the body had turned up so quickly. They could thank the dog walker for that.

Keane stood among the trees, the stillness of the woods pressing in around him, trying to get some whiff of retrocognition to tell him what had happened here. It had suddenly become so quiet that the buzzing from the gnats was audible. He realized that even if Galarza had shouted for help, it was possible that no one could have heard him. A gunshot would have been much harder to ignore, but a shot fired from a small-caliber pistol would have been fairly muffled back in here. Or from a gun with a silencer, he thought.

He waited, hoping for something to come to him in this sinister place, but in the end, it was not his sixth sense that filled in the details, but his imagination. It was simple enough to picture how someone had forced Galarza off the trail at gunpoint, marched him back into the underbrush, and shot him. The sordid detail about his trousers being down around his knees would have been easy enough to arrange once the man was dead.

Again, the question was, why would someone kill Galarza?

None the wiser, he retraced his steps to the trail and then back to the car. Keane's shoes were now dusty, so he took a rag from the trunk of the Corvette and wiped them down. His hike had taken him no more than an hour, but his shirt was soaked through, so he dug his previous day's shirt out of his kit bag and put it on. Maybe Biesty had been right about him wasting his time. He hoped to have better luck at his next destination.

17

B y lunchtime, Keane was on the road to Baltimore in order to pay a visit to the Enoch Pratt Free Library, where Lindermann had worked. His preferred route between Washington and Baltimore was the heavily forested Baltimore-Washington Parkway, a throwback to an idyllic era when highway planners had thought that roads should be more scenic and connect motorists with nature.

Although the highway was thoroughly modernized and Keane whisked through at sixty miles per hour, he still found the uninterrupted sight of trees peaceful. The signage was the familiar brown-and-white of the National Park Service, which had jurisdiction over the parkway.

One drawback was that the parkway with its natural surroundings offered nowhere to eat, so after reaching Baltimore he stopped at a pub on Pratt Street for fish and chips, before heading on to the Enoch Pratt.

He was stopped at a traffic light when the driver of a car next to him rolled down his window and shouted, "Go O's!"

Keane gave him a thumbs up before the light turned green. It wasn't the first time that someone had seen his "OSAY" license plate and pegged him as an Orioles fan. When singing the National Anthem before the start of a game at nearby Camden Yards, the fans were famous for shouting "O!" when the song entered its rousing final line. Not only did the O stand for Orioles, but it was also a nod to the peculiar nasal way that "O" was pronounced in the local Baltimore accent. Keane wasn't much of a baseball fan, but he was a big National Anthem fan.

Keane parked the Corvette in a garage adjacent to the library and crossed Cathedral Street to enter the library. The Enoch Pratt Free Library bore the name of the city library system's original benefactor, a wealthy Baltimore merchant who had donated the equivalent of twenty-two million dollars to found the city library. In those early days, Andrew Carnegie had also donated substantially to the cause, enabling the magnificent structure to be built in 1933.

The Enoch Pratt Free Library remained the crown jewel of the entire state's library system. Architect Clyde N. Fritz had said that he intended to build a structure that was stately but friendly. To Keane's trained eye, the result was a timeless building that still served the public well, especially after a complete renovation in 2016.

Downstairs, the vast space was dotted with reference desks and public-use computers. The librarians here seemed mostly in their twenties and thirties, and most were women, although there were several uniformed security guards present as well. The usual population of homeless people lounged on benches or chairs. Officially, sleeping in the library wasn't allowed, but many of the homeless had their eyes closed. It was the one place where they could get a respite from life on the streets and feel just a little more human.

Keane's destination was on the second floor. On the landing at the top of the stairs, he passed an old card catalog on display, with a light shining down to illuminate it like a museum piece. The card catalog came from an era when beauty and function were blended into one. The catalog was made of oak, with brass detailing and handles on the rectangular drawers worn smooth by a hundred years of searches. Now, of course, no one needed a card catalog. There was barely a need for a library in which actual books were housed. Keane was glad that libraries were still around.

If the first floor was rather noisy, the research area upstairs still managed to maintain the hushed tones one traditionally expected of a library. No homeless people were evident. A few people sat at tables, open books in front of them, reading or taking notes on paper or on laptops.

Keane approached the reference desk and introduced himself to the librarians working there.

One was a woman in her forties with reddish hair and the nearly alabaster skin of someone who rarely braved the sunshine. Her name badge identified her as Lois. The other librarian was an African-American woman in her fifties whose face seemed dominated by heavy, red-framed eyeglasses and a scowl. Her name tag identified her as Mrs. Goins. The upstairs reference desk was intended for serious researchers and equally serious librarians.

"What can we help you with today?" Lois asked.

"I'm here to learn something about your colleague, Bob Lindermann."

"Poor Bob," Lois said, her helpful public face collapsing into sadness. "Murdered! I can't believe it."

Mrs. Goins shook her head. "What's the world coming to? I heard he was beaten to death with a cannonball."

Lois gasped.

Beaten to death with a cannonball? Keane never failed to be fascinated by how legends were born. He did not bother to inform Mrs. Goins that Lindermann had been shot, execution-style.

"Did he have any enemies to you know of?"

Mrs. Goins looked pointedly at him. "Are you a police officer?"

"No, ma'am, I'm not."

"Didn't think so. But who are you again, exactly, and what's your interest in our colleague?"

"My apologies. I should have introduced myself right away. My name is Franklin Scott Keane, and I am a senior field officer for the Great American Preservation Society." Quickly, Keane added an explanation for why he might be asking about the deceased librarian. "Unfortunately, Mister Lindermann was killed at the Cannonball House in St. Michaels, which is a property that GAPS is consulting on."

"I've heard of you," Mrs. Goins said, frowning at him. "And the last I heard, *you* were the one being investigated."

Keane didn't want to be drawn into that particular discussion. "Do you know anything about what he was researching?"

Both Lois and Mrs. Goins laughed.

"What *wasn't* Bob researching!" Lois said.

"That man was into everything," Mrs. Goins said, shaking her head. "Lois, do you remember how he dug up all that information about Barbara Frietchie? The good people of Frederick were not happy with him, I can tell you that!"

Keane knew that *Barbara Frietche* was the title of a famous poem by John Greeneaf Whittier, published in *The Atlantic* in 1863. The poem recounted how an old woman named Barbara Frietchie had defied Confederate troops marching through that Maryland city by flying the Union flag. Well into the twentieth century, when children still had to memorize poems for school, it had been one of the most familiar poems in the classroom. Her popular legend remained a tourist draw, although, as with the St. Michaels legend, there was little proof that any of the events in the poem had taken place.

"*Shoot if you must, this old gray head, but spare your country's flag, she said,*" Keane quoted.

Mrs. Goins nodded. "I think it was Bob they wanted to shoot, once he got through with that one."

"Oh, and what about the Snallygaster?" Lois asked.

Mrs. Goins nodded emphatically. "Yes, that was another good one!"

Keane was at a loss. "Snallygaster?"

"What, you mean you've never heard the legend of the Snallygaster?"

Keane had not.

"You see, there's this creature that's been seen for years down around Sykesville in Carroll County," Lois explained. "It's very wild down there in the Patapsco River valley. It's called the Hugg Thomas Wildlife Area. There are hundreds of acres of woods along the river."

Mrs. Goins interrupted. "Anyhow, for years and years, people have reported seeing a mysterious creature there."

"That was the legend, anyhow," Lois continued. "Bob researched it all and found that there were only one or two sightings, and those came about only after an article had appeared in the *Sykesville Herald*, the weekly newspaper, back in October 1965. Only it wasn't really an article—the reporter had written a spooky story to entertain readers for Halloween. He'd made up the whole Snallygaster business, but people took the article to be true, and what do you know, they started seeing the Snallygaster."

"Bob burst that bubble, too. Didn't win him any friends in Sykesville!"

"How was he to work worth?" Keane asked.

Lois and Mrs. Goins looked at each other, as if deciding how to answer that.

Finally, Mrs. Goins spoke up. "I never had any problem with Bob, but he was a strong flavor."

Keane smiled. "Licorice?"

Mrs. Goins made a face. "More like asparagus. Or brussels sprouts."

"The thing about Bob was that he didn't suffer fools," Lois said. "He was not interested in helping a high school student with a research paper, or even a college student, for that matter."

"Pardon my saying so, but wasn't that his job? He was a research librarian."

Lois shrugged. "Bob passed them on us. Now, if someone came in who needed help with real, actual research, maybe a graduate student or an author, he bent over backwards to help them. He enjoyed it, and he was good at it. Most of the time, honestly, he worked on his own projects."

"Liver and onions," Mrs. Goins said. "Hmm. Broccoli."

"I think I get the picture. Didn't you mind that he dumped the work on you?"

"How busy do we look, Mister Keane? Ever hear of Google?"

"I see your point."

"Now, Bob wasn't all bad, let me just be clear. You ought to ask Lois about that."

The red-headed woman blushed. "Well."

"I'll bet you've still got that key to his place, don't you?"

Lois turned an even deeper shade of red.

"Key?" Keane asked.

18

L indermann's condo was located on the fourth floor of
  what had once been a single-family home in Mount
Vernon, one of Baltimore's trendy neighborhoods. In addition
to being close to shops and restaurants, the condo also
happened to be within walking distance of the Enoch Pratt
Library. A modest condo such as Lindermann's sold for a
couple hundred thousand dollars, which was attainable even
on a librarian's salary.

Lois, who had been Lindermann's colleague and apparently
something more in the past, had agreed to give Keane the key
to take a look around, if it might help to catch the killer. She
told him to leave the key with the maintenance office when he
was done.

There was no elevator, so between climbing the stairs and
walking to work, the librarian must have been in fairly good
shape. Keane unlocked the door, and right away, he noticed two
things.

The first was that someone had been there before him.
Every drawer in the kitchen was open, with its contents spilled

on the floor. The same was true of the cabinets. The condo had an open floor plan, and the adjacent living area also had been rummaged, with the sofa and chair cushions strewn across the carpet, and in some cases, sliced open as if someone was searching for something.

The second thing Keane noticed was a fluffy gray cat, mewling in the kitchen beside his empty food and water dishes. Whoever had ransacked the condo hadn't harmed the cat, but had left the poor creature hungry and thirsty.

Keane stepped inside and shut the door.

"You poor thing," he said. "You must be starving. Let's see if we can find something for you."

Keane owned two dogs, which he much preferred to cats, but he couldn't abide seeing an animal suffer. Gingerly, he stepped around the broken plates and scattered cutlery. The contents of the cabinets had been pulled out, and he poked around until he found a can of cat food.

By now, the cat was rubbing frantically against his leg, and meowing insistently. Keane emptied the food into the cat's bowl, then refilled the water bowl from the tap and set it down. The cat ate ravenously.

He had gone to the apartment not looking for anything in particular, but only to get a better sense of who Lindermann had been. However, this was not the time or place to use his retrocognition abilities. Instead, he would rely on old-fashioned snooping.

Looking past the damage, it was apparent that the condo was surprisingly tasteful, although the exposed conduits and pipes meant to give the condo an urban loft feel were, in Keane's opinion, an unsightly distraction. The single bedroom contained floor-to-ceiling windows providing a view of the street below, and a full-view glass door led to a narrow balcony filled with potted plants and iron patio furniture. The balcony railing had been strung with festive Japanese lanterns. It would be quite a pleasant spot to enjoy a cup of coffee or a cocktail, and apparently, Lindermann had enjoyed entertaining on occasion. After giving him the key, the librarians had explained that he'd sometimes had people over. The man was known for his bombastic personality, but there seemed to have been a few people who didn't find him completely unbearable. His colleague, Lois, for starters.

How different Lindermann had been from Esteban Galarza, whom his co-workers had painted as a loner.

The bedroom had received the same treatment as the rest of the condo. The covers were torn off the bed, and the mattress had been shifted partially onto the floor so that someone could get at it with a knife. The search had been thorough. Was this the work of a burglar, or was it related to Lindermann's murder? What on earth had someone been looking for?

He felt something brush against his ankles and nearly jumped.

"Ah, there you are," he said to the cat. "Come to help?"

Keane now felt that he should be looking for something, too. But what? He did a cursory inspection of the debris on the floor and the ransacked closet.

He returned to the living room, with the cat in tow. Having fed the cat, he now seemed to have a new best friend.

Lindermann had a work area set up in one corner, with a good-sized desk made from reclaimed wood, a high-end Epson printer, and expensive Bose bookshelf speakers. Thieves could have gotten good money for those speakers, yet here they were.

What was missing was any sort of computer. Had the intruder taken that? Had Lindermann packed it to take to the War of 1812 symposium? That was a question that the police might be able to answer, but there was no way that he'd be getting that answer out of Detective Crawford.

The work area was neat and business-like, except for the fact that a pizza box sat in the middle of it. Whoever had ransacked Lindermann's place hadn't bothered with a stale pizza. Keane flicked the box open out of idle curiosity, wondering if Lindermann had been more of a pepperoni or Hawaiian pizza guy.

However, the box did not contain a pizza. Inside was a piece of battered fabric, yellow with age. Spread out, the scrap of fabric fit perfectly inside the pizza box.

The scrap was in the shape of a star.

Keane stared. The star was about two feet across, and clearly quite old. Though now faded, the star had once been a brilliant white. To anyone else, the star might have appeared to be just a decoration or old-fashioned oddity, to be tossed out in the trash along with the pizza box.

But Keane wasn't just anyone. He had spent most of a life-time studying history, with a particular interest in the War of 1812. He knew very well the legend of the lost star, the fifteenth star that disappeared from the Star-Spangled Banner sometime before the Civil War. Where it had gone, no one knew.

The Smithsonian director had intimated that Lindermann and Galazara had come across the star, but Keane had had his doubts. However, this scrap of fabric in Lindermann's condo appeared to have the correct dimensions and a patina of age. The puzzle pieces quickly fit together. *Was this the lost star?*

Keane gulped, and shut the lid.

If someone had, in fact, come to Lindermann's condo looking for the star, Keane decided that the last place they would look would be inside an old pizza box. Lindermann had likely used the box because it was a perfect fit. Perhaps unin-tentionally, it had become the ideal hiding place.

In the trash can beneath the desk was a jumble of brown wrapping paper and a packing slip. With a jolt, Keane saw that

Lindermann had bought the star on eBay. He stuck the packing slip in a pocket.

Keane left the box and went in search of something he had seen earlier. There it was, pulled out of the bedroom closet. A cat carrier.

The cat went in without much argument.

Keane walked out of the condo, shut the door behind him, and started down the four flights of stairs with the pizza box in one hand and the cat carrier in the other. He slipped the key into a slot at the maintenance office.

Out on the street, he nearly collided with a man who seemed to be waiting for him, or at least, waiting for someone, to walk out. The man's hair was shaved in the high-and-tight fashion favored by military types. He was a big man, even taller than Keane, and much broader through the shoulders. He would have been a match even for Beau.

"Who are you?" the man demanded.

"I beg your pardon?"

"Do you live here?"

Keane thought quickly. If someone had gone to the trouble of ransacking Lindermann's condo, it wouldn't be surprising if it was still being watched. He thought about running, but he wouldn't get very far dragging a cat and a pizza box.

Keane put a warm smile on his face. "You must be one of the neighbors. Dad told me how everyone in the building looks out for one another. I brought my father over a pizza, but he can't finish it. Care for a slice?"

The big man just stared, as if trying to make up his mind about Keane.

Keane lifted his other hand, which held the cat carrier. "Dad's cat needs to go to the vet for his shots."

To Keane's surprise, the big man smiled and peered more closely at the cat through the plastic grid on the front of the carrier. He made kissy noises at the cat.

"Your cat got a name?"

Keane grasped the first word that came to mind. "Star."

"Uh huh," the big man said, straightening up. "We've had some trouble lately with break-ins in the neighborhood."

"Well, thanks for keeping an eye out. Have a good evening."

Keane forced himself to walk away as normally as possible. His heart was hammering. He was fairly certain that he had just come face to face with whoever had ransacked Lindermann's condo.

He felt the big man's eyes on him every step of the way until he rounded the corner, as if he hadn't quite made up his mind to let Keane walk away. Keane was glad that he had been forced to park on a side street. He quickened his pace until he reached the car. The pizza box went into the Corvette's minuscule trunk. The cat carrier went on the passenger seat.

He turned onto St. Paul Street and drove toward the Inner Harbor area and the entrance to the interstate.

As he finally entered the harbor tunnel, he realized that he had just absconded with a dead man's cat.

And far more shocking than that, he now had what might have been lost for nearly two centuries, the missing star cut from the Star-Spangled Banner.

* * *

KEANE WAS HEADING up I-95 when he got a call from Elizabeth Graham. The Maryland House rest stop was coming up, so he pulled off to get coffee and call her back—a 1979 Corvette did not have a Bluetooth connection for a mobile phone. The cat had fussed part of the way, not so happy about riding in a car, but was now curled up and sleeping contentedly in the carrier beside him.

"This is Franklin. How are things there?" he asked, once she picked up.

"The Cannonball House is still closed," she said. "The police won't even let me in. That detective was there again and I tried to get some answers from him, but he was not very helpful."

"I don't think that he wants to hear from me, but I'll ask Charlene Dearborn to give him a call and put some pressure on."

"That would be awesome. I can't wait to get to work," Elizabeth said. "Listen, I did some more research into the attack on St. Michaels. I can't find any contemporary accounts stating that lanterns were hung in the trees to fool the British, although that doesn't mean it didn't happen."

Keane laughed. "It sounds as if you have already become an apologist for the legend behind the Town that Fooled the British."

"Well," she said. "We'll see about that. What I did find out was that three townspeople died in the bombardment. Those records are fairly definitive. Two of the men were older, members of the militia defending the town. It doesn't say how they died, though. But get this. Remember how you mentioned that ghost walk in town? The third person killed in the bombardment was a twelve-year-old boy named Tommy Tilghman. He was killed by a cannonball. Maybe that's who they're seeing on these ghost tours."

Keane felt a chill run through him. Had he seen the presence of Tommy Tilghman at the Cannonball House two nights ago?

"Interesting," he said. "When the Cannonball House does re-open, you will have some new material to share with visitors."

"What am I supposed to do until then?" she asked.

Keane thought about it. Elizabeth was obviously a capable and dedicated researcher. If she had a few days free until the Cannonball House re-opened, he could use some help researching the star that he had found in Lindermann's condo. However, it was not something he wanted to discuss over the phone. Maybe Elizabeth would be able to come up to World's End.

"How are you with cats?" he asked.

19

A s dusk settled over the countryside, Keane's headlights picked out the brick pillars that flanked the entrance to World's End. As always, it was with a great sense of relief that he turned into the lane.

The place wasn't called World's End without reason. The sunken lane meandered for two miles through woods and fields. In places, the ancient Osage orange trees had weaved together overhead to create a sort of tunnel that the Corvette passed through, like a time warp. Keane took it slow—try as they might, it was almost impossible to keep up with the road repairs. In places, the lane was pockmarked with stones, holes, and even tree roots. He and Beau had talked about paving the road and finally decided against it. The unpaved lane kept unwanted visitors out, and while it was inconvenient in the winter and through the rainy spring, the lane was part of what made World's End so special. Getting there was a journey.

Shapes flickered past him on the other side of the trees. Deer. Keane sometimes counted them as he drove in and out; it was not unusual to see fifty or sixty deer. As the twilight deepened, a beautiful red fox darted into the lane ahead, turned momentarily to glance at the car, and then disappeared into the hedge. Keane was already glad to be home; now his spirits lifted yet again at the sight of the fox. Sadly, foxes were becoming rare as coyotes moved into their Eastern Shore range, but the population seemed to be holding its own at World's End.

Finally, he rounded the last bend in the lane and passed between the long row of majestic sycamore trees leading to the house itself.

Located in southern Cecil County, World's End was a brick manor house built about 1740, during the property's heyday as a tidewater tobacco plantation. The plantation was located on a point of land that jutted into the Sassafras River. Long ago, the plantation master had owned a schooner that sailed from the wharf to England, returning with goods such as fine cloth and furniture. Some of the pieces had even survived more than two centuries in the manor house.

The property's European history originated in a land grant from Lord Baltimore in 1653 to a fur trader from nearby New Sweden—what was now known as Delaware. The trader must have developed a relationship with the Tockwoghs and Susquehannocks in the area, probably building a log trading post, now long gone. Back then, the river was known as the Tockwogh, after the large Native American village that had existed just upstream from World's End. English settlers had re-named it Sassafras, for the thick copses of the medicinal tree that grew along its banks.

Keane's grandfather had bought the place in 1970 after many years of abandonment. The lane was overgrown and nearly impassable. Keane had wanted a country getaway within a reasonable drive of Baltimore. The opening of Interstate 95 in 1963 had made the upper Eastern Shore more accessible. Still, the old man had gotten the place for a song.

Bats and field mice were the only occupants of the crumbling manor house back then. For all his faults, Jack Keane did have a sense of history, and instead of bulldozing the house—which sensible friends advised him to do—he'd had it restored from the foundation up. With any luck, the house might last another 200 years.

The ancient tobacco prize house had been rebuilt, as had the wharf on the Sassafras River. Beau kept his fishing boat tied up at the wharf now. Keane used to keep the sailboat there as well, but he had sold it not long after the investigation wrapped up. After what had taken place, he had no desire to go sailing again.

Keane parked near the boxwood garden and walked toward the house. In the distance, through the trees, he could just see the lights of Beau's house on the river.

Before he had taken a step, two massive shapes galloped toward him out of the dusk, then greeted him with excited barking. These were his Irish wolfhounds, Boru and Danu. Visitors sometimes mistook them for ponies.

He reached down to scratch their heads, but he did not have to reach far. When Boru lifted his head, his nose nearly brushed Keane's chin. If Boru had been able to stand on his hind legs, he would be more than seven feet tall.

"*Madra maith*," he said fondly in Irish. "Good dog."

His grandfather, a fanatic for all things Irish, had kept three or four of the beasts at one time, to the terror of any trespassers. Keane had kept the tradition going, but found that two of the massive dogs were enough to handle. One dog wasn't enough. Boru and Danu kept each other company.

"Meet your new friend," he said, lifting the cat carrier as high as he could above their heads. They sniffed curiously. From the interior of the carrier, Star emitted a nervous yowl. Keane laughed. "Don't worry. There's plenty of room here for everyone."

The door opened—technically, this was the back door,

overlooking the boxwood garden—framing the man who stood there in a rectangle of warm yellow light. Classical music drifted out. Debussey.

"We're out of bread and eggs," the old man in the doorway said by way of greeting. He had a distinctly English accent.

"You should have texted me," Keane said.

"And how would I do that?"

Keane smiled. "We'll survive the night somehow without a loaf of bread. It's good to be home. How are you, Ed?"

"Enjoying a quiet evening until now. Those dogs make a ruckus when they hear you driving in. You spoil them, you know."

"Have you had dinner?"

The old man waved a hand dismissively. He was rail-thin, with skin gone wrinkly and brittle, like crumpled up paper. Neither he nor Beau really knew how old Edward Kirby was. Since childhood, they had called him by his nickname, English Ed. More and more, Ed made cryptic references to events and things from another age, such as ration stamps, Churchill, Oleo, and MGBs. It was as if he was going back in time the older that he got.

He had taken up residence at World's End long before Keane or Beau. Their grandfather, who had begun life as a penniless Irish immigrant, took delight in having an English butler. Jack Keane had never cared whether or not English Ed did a lick of work around the mansion, or what he wore, unless there were dinner guests. In that case, English Ed was expected to appear at six o'clock, wearing his black morning coat and white gloves, to announce to guests in his poshest accent, "Dinner is served." He then put on quite a show in pouring wine and bossing around the maids hired for the night. These days, it was Keane and Beau who waited on the aged butler.

He handed English Ed the cat, and went into the kitchen to see what he could rustle up for them.

He paused for a moment, simply glad to be home, and looked out the window at the silhouette of the Corvette, trying not to think about the fact that, out in the trunk of the car, there could be a piece of the Star-Spangled Banner. He poured English Ed a glass of pinot noir, but skipped the wine himself; after dinner, he might have a small glass of cognac while he reflected on the day's events. The lost star wasn't going anywhere. Besides, he had found that sometimes, history and legends were better dealt with by light of day.

20

Keane was no Thomas Jefferson, who was said to have gone for a period of fifty years when the rising sun never caught him in bed, but he always woke earlier at World's End. Something about the country setting did not encourage sleeping in. Before sunrise, he went down and made coffee, then brought it outside and sat in the boxwood garden to listen to the birds wake up. After the noise of Washington and Baltimore, the utter quiet was welcome.

A few minutes later, he heard Beau's truck start, and the ancient Ford pickup soon came into sight, bouncing up the gravel road toward the manor house.

Keane held himself perfectly still to see if Beau would notice him. The two had been testing each other like that since boyhood, and old habits died hard.

Not much got past Beau, though. He saw Keane sitting there still as a statue in the morning gloom, rolled down the window, and pointed a thick finger and thumb at him like a gun.

"You'll have to do better than that, Cuz."

"Are the fish biting?" Keane called.

Beau laughed. "I don't know about the fish, but I've got a

nice charter on the hook. I've got to run down to Rock Hall to pick them up."

He gave Keane a wave, and drove on toward the wharf. A few minutes later, Keane heard the big diesel engine start on *Rascal*, Beau's 38-foot Chesapeake Bay deadrise. It was rockfish season, so Beau would be out on the water every day with a charter of fishermen who paid several hundred dollars. Keane knew for a fact that Beau could afford to go fishing whenever he wanted, anywhere in the world, but took pride in the fact that it was the charter business that paid for the boat and fuel. Like Keane himself, Beau believed in having a useful purpose. This wasn't the nineteenth-century, when the gentry who lived at World's End never considered doing a day's work.

Rascal left the wharf, and for a long way off Keane could hear the powerful diesel engine taking her out toward the Chesapeake. Then the silence and the birds returned. Keane finished his coffee and went back inside. He had work of his own.

*　*　*

GROWING UP, he and Beau had been more like brothers than cousins. They went everywhere together and did everything together. They had been lucky to live through some of their adventures. The r-shaped scar just below Keane's right cheekbone had come courtesy of his cousin, when the two boys had foolishly played war across the woods and fields using .22 rifles, seeing who could shoot closest to the other. Jack Keane normally took a "boys will be boys" view of such things, but the sight of his grandson's cheek laid open by a ricochet had prompted him to take away their guns for an entire year.

Despite the fact that there was plenty of space at World's End, they had even shared a bedroom. Keane still recalled fondly how they had stayed up late reading comics books by flashlight, long after their grandfather or English Ed had shouted at them to turn off the damn lights and go to sleep.

That all began to change once they were teenagers. Keane had always gravitated toward being more bookish and in high school he hadn't minded being assigned *Don Quixote* or having to write an essay on the causes of World War II. Sports had not interested him beyond the fencing club.

Just the opposite was true of Beau. He had been a standout in football, basketball, and baseball. As a good-looking jock, Beau had also been popular. He went through so many girl-friends that it was hard to keep track of their names, whereas Franklin barely had the courage to so much as talk to a girl. Most Friday and Saturday nights, Beau was out at a party, sometimes sneaking back early in the morning. Keane's big night out was catching a movie with a group of friends or reading *The Count of Monte Cristo*.

Their grandfather seemed to revel in Beau's exploits on and off the field. He loved a good hell-raiser, having been one himself. On the other hand, his bookish grandson Franklin left him mystified.

One summer night, Keane had let himself be talked into partying with Beau's group of popular kids.

"Come on," said Beau. "It'll be fun."

Even then, Keane might not have gone if it hadn't been for the fact that one of the group was Cindy Jensen, a girl whom he had a secret crush on.

"Come with us, Franklin," she had said, and that was all it took.

They piled into canoes with coolers and a boombox, then paddled across the cove to an empty beach, where they gathered driftwood and built a bonfire. Some of the kids stripped down to swim on that muggy summer night.

As it turned out, Beau's so-called fun came from trying to get his cousin drunk on cheap beer. But Keane had stubbornly refused more than two beers, much to Beau's disappointment.

"You are such a pussy," Beau scoffed.

Coming from his cousin, the name was like a physical blow. "What?"

"You heard me. I said you were a *pussy*."

Franklin retreated to the edge of the firelight and sulked. A summer thunderstorm had started to blow up, lightning flickering on the horizon. They scattered the bonfire and started back across the cove, laughing and whooping, just ahead of the storm.

Once they were safely back on shore, Cindy had put a hand to her mouth and exclaimed, "Oh no! I left my locket over there! I took it off to go swimming and hung it on that big driftwood tree. It might wash away in the storm!"

"Don't worry about it," Beau growled. "Your dad can buy you a whole truckload of jewelry."

"But you don't understand, Beau. That was a present from my grandmother. It's like a family heirloom. I can't just go out and buy a new one."

"I'll go back and get it," Franklin heard himself say.

"No way!" Beau protested. He was still holding a canoe paddle. "This storm is about to kick our asses!"

He wasn't exaggerating. The wind had picked up, whooshing through the dark trees. Now and then, a streak of lightning forked through the night sky to the west.

He knew that Beau was right. The smart thing to do was to get back to the house. But some part of Keane not only wanted to impress Cindy, but also to prove something to Beau.

"It's just a thunderstorm," Keane said, trying to sound nonchalant. "Anyhow, I'll be there and back before it hits."

Keane reached for the paddle in Beau's hand, meaning to take it from him and paddle one of the canoes across the cove.

But Beau wouldn't let go. Keane tugged harder, but there was no breaking Beau's grip.

"It's about to storm, Franklin."

"Fine," he said. "I'll swim."

The other kids jeered at him, until Keane shucked off his shirt and waded out into the water.

"Hey, come back!" someone shouted.

"Dude, this isn't cool! Look at that lightning!"

Keane ignored them and slogged out until the water was waist-high, then slid into the water and began to swim. Having grown up around boats and the water, and being long and lanky, he was a strong swimmer. He was soon out in deep water.

But the storm was coming on. Thunder clapped, and he felt the vibration along his entire body in the water.

Another ten minutes sooner, and he could have made it. But halfway across, the storm struck. Lightning snaked overhead, and in the flash, he saw that the calm surface of the cove had now erupted in whitecaps. The wind howled like a tornado.

His arms flailed at the frothy waves. He was halfway across, but he realized that he wasn't going to make it. He sucked in a big lungful of water, then another, and no matter how hard he kicked, he felt himself sinking into the dark water of the cove.

Keane was moments from drowning when strong hands suddenly grabbed him from above. He glimpsed Beau in another flash of lightning. Keane found himself being hauled into the canoe. He managed to get over the side without capsizing them both and lay in the belly of the canoe, sputtering, as the storm broke all around them. Beau kept the bow of the canoe pointed into the wind as they were lashed with rain. Keane struggled to his knees and found another paddle. Between the two of them, they managed to keep the canoe from capsizing until the worst of the storm had passed.

As quickly as it had struck, the fury of the storm rolled on across the fields and rivers. The worst of the waves subsided.

"What were you thinking?" Beau screamed at him, now that the wind had let up. "That was so fucking stupid."

Keane found that he was angry at Beau, rather than grateful for being rescued. "You called me a pussy!"

"Jesus Christ, Franklin! Is that what this is all about? You don't get it, do you? You could have drowned. You could have died, Franklin!" Beau's voice was suddenly plaintive and grief-stricken. "What would we do without you?"

Lightning still flickered, and he noticed Beau swipe at his eyes with the back of a hand. He thought that his cousin's face was wet with rain, but in another flash of lightning, he saw that those were tears on Beau's face. His big, tough cousin the jock was crying.

That was one of their last summers as teenagers. Beau graduated and drifted through a series of roughneck jobs before joining the military. Keane had gone to college and graduate school. Now, they were back at World's End where they belonged, close as they'd ever been as boys.

21

K eane walked back up to the house, careful not to let the cat escape when he opened the door. Star remained skittish, and who could blame him? This was a strange house with grounds patrolled by Irish Wolfhounds. Keane poured some milk into a saucer and left it out for the cat, hoping to make him feel welcome. He had retrieved the pizza box from the trunk of the Corvette, and he put it now on the huge dining room table that took up much of the living space.

Keane occupied the wing of the house built in 1939 and remodeled over the years to retrofit modern conveniences. The downstairs of what he liked to call the "colonial" portion of the house wasn't lived in these days, but was more of a showcase for the antiques that his family had collected over the years. It was also a good setting for the occasional GAPS fund-raiser for the more exclusive donors.

English Ed still occupied a bedroom on the second floor, insisting that he was plenty spry enough to climb stairs for some years to come. Keane wasn't so sure; he and Beau had talked about building a small one-level house on the property, or perhaps some version of an in-law suite added to the manor house for the day when stairs became too much for Ed.

The two-story modernized wing suited Keane. He and Amanda had lived there quite comfortably. Downstairs was a combination living and dining room with that massive table. A screen porch off to one side made a pleasant place for dining and reading in the warmer months. The kitchen remained in the older part of the house, but was easily accessible—not that Keane did much cooking these days.

Upstairs were two bedrooms and a bathroom. He had converted the second bedroom into an office, although he found that he did most of his work spread out on the big trestle table downstairs. Guests stayed in the original part of the house, which gave everyone their privacy—and made them feel like lords of the manor, to boot.

Not that privacy mattered much to English Ed, who came and went to whatever part of the house he pleased.

Keane was just finishing his second cup of coffee of the day, wondering how to proceed with the discovery that he had made at Lindermann's condo, when English Ed appeared in the doorway.

"There is a young lady to see you," he announced, using his butler's voice.

"Oh, that must be Elizabeth," Keane said. He had forgotten to mention to English Ed that he was expecting her.

"She's a rather attractive young lady," Ed said with a wink.

"It's not like that," Keane said hurriedly. The old butler had a knack for making him feel like he was sixteen again and having a girl over for a study date.

"What a shame," English Ed said. "You could do with a little company."

After so many years at World's End, English Ed was more than his grandfather's old butler; he was family. He had urged

Keane not to become a lonely old bachelor, but Keane kept insisting that he wasn't ready.

"I will say it again, Ed. It's not like that."

"In that case, you won't mind if I ask her out?"

"You do that, Ed." Keane suppressed a smile. "Where is she, by the way?"

"Waiting in the foyer. Is that all right? Since 'it's not like that,' as you put it, do you want me to send her around to the servant's entrance?"

"Ed!"

"Sorry, that's just a little butler's humor."

English Ed left, then returned a few moments later with Elizabeth Graham. Keane felt his heart skip a beat when he saw her. *What was wrong with him?* Still, Keane managed to introduce English Ed, and then the old man left them alone.

"Two things," she said. "First, you have an English *butler*? Just how rich are you, anyhow?"

"He came with the house, I'm afraid," Keane said. "He's sort of like built-in furniture. What's the second thing?"

"What's this about a cat?"

"It's kind of a complicated story," he said. "Better have some coffee first."

Call it intuition, but Keane felt that he could trust Elizabeth completely. She listened intently as he explained about the meeting at the Smithsonian, and then his visit to the Enoch Pratt Free Library and Lindermann's condo. He stopped short of revealing his discovery of what might be the lost star from the Star-Spangled Banner.

"This is insane," she said. "Just how long does the Smithsonian plan on keeping this quiet?"

"It sounds as if the curator is going to make good on her pledge to notify the media," he said. "The anniversary of the Battle of Baltimore is going to be in three days. It's better this way, anyhow. The Smithsonian could not keep this quiet indefinitely. If it's just a few days, they can spin it as part of the criminal investigation. If they wait any longer, it would look like a coverup."

Elizabeth nodded, thinking. "The fact that the flag was stolen must be connected to the two murders. What were those two mixed up in?" she wondered. "Someone killed Galarza and Lindermann to keep them quiet."

"It certainly looks that way," Keane said.

"But you didn't find anything?"

"Actually, something interesting that I found at Galarza's desk at the Smithsonian was a signed copy of Charles Montgomery's new book. The FBI left it there, so I guess they weren't interested." He showed her the book and the inscription. "I have no idea what the significance of Anacreon might be, but whatever it was, Galarza seemed to be a part of it."

Elizabeth frowned. "Anacreon? Where have I heard that before?"

"Well, each time you hear *The Star-Spangled Banner* being sung, you are hearing the tune *To Anacreon in Heaven*, an old English drinking song."

Elizabeth snapped her fingers. "That's where I've heard the name! Who or what on earth is Anacreon? I should probably know this, but you'll have to refresh my memory."

"Anacreon was a minor Greek poet who wrote rather ribald poems celebrating wine and love and drinking. He was a court favorite who lived to a ripe old age, so perhaps he was on to something with that lifestyle."

"I've seen Charles Montgomery on TV," Elizabeth said. "He is not the ribald type."

"Then what could Anacreon have meant to Montgomery and Galarza?"

"Let me noodle around online when I have some time," she said. "The interwebs will reveal all."

The cat made an appearance, having scurried under the

furniture at her initial arrival. Now, Star came out and rubbed against Elizabeth's ankles.

"Meet your new friend," Keane said. "His name is Star. I'm hoping that you will be taking him home with you."

"Really, Franklin? I'm starting a new job, you know. The last thing I need now is a pet."

"Where else is he supposed to go? I have two dogs, and they're on lockdown right now until I figure out what to do with this cat."

Elizabeth looked at him and laughed. "The Star-Spangled Banner has been stolen, you've been asked by the Smithsonian to help find it, and you're so concerned about a cat? Don't worry, by the way, he's got a home with me, at least temporarily. But is this really why you dragged me all the way up here?"

"There is something else." Keane pointed at the pizza box.

"Pizza?" Elizabeth gave him a puzzled look. "I would have thought you'd have your butler whip up some salmon croquettes or crumpets or whatever."

"There's no pizza in the box. Take a look. You may want to put these on first." He handed her a pair of white cotton conservator's gloves, then pulled on a pair himself.

Elizabeth put on the gloves, and almost gingerly, opened the box. She stared for a long moment. "Wait a minute. If the Smithsonian assistant curator was a nineteenth century fabrics expert, and he was teamed up with a historical researcher like Bob Lindermann ..." She fell silent, staring at the star. "Is this what I think it is?"

"I can't be one hundred percent sure. Unfortunately, the one man who might have verified at a glance what we are looking at here seems to be dead."

"Where did you find this?"

"Lindermann's condo. Whoever ransacked the place probably thought what I did at first—that it was just an old pizza. I don't think Lindermann was intending to camouflage it, but it was the perfect hiding place, no matter how unintentional."

Elizabeth took a step back from the box on the table. "Oh, Franklin. What's going on here? Is this why those two men were killed?"

"I'm not sure."

"Where did Lindermann find it?"

"There was brown wrapping paper and a shipping label in his trash. He bought this on eBay."

"You've got to be kidding me. Franklin, this could be evidence. You have to tell someone!"

"I will, in due time. But first, I wanted to be reasonably sure that I was looking at the real thing."

"You think it might be a forgery?"

"Lindermann was no fool. I don't think he would have bought this online if he didn't have at least some inkling that it was real." He nodded at the star. "Take a look and tell me what you think."

Elizabeth reached into the box and lifted the star gingerly. Once white, the fabric appeared almost tea-stained by age. Bits of blue fabric appeared at the fringes, as if the star had been hacked from the fabric surrounding it with something like a knife, rather than scissors. Obviously, the fabric itself was old.

"Do you have a magnifying glass?" she asked.

Keane retrieved one and handed it to her. "What are you looking for?"

"I would say that this is a woolen fabric, rather than cotton. Do you think that matters?"

"The original flag was made of English wool bunting, smuggled through the Royal Navy blockade. The seamstress was Mary Pickersgill in Baltimore. She made nautical flags for a living, and she knew more than one wily sea captain who could have obtained this fabric."

"See how these fibers look fuzzy? It's definitely wool." Elizabeth nodded, and flipped the star over. "Someone has drawn a star in ink on this point of the star. There's some kind of writing here as well. I think it says ... *Three paces*."

"But three paces from what?" Keane wondered. "I think we're looking at a map of some sort, but there's no point of reference."

"It's got to be a map," Elizabeth agreed. She handed him the magnifying glass. "You need to see this for yourself."

Franklin took the magnifying glass and peered closely. The *Three paces* was penned between the point of the star and the star that someone had drawn. Beneath it, he could just make out a set of faded initials and a date.

FSK Oct 12 1834

"FSK," he said. He could think of one individual with those initials who also had a very strong association with the Star-Spangled Banner flag. "Francis Scott Key."

22

"This is a beautiful place," Elizabeth said. "If I were you, I don't think I'd ever leave."

"Marcus Aurelius once said that the best retreat was to be found in one's own mind," Keane replied.

"He never had the opportunity to visit World's End."

"I suppose not, considering that he died in the second century AD."

Elizabeth laughed. At the sound, Keane felt something shift inside him, almost like the way that a frozen river begins to thaw in spring. She said, "And here I thought that *I* was the history geek! Is there anything about history that you don't know?"

"Sorry," Keane said. "You must think that I'm a bore."

"No, not at all," she said. She grabbed his arm. "Please tell me more about Marcus Aurelius!"

"Only if you beg," Keane replied, laughing. He noticed that Elizabeth took her time letting go of his arm.

They were strolling up the long gravel lane, taking Boru and Danu for a walk. No need for leashes out here. The dogs charged off into the fields and woods, then ran back periodically to check on their human escorts, before chasing off again.

"These two weigh more than me and you put together," she said. "I have to admit that it's a little disconcerting, although they seem friendly enough."

"They like you," Keane said, watching as the dogs burst across a field. They were beautiful runners, not at all lumbering as one might expect from such large dogs. "I have always found that wolfhounds are excellent judges of character."

"That's a good thing," Elizabeth said. "I don't want to become a Scooby snack. I'd pity anyone who came snooping around here."

"Scooby was a Great Dane, you know," Keane said with a grin.

"There you go again," she said. "Although, technically that was a pop culture reference."

"Sorry," Keane said. "I just wanted to make the point that Irish wolfhounds aren't very good watchdogs. They have a very trusting nature, even toward strangers. However, they are extremely loyal. Once they got to know you, no one would be safe if he put a hand on you."

"What I do want to know is something about this place. How in the world did your family end up here?"

"My grandfather bought it for next to nothing," Keane said. "Of course, he had to put a lot of money into it. The house was about to fall down. Back then, this road was almost impassable."

"Unlike Marcus Aurelius, he wanted a retreat?"

Keane laughed again. This was the best he had felt in a long time. Momentarily, he had forgotten all about the missing flag and the lost star. With a guilty pang, he realized that he had even forgotten about Amanda. "Once he'd made his pile of money with Keane Silver, he decided that he wanted to live the life of a country squire."

"Complete with English butler?"

"Exactly."

"My mother still has her Keane Silver that she takes out for Thanksgiving and Christmas."

"Hang onto it," he said. "Some of the older sets of Keane Silver are starting to become collectible. Where do your parents live?"

"It's just my mother now. I grew up in Columbia, in a neighborhood that my father used to call 'The Plywood Village.' He worked for the federal government. Your typical, uneventful suburban childhood in Maryland's most famous planned community, which also happens to be hugely boring from a historical perspective."

"And yet, you became enamored with history."

"I guess I love a good story," she said. "Speaking of which, how in the world did your grandfather ever get into the silverware business? Was he a craftsman in Ireland?"

"Ha! The only thing crafty about Jack Keane was Jack Keane himself. Believe it or not, distant relatives in Ireland did own a modest silver mine, so I think that silver held some sort of fascination for him. My grandfather had a gift for putting the right people in the right place at the right time. Baltimore was a steel town—all gone now—and he found some of the really skilled metalworkers who become bored with making steel beams. He gave them a chance to be artisans."

"But still, to get started in the silver business couldn't have been easy—I guess I'm always fascinated by entrepreneurs."

"My grandfather would never admit it, but there is a family legend that he stole the silver to get started."

"*What?*"

"During World War II, all sorts of precious metals in bulk moved through Baltimore by train or ship, being shipped for the war effort. Most of it would be melted down and turned into something else. The story goes that a few crates of old silver dollars went missing. In the end, it was blamed on a paperwork mixup because an outright theft would have looked bad for all involved. The question is, did my grandfather steal the coins himself or did he knowingly buy or trade stolen goods that someone was eager to get rid of at a huge discount? We're not talking about a fortune in coins here, but those coins would have been enough to get Keane Silver going right after the war."

"You mean my mother's silverware and punch bowl are made out of stolen goods?"

"I hate to say it, but it's just possible."

Elizabeth laughed again. "Go figure."

"By the seventies, the market was already drying up. Cheaper imports made it hard to compete. The smaller department store chains like Montgomery Ward that sold Keane Silver were slowly going out of business. He sold the business and moved here permanently. It was my mother who married into the family, but her marriage was troubled. My cousin Beau and I spent most of our time here, growing up. Basically, our grandfather raised us."

"You must miss him."

"It's complicated," Keane said. "Jack Keane was always a little larger than life, which meant that he wanted the starring role in everyone else's life. He wasn't always an easy man to like."

They walked for a while in silence, watching the dogs run.

"What happens next?" Elizabeth asked.

"I am going to stay at World's End for a couple of days and do some research into the flag. I'll try to determine how and why Francis Scott Key might have had a piece of it, and why he used it for a map."

"What about the Smithsonian?"

"The best way to help the Smithsonian and find the Star-Spangled Banner may be to find out what Lindermann and Galarza were up to."

"I'll try to find out who sold the star to Lindermann and where they got it," Elizabeth said. "I'll also see what I can find out about Anacreon."

"This means you're in?" he asked, unable to keep the tone of amusement out of his voice.

"I'm in," she said.

"On one condition," he said.

"What's that?"

"The cat goes home with you."

23

B ecause Keane didn't have any cat food on hand, he opted to make the four of them—Keane, Elizabeth, English Ed, and Star—tuna sandwiches for lunch. The humans also enjoyed Herr's potato chips and bottles of Stewart's Cream Soda. Over lunch on the screen porch, English Ed regaled them with tales of some of the wilder parties that had taken place at World's End back in Jack Keane's 1970s heyday, including one that involved fireworks, skinny dipping, and a rabid raccoon.

Keane had heard them all before, but he was pleased that English Ed's stories made her laugh out loud. It had been a long time since the mansion had echoed with laughter.

Once Elizabeth had gone, World's End felt curiously hollow and empty.

"I should hope that we'll be seeing more of her," English Ed remarked. "Lovely girl."

"Don't you have to go polish the silver or whatever it is that butlers do?"

English Ed harrumphed and left him alone.

Keane spent the early afternoon researching the history of

the Star-Spangled Banner. He knew the story, of course, because Francis Scott Key was his most famous ancestor.

But there was always something new to learn and some detail he had forgotten. Keane had an extensive research library of journals and diaries that could not be found anywhere online. He dipped into them now, hoping to uncover some hidden clue as to the history of the flag and the missing star.

His research was interrupted by a telephone call from Roger Biesty at the Smithsonian. His voice crackled with stress and exhaustion.

"Any news, Franklin?"

"Nothing yet, I'm afraid. Has the FBI found anything?"

"They found the fire truck parked in a cul de sac in Montgomery County. It had been stolen the day before from a volunteer fire company in Odenton. But there wasn't so much as a fingerprint on it, and no sign of the Star-Spangled Banner."

Keane thought it wise not to mention the star until he had determined its significance—and whether or not it was even real. "Did you know that your deceased curator was a fan of Charles Montgomery?"

"What, that talking head on TV? That Charles Montgomery?"

"I found a signed copy of Montgomery's new book on Esteban Galarza's desk."

"I didn't know that Esteban was such a fan." Biesty paused. "Anyhow, what he read or did on his own time was Esteban's business. But do you think it has something to do with the disappearance of the Star-Spangled Banner?"

"I doubt it," Keane said. "It's just curious, is all."

"Well, keep me posted. The clock is ticking."

"What do you mean?"

Biesty snorted in disbelief. "Did I appoint the right investigator? I would think that you of all people would notice that

September fourteenth is in a few days. You know, the anniversary of the Battle of Baltimore and the Star-Spangled Banner?"

"Oh, that."

"It seems significant in some way, don't you think? Listen, I've got to go. Keep me posted, OK?"

"Will do."

Keane was not surprised to have heard from Biesty. He made a mental note to do a better job of keeping the Smithsonian director abreast of what he learned in the future.

The one person he had not heard from was the GAPS director, Charlene Dearborn, which was a mixed blessing. He decided that if there was anything pressing, then she would contact him.

Keane returned to his books, hoping to find some new nugget of information. He was annoyed at himself for not making the connection earlier to the anniversary coming up. He was not sure of its significance, but Biesty was right; something about that date now nagged at him.

On September 14, 1814, his famous ancestor had watched the bombardment of Fort McHenry as a prisoner aboard *HMS Tonnant*, the flagship of Rear Admiral George Cockburn. Contrary to popular legend, it was a smaller storm flag sewn by Mary Pickersgill that flew over the fort during the battle. The massive Star-Spangled Banner was raised only as the British fleet sailed away in defeat, although it was just possible that at least one final cannonball had perforated the flag as the British fired a parting shot.

Francis Scott Key's poem, originally entitled *The Defense of Fort McHenry*, came to be known as *The Star-Spangled Banner*.

O say can you see, by the dawn's early light,
What so proudly we hailed at the twilight's last gleaming,
Whose broad stripes and bright stars through the perilous fight,

O'er the ramparts we watched, were so gallantly streaming?
And the rockets' red glare, the bombs bursting in air,
Gave proof through the night that our flag was still there;
O say does that star-spangled banner yet wave
O'er the land of the free and the home of the brave?

IN MANY WAYS and on many levels, it was a beautiful and powerful poem. The words had managed to move generations of Americans.

Later, Key had composed a total of three more stanzas that took on a darker tone, including these lines:

THEIR BLOOD HAS wash'd out their foul footstep's pollution.
No refuge could save the hireling and slave
From the terror of flight and the gloom of the grave

AN UGLY TRUTH about Key was that he had been a slaveholder and proponent of resolving the slavery issue by colonizing former slaves in Africa. This rankled Keane's sense of social justice. In Francis Scott Key's defense, he had been a man of his times, perhaps even somewhat less racist than the rest of the white gentry.

In the case of *The Star-Spangled Banner*, Key had surely meant the word "slave" in a more figurative sense—hired guns and mercenaries who fought for the King's shilling against free Americans. In some ways, the National Anthem was also a Deadly Anthem, threatening vengeance and destruction upon America's enemies.

However, his research today was not about the poem. What he wanted to do was delve more into what had happened to the flag after the battle of Baltimore. He knew that the flag was given to Major George Armistead, commander of Fort McHenry. The commander had poured all of his energy into the fort and was afflicted by chronic illness as a result. He could almost be counted among the casualties of the battle. When Armistead died in 1818 at age 39, the flag passed into the care of his family. Along with Key, Armistead was seen as a true patriot and hero—never mind the fact that his nephew, Confederate General Lew Armistead, would carry his black hat atop his sword as he led the gray waves to crash against the Union lines at Pickett's Charge in the 1863 Battle of Gettysburg.

The flag remained in the care of the Armistead family for ninety years. During that time, a curious tradition took place. Bits and pieces of the flag were given away over the decades. Some were given to dinner guests or friends of the family. Most of the pieces from the flag were given to War of 1812 veterans who requested that a piece of the flag be buried with them. The Armistead family never turned down such a request, and bit by bit, the once-great banner was diminished.

It was a curious habit that horrified some today, this idea of a symbol as important as the flag quite literally being cut to pieces. Yet all through the nineteenth century, such souvenirs and keepsakes were very popular. Famous and celebrated people were asked for everything from bits of uniforms to locks of hair to autographs. It was a way to make a connection. Keane supposed it wasn't much different from following a celebrity on social media today.

For example, Confederate General Robert E. Lee's uniform coat was reduced to what appeared to be a moth-eaten scrap as he cut away pieces and mailed them to admirers. A veteran might receive a button or a bit of braid from his sleeve, the so-called "chicken guts" that decorated an officer's uniform.

Keane himself owned a piece of the last Confederate flag flown over Richmond, given to him by an auctioneer friend.

Certainly, Francis Scott Key had been an occasional guest of the Armistead family over the years. Although there was no record of it anywhere that Keane could find, it was possible that the author of *The Star-Spangled Banner* had asked for, and received, the greatest flag relic of them all—an entire star roughly shorn from the blue field of the flag.

Mercifully, the diminishing of the flag had ended for good when Armistead descendent Eben Appleton made a gift of the flag, by now quite famous, to the Smithsonian in 1912—in honor of the centennial of the War of 1812.

Key died in Baltimore in 1843 at age 63 and was buried in his hometown of Frederick, Maryland. Keane wondered what secrets had died with him? Had he left behind this star as a token of unfinished business?

If it was indeed a map, what was it a map of?

Had Lindermann actually stumbled upon the star up for sale in an online auction? It was just possible, considering Lindermann's acumen as a researcher. After all, it wouldn't be the first piece of American history that had turned up in an attic or old trunk, only to be sold to the highest bidder.

Needing a breath of air, Keane went for a short walk to stretch his legs. Boru and Danu stirred themselves and kept him company, romping on the front lawn. Keane walked the boundary of the lawn where it met the edge of a soybean field rented to a local farmer. Looking back at the house, he paused to admire the two flags flying from the tall pole in front of the house. The second flag was the colorful Maryland state flag derived from the coat of arms of the aristocratic Calvert family, barons Baltimore, who had founded the colony during the reign of James I. The flag at the top of the pole was a 15-star and 15-stripe United States flag, a replica of the Star-Spangled Banner.

Beyond the house, a cloud of dust indicated that a vehicle was coming up the long lane. A moment later, Boru and Danu began barking. A black SUV was approaching. The vehicle had an official look that made Keane think, *Uh oh.*

When he got closer to the house, he saw two figures had gotten out of the SUV and stood there, waiting for him. Both wore dark suits. Both wore sunglasses. One was a tall black man. The other was a tall blonde woman.

The need to flash a badge at him as he approached was almost redundant because everything about their appearance screamed FBI. Flanking him, Boru and Danu sniffed the air warily, but stopped short of growling. That was exactly how Keane felt about the FBI agents. He noticed they did not introduce themselves, which Keane decided was some sort of intimidation tactic.

The agents kept their eyes on the massive dogs, rather than on Keane.

"Mister Keane, we want to ask you a few questions about the Star-Spangled Banner. Can we go inside? I think we'll all be more comfortable if the dogs stay out here."

"I fed them this morning, so it's probably safe," Keane said. "Nonetheless, we may certainly go inside."

With Keane leading the way, they went into Keane's apartment. He spotted the pizza box on the table, and froze.

He had forgotten about the star. One of the agents nudged the pizza box as if debating to see if it was pepperoni or sausage. Keane felt his heart thump in this throat. He did not want to explain that he had taken it from a murder victim's apartment.

"Hungry? I could heat up a slice for you."

"What kind?" the female agent asked.

Keane thought fast, sizing her up. He didn't think an FBI agent would be much of a vegetarian. "How about mushroom and broccoli?"

The agent wrinkled her button nose. "No, thank you."

Her partner gave her a look. "Listen, we understand that the

Smithsonian has engaged you to look into the disappearance of the Star-Spangled Banner."

"That's correct."

"I've got to tell you, we're not really happy about that. The FBI prefers to do its own investigating."

Keane nodded. "I understand that, but the Smithsonian has every right to appoint its own civilian investigator. There may be something that escapes your notice that a trained historian would be more likely to see."

That comment made them bristle. The female agent looked like Danu when she got a whiff of a fox.

"Leave the investigating up to us, Mister Keane."

"It's Doctor Keane, actually."

"Fine, *Doctor* Keane. Just see that to it that you stick to the history books and share any information with us."

"Of course. What have you found out?"

"Nothing we are at liberty to share. What have you found?"

"Nothing that I am at liberty to share."

"Don't play games with us."

"Look, all I want is for the Star-Spangled Banner to be returned."

None of them had much more to say to one another. Keane walked them out, where he found the dogs waiting. He reached out and took both dogs by their collars.

If the dogs had managed to read his mind, he wasn't so sure that Boru and Danu would grant the agents safe passage. Standing there, an immense Irish wolfhound gripped in each hand, he watched the FBI agents drive off.

Somehow, Keane felt that his role in the investigation had just become more complicated.

24

Dusk had fallen by the time Keane emerged from his research again. The hours spent paging through old books had been pleasurable, but not very rewarding. He had found nothing of interest, other than reacquainting himself with the sometimes bloodthirsty lyrics of the lesser-known stanzas of the National Anthem. *Their blood has washed out their foul footsteps' pollution.* It was hard to reconcile the image of his genteel ancestor with those violent words.

Feeling the need for fresh air and exercise, he took the dogs for a walk down to the wharf, about half a mile from the house. Leaving the wolfhounds to carouse on shore and terrorize the local wildlife, he walked to the end of the wharf and sat on a bench there. The sun had already gone down, leaving the sky painted with dull red fire. A slight breeze blew off the water, but it was refreshing rather than chill. September was an extension of summer weather.

The stillness and quiet seemed to gather around him. As the shadows grew deeper in the woods, he became dimly aware of ghostly shapes moving along the shoreline, apparitions out of the past. He ignored them. Sometimes, his talent for retrocognition manifested itself unbidden. The dogs ran among the apparitions, apparently oblivious to the phenomenon. Keane shifted on the bench so that his back was to the shore. He preferred not to put retrocognition into practice at World's End. In fact, he lived in terror of seeing Jack Keane's apparition.

Instead, he focused his attention on the present, and the fading light of a beautiful evening.

Not so long ago, he and Amanda might have taken the sailboat out for a short cruise on an evening like this.

He was not sure, exactly, what had made him think of Amanda just now, although, truth be told, his thoughts never strayed far from her.

Or far from that awful night.

Even Keane was not really sure what had happened. They had taken *Miranda* out on a beautiful summer day and sailed down the bay. Finally, they anchored in a secluded spot to spend the night. Not so much as a light shone on shore. That was the thing about the Chesapeake; you could still find remote places where you were utterly by yourself.

They went for a swim before dark. They were both strong swimmers, but while Keane had a tendency to try to wrestle his way through the water, Amanda was graceful and lithe. The surface of the water was still as glass and clear to the bottom.

Climbing back aboard *Miranda*, they stretched out on a blanket. Keane opened a bottle of wine for them. They sipped the sweet white Riesling and watched the stars come out. Their conversation was limited to an occasional murmur. Amanda gave him a smile—an invitation, really. Her hand drifted down his flat belly and slid beneath the waistband of his trunks.

Things had been difficult between them romantically since discovering that they could not have children. Keane had reassured her that they could adopt, but the news had left Amanda deeply saddened. What had once been a beautiful act that might result in the miracle of a child now felt as hollow as a treadmill workout. It didn't help that Amanda's melancholy was draped over them like a scratchy wool blanket whenever they dutifully went through the motions, rare as that had become.

Tonight was different. They made love, slowly and tenderly. Then they lay back on the deck, finishing the wine and admiring the clear night sky.

Amanda had been the first one to notice the lights.

Approaching from across the marsh, several glowing orbs drifted out over the water. It was immediately clear that these lights were nothing that had been generated by man. Keane guessed that each light was maybe the size of a cannonball, burning from within with a blue-white fire. The lights hovered offshore, then seemed to chase one another across the water. None of them came close to the boat.

"Have you ever seen anything like that before, Franklin?"

"Never. They must be will o' wisps."

"They're so beautiful.

Keane had never seen a will o' wisp before, although he had come across descriptions of them in regional histories. On the Eastern Shore, the old-timers had called them Jack o' lanterns. It seemed that they had once been a common sight, but were rare these days.

After a while, watching the lights, they grew sleepy. And cold.

They went below and made love again to warm up. The last thing Keane remembered was feeling pleasantly sleepy from the wine and the afterglow of making love to his wife, his body entwined with Amanda's under the soft fleece blanket. He slipped into a dreamless sleep.

When he woke, the sun was already up, but it was hidden by mist. Through the portholes, he could see that it was a gray morning. With any luck, the mist would burn off later that day.

Amanda was not in bed, but Keane didn't think much of it,

supposing that she had gone up on deck. His head felt a bit wooly from the wine, because it was more than he normally drank. He pulled on a pair of boxer briefs and made coffee for them in the galley, carrying two steaming mugs up the ladder.

He fully expected to find Amanda on deck, enjoying the morning quiet. But she was nowhere in sight.

"Amanda," he said aloud, a little stupidly. *Miranda* was just thirty-five feet in length. His eyes swept the length of the boat in a single glance. Amanda was definitely not on deck.

A tiny frisson of fear touched him.

He set down the mugs of coffee and returned below. The sailboat had a tiny head, and it was just possible that Amanda was in there. Surely, that could be the only explanation. He knocked.

"Hon?"

He listened at the door. When there was no answer, he turned the latch and peeked inside.

Empty.

He stuck his head back into the bedroom, in case he had somehow missed his wife among the sheets and pillows, but no one was there.

He noticed Amanda's smartphone beside the bed. She rarely went anywhere without it, even on the boat.

Now, fear jolted him like an electric current, but it felt icy cold, rather than hot.

Absurdly, he opened some of the storage cabinets in the cramped galley, as if she might be hiding there. Nothing there but spare lifejackets and cleaning supplies.

Keane went back on deck. Their dory was secured to the bow. Amanda's swimsuit lay on the blanket alongside his trunks, right where they had shed them last night.

It wasn't like Amanda to go skinny dipping in the morning light, but it seemed to be the only possible explanation. A little feebly at first, and then louder and louder, he called out over the lonely water, "Amanda! Amanda!"

No answer came back from the gray mists. His beautiful wife, Amanda Keane, was gone.

* * *

KEANE REMEMBERED the days and weeks that followed like scenes from a movie, more as something that he had watched rather than something that had actually happened to him. He had called 911 and waited in growing terror until the Maryland Natural Resources Police arrived in a single small boat. After that, things quickly escalated.

More DNR police arrived, and then the state police. Keane had been taken ashore and questioned, first with sympathy, and then with growing suspicion.

Even Keane knew that it was highly unlikely that his wife had simply vanished.

When he tried to explain about the lights they had seen, no one was interested in his descriptions of the will o' wisps, except as it related to his sobriety.

"How much did you two have to drink last night?"

"We shared a bottle of wine, but I don't think we finished it."

"Any drugs?"

Keane recoiled. "No, of course not!"

The bottle of wine was found, there on the blanket. They had polished off a little over half the bottle. Embarrassed, Keane had been forced to explain about them making love.

"Did things maybe get a little rough?" the state police detective had wanted to know. His name was Crawford. This was the same detective that Keane had just seen again in St. Michaels at the Cannonball House.

"Dear God, no."

"But then you went below and did it again?"

He'd been forced to share the story with more than one investigator. Somehow, the details of what had been a romantic evening seemed to become more sordid with each retelling.

A theory began to evolve that his wife had too much to drink and had fallen overboard in the dark. Maybe she had hit her head in the process. Keane must have slept right through it.

There was also the possibility that Amanda had been more depressed than Keane had realized about their inability to have children. The theory that Amanda had committed suicide was something that the police didn't seem to put much stock in, but Keane wasn't so sure. He doubted that Amanda had intentionally drowned herself. But if she had gone overboard by accident, it was just possible that her melancholy had been like chains around her legs, making her give up too easily on life. Keane felt deeply guilty that he might not have seen these signs and tried to help her. He felt even worse about the fact that maybe she had fallen in, and that he'd been too drowsy from wine and sex to hear the splash and her cries for help. In her time of need, he had failed her.

Search parties combed the marsh, in case she had gone overboard and swam toward shore. Nothing was found.

Another explanation arose, which was that Keane had killed her. No one came out and accused him directly, but he sensed it in some of the looks he was getting. *Maybe the husband did it.* Keane was no expert, but he knew from reading crime novels and watching TV shows that the husband was often the first person that the police looked at in cases like this.

Yet more police arrived, and a boat from the local volunteer fire company. This boat had a grappling hook, and began to drag the bottom.

Horrified, Keane watched the muck and mire being pulled up, afraid that he would see Amanda's lifeless body gripped in the iron tines.

The searchers found old tires and rusting crab pots, but no sign of his wife. Keane turned away.

But then there came a shout. The hooks had snagged something. As Keane looked on, the grappling hooks came free of the water, along with a pale, naked body clutched in the muddy hooks. There was no doubt that it was Amanda. Keane gasped.

He felt someone touch his shoulder. "This probably isn't the best thing to watch," a voice said. Keane looked up at a DNR officer he didn't recognize, and allowed himself to be led away before he could see more. Although he was grateful to that officer to this day for that act of kindness, he sometimes wished that the man had turned him away just a minute before. He would have been spared any number of nightmares.

In the end, Amanda's death was declared accidental, although not everyone was convinced. An autopsy revealed no trauma of any kind. The cause of death was determined to be drowning. The likeliest explanation was that Amanda had somehow fallen overboard and drowned during the night—all while he slept off the wine below decks.

There was another explanation, of course. Detective Crawford and more than a few others thought that Keane was getting away with murder, but they found no evidence to charge Keane with any crime. In a sense, that didn't even matter. People believed what they wanted to believe about what had happened that night. As a result, Keane would always be tainted by Amanda's death.

It was his desire to know what had happened to Amanda that night that had pushed Keane to develop his skill for retrocognition. Something about those lights that night had seemed so otherworldly. What had the lights meant? Where had Amanda gone? He hoped that he might be able to discover that through retrocognition. So far, although he had tried many times, he had seen nothing of that night. It was as closed off to

him as if a curtain was drawn across the stage or a thick door
had been shut.

When it was fully dark, he whistled for the dogs and made
his way back toward the house.

25

K eane woke early and expected to spend the day doing further research into Charles Montgomery and any connection he might have with Esteban Galarza or the Star-Spangled Banner. That had been the plan, anyway, until the phone rang during his second pot of coffee. He might have ignored the phone, until he saw that the caller was Charlene Dearborn.

"Franklin, I need you to get down to Easton," she said without preamble. "We have an incident there."

"An incident?" Keane was puzzled; GAPS had no properties in Easton at the moment. The Cannonball House was the nearest GAPS affiliate. Wasn't the recent murder incident enough?

"A protest," she said.

"What protest?"

"It's that damn Confederate statue," she elaborated. "The one in front of the county courthouse."

Keane knew exactly what statue she meant. He had passed by it recently, during the War of 1812 symposium. Even then, he had noticed two protesters with hand-lettered signs, camped out on the courthouse lawn. Scarcely anyone had paid attention to them at the time, but their protest had gained momentum.

"Charlene, what does this have to do with GAPS?" he wanted to know. "We don't have a dog in this fight."

"When it comes to history, we always have a dog in the fight," she pointed out. "I need some bodies here. We need to show solidarity."

"Solidarity for what? For whom? The Old South? The so-called Lost Cause? That Confederate monument should come down, Charlene, if that's what people today want."

"Then let me ask you, where do we draw the line? Is there going to be a committee that decides what is acceptable history that doesn't muddy the narrative? History shouldn't be decided by half-wits waving signs and shouting slogans."

"Tell that to Czar Nicholas ... or maybe to King Louis and Marie Antoinette."

"Political correctness is a slippery slope, Franklin."

Keane sighed. "We could debate this all day, but the last time I checked, we are not in the monument business."

"No, but I don't think that I need to remind you that we *are* in the history business," she said. "Just get down here, please."

"All right. Try not to get arrested in the meantime."

It was a ninety-minute drive down to Easton. He decided to take the Corvette. Keane checked in with English Ed to let him know that he wouldn't be home for dinner, after all.

"In that case, it looks like some microwaved beef stroganoff, a large Pimm's and lemonade, and Netflix for me, old chap."

"Sounds like the perfect evening."

"The only way it could get better would be for you to send that lovely Miss Graham to keep me company."

Keane grinned. "Dream on, old man."

Before he left, Keane called Elizabeth, but not to invite her to dinner with English Ed. Ostensibly, the call was a heads up about the protest. But he wouldn't mind seeing her again, either.

"Listen, I have some news for you about the star," she said. "I did some sleuthing around on eBay, based on the packing slip you found at Bob Lindermann's place. It turns out that Lindermann bought the star from a guy named Jeff Coe. I tracked him down and gave him a call. He was very nice about explaining where he'd gotten the star."

"OK," said Keane. The name did not ring any bells.

"Guess what? Coe's grandfather worked on the construction crew that dismantled Francis Scott Key's house in Georgetown in 1947."

Keane snapped his fingers. "His grandfather decided to keep a souvenir," he said.

There was some well-known controversy over what had become of Key's house a few years before when the Washington Post published a story about it. The Georgetown house was no mansion, but had been a substantial upper middle class brick home that served as Key's residence for much of his life. He had been living there when the British burned Washington and it had been from here that Key traveled to Baltimore to end up as a witness to history.

"His story made sense to me," Elizabeth said. "This guy said he was cleaning junk out of his grandparents' house and decided to sell the star online. He wasn't exactly sure what he had, but Lindermann pounced on it."

"The National Park Service oversaw the dismantling of the house to make room for a highway," Keane said, sharing the details that came to mind. "Technically, I'm sure that Coe's grandfather wasn't supposed to keep anything for himself. All of the materials were put into storage, but the Park Service lost track of them over the years or used them in other restorations. There are probably pieces of Key's house all over Georgetown."

"Maybe he broke the rules, but it sounds as if we can thank that construction worker for actually saving a piece of history," Elizabeth said.

26

When Keane arrived in Easton later that day, he was more than a little surprised to see the crowd on Washington Street. Normally, this was a relatively sleepy Eastern Shore county seat, but not today.

Earlier, he had checked social media to discover that protesters had worked up their supporters on both sides to a fever pitch. Signs bobbed up and down on the courthouse lawn. This was not going to be the place for intelligent debate.

He left the Corvette parked near the county library—well away from any possibility of being struck by thrown rocks or hurled bottles, just in case the crowd spiraled out of control—and walked a couple of blocks to the scene of the protest. He passed several police officers watching the protest. One of the officers was Detective Crawford, who glared at Keane.

"I should have known that you of all people would show up," the detective said. "You know what they say about flies on shit."

"Nice to see you too, Detective."

Keane moved on, feeling Crawford's eyes stabbing into his back. Elizabeth was already there, on the sidewalk in front of the courthouse. "This does not look good," she said. "Can you please tell me what we're doing here?"

"I'm here to make sure my boss doesn't get arrested," Keane explained.

"Good luck with that," Elizabeth said, nodding toward the scene of bedlam surrounding the courthouse.

Built in 1794, the Talbot County Courthouse was no stranger to controversy or violent protests. During the War of 1812, the last British prisoners of war were taken to the courthouse after the Battle of the Ice Mound, but released days later once word arrived that the war had ended nearly two months earlier. During the Civil War, in 1862, Union troops surrounded the courthouse and forcibly arrested a pro-Southern county judge for refusing to sentence local men for protesting the Union. The outspoken judge was pistol-whipped and taken to Fort McHenry, to be held there with other Southern sympathizers— including one of the relatives that he and Francis Scott Key shared. It was probably the granddaddy of all ironies that one of Key's family members was imprisoned for treason at Fort McHenry, of all places. Then again, there was the additional irony to consider that all of Francis Scott Key's descendants had fought on the Confederate side of the Civil War.

Back in 1913, nearly fifty years after the Civil War, local citizens erected a statue to "The Talbot Boys" for their service to the Confederate States of America. The monument depicted a young man carrying a furled Confederate flag. Union veterans didn't get a monument, but directly across from the young Johnny Reb was a statue of Frederick Douglass, born nearby in 1818. The statue of Douglass had been erected in the late twentieth century.

If the statues were vastly different, the protesters themselves continued this dichotomy. They had taken sides like two opposing football teams, with the statues serving as their goalposts.

He spotted Charlene in the crowd near the Talbot Boys and made his way toward her. She was a tall and attractive woman in her fifties, handsome rather than pretty. With her height and scowl, there was always something formidable about Charlene's appearance, and today was no exception. She had positioned herself near the foot of the Confederate statue.

"Have you reached the conclusion yet that this is a bad idea?" he said into her ear, having to raise his voice to be heard above the shouting and chanting.

"It's about time you got here," she replied.

Keane introduced Elizabeth to the GAPS director, then said, "This is foolhardy, Charlene. Nobody in either one of these groups is interested in meaningful dialogue today. You do remember what Mark Twain said about arguing with a pig?"

"He said, 'You'll both get dirty, and the pig enjoys it,' " Charlene responded. "You know what else Mark Twain said? He also said that a patriot is the person who can yell the loudest without knowing what he's yelling about."

"Then this is surely a gathering of patriots," Keane said.

He was proven right when a big man with a shaved head approached them. "Hey lady!" he called out. His face contorted with anger as he shouted, his eyes spinning like marbles, but it was clear that his gaze was directed at Charlene. He was like a poster child for the mentally unbalanced. "You sure you're on the right side?"

There was no doubt that he was calling attention to the fact that Charlene was African-American. Keane stepped between Charlene and the angry protester, but she was having none of it. She came around from behind Keane and jabbed a finger at the man. "What do you mean by that?"

The confrontation was quickly becoming a magnet for more crazies. Keane looked around for the police, but their attention was elsewhere. Besides, he was fairly certain that the police wouldn't be of much help, if Detective Crawford had any say in the matter. They were on their own.

Another man appeared beside the individual whom Charlene was chewing out. This second man had a short crewcut in an almost military style. He wore a T-shirt with a single word on it, *Anacreon*.

Keane stared. This was the second time in recent days that he had come across that word. Esteban's book had recognized him as a member of a group called Anacreon, and had been signed by Charles Montgomery. Was this another one of Montgomery's followers?

On a whim, Keane asked the man, "What is Anacreon?"

The protester stared. "If you're with her, then it's none of your damn business!"

This was going downhill quickly. He turned to Charlene. "We need to get you out of here."

Hanging back, Elizabeth clearly looked confused and frightened.

Seeing Elizabeth's expression and the two angry men confronting her, Charlene seemed to come to her senses. "All right," she said. "Let's get out of here."

But escape wasn't that easy. The crowd pressed in around them, and they found themselves trapped against the base of the monument. The two protesters now seemed angrier than ever. Keane didn't like this situation at all.

"Hey!" the protester shouted. "I'm gonna kick—"

Keane lost the rest of what the man said, but his intentions were clear enough. He saw him start toward them purposefully. The man suddenly stopped. Keane was aware that someone had appeared at his own shoulder, standing beside him. The presence was so familiar that he knew who it was without looking.

Beau.

His cousin stood with his hands at his side, but there was

nothing casual in his body language. Beau and Keane were the same height, but where Keane was thin and angular, Beau possessed shoulders like sacks of grain and biceps big around as most people's thighs. Beau's dark eyes stared the man down. His face, already tan from tours of duty under foreign suns and days spent on the Chesapeake, grew darker as if a storm was blowing up from somewhere within him. Perhaps most disconcerting of all was the fact that he was smiling.

"Beau," Keane said. "It's not worth it."

"That's for this asshole to decide," Beau said. He asked the protester, "Is taking one more step really worth a week in the hospital?"

The protester hesitated, then glared at Keane. "Good thing for you that you brought your bodyguard," the man snapped. Then he and the man with the Anacreon T-shirt melted away into the crowd.

Keane took Charlene firmly by the arm and force-marched her away from the protest. At this point, he didn't much care if she was his boss, or not. Beau went ahead of them like an icebreaker.

Once they had reached the relative quiet of the sidewalk on Washington Street, Keane turned to his cousin.

"It's not that I'm not glad to see you, Beau. But what the hell are you doing here?"

"English Ed said something about you going to a protest with Charlene. That kind of got my attention. The Charlene part, especially."

"It's nice to see that you've finally taken an interest in history," Charlene said.

"My main interest was in seeing that my cousin and his boss didn't get torn apart by an angry mob," Beau said. "Although I've got to say, I really wanted that blockhead to try something."

"I'm fairly certain that blockhead was one of Charles Montgomery's followers," Keane said. "His Anacreon T-shirt was a dead giveaway."

"Charles Montgomery?" Beau wondered. "Isn't he that political commentator? I'm kind of surprised that you even know about him."

"It's a long story," Keane said.

Charlene sighed. "You know what we need?"

"Baseball bats?" Beau suggested.

"Actually, I was thinking of ice cream cones," Charlene said. "It's the best I can do since I quit drinking."

"Now that you mention it, I could use two scoops of rocky road on a sugar cone with rainbow sprinkles," Beau said. "That is, as long as you're buying."

27

I t was mid-afternoon the next day when Keane drove back down to St. Michaels and picked up Elizabeth. All was quiet in Easton after the previous day's protest, and Keane was relieved by the fact that Charlene had returned to DC the night before.

Seeing the man with the Anacreon T-shirt had prompted Keane to put in a call to Charles Montgomery. The man seemed to have gathered quite a following and Keane wanted to meet him in person.

To his surprise, Keane lucked out. Montgomery was at his home on the Choptank River rather than at his office in DC. Like many of the Washington elite, Montgomery had found a country getaway on the nearby Eastern Shore. Apparently, Montgomery had not read Marcus Aurelius. Even luckier for Keane was the fact that Montgomery's getaway happened to be a manor house called Tailwinds that dated back to colonial times. Keane had arranged a meeting under the premise of wanting to learn more about Tailwinds. Montgomery, it seemed, was only too happy to show off his historical gem.

"How much do you know about Charles Montgomery?"

Elizabeth asked as Keane drove the Corvette toward Dorchester County.

"Not much beyond the bio on his website. He's a retired Army colonel. For four years, he was the secretary of transportation on the cabinet of Governor White in North Carolina."

"Governor White? Didn't he want to bring spanking back to the public schools?"

"I think that was one of Governor White's gentler reforms," Keane said. "From what I understand, he lost re-election by a whisper. It sounds as if he and Montgomery are birds of a feather. The former governor has sort of faded into the woodwork, but Montgomery took his career in a different direction. He's on TV talk shows a lot. His last book was a bestseller."

"His message must resonate with somebody," she said.

"It must have resonated with Esteban Galarza because he had a signed copy of Montgomery's book in his office."

"What does that tell us?"

Keane smiled at Elizabeth's use of *us*. "I'm not exactly sure, other than the fact that Galarza must have liked what Montgomery had to say. I wonder how he got mixed up with Anacreon? From what I understand, it's the club for Montgomery insiders."

"Then that's what we need to go talk to Charles Montgomery about," Elizabeth said. "What's our plan here?"

"It turns out that Montgomery happens to have a love for history. It's why he bought an old estate near Hurlock in Dorchester County. The house dates to 1760. It wouldn't be untoward of a senior field agent for GAPS to be curious about his property, now would it?"

"And if you just happen to bring up Esteban Galarza and Anacreon—"

"Exactly."

"Hold on, Franklin. You don't think that Montgomery—"

"Stole the Star-Spangled Banner? Killed Galarza and

Lindermann?" Keane shook his head. "This is a former United States colonel and public official we're talking about. He's the former secretary of transportation for the state of North Carolina. He's a minor media celebrity. Somehow, I doubt that he masterminded the theft of the Star-Spangled Banner and two murders."

"OK, I don't disagree with that assessment," Elizabeth said. "But just to be on the safe side, does anyone else know we're going to interview him?"

"No. Why?"

Elizabeth took out her phone. "Give me your cousin's number. I'm texting him that if he doesn't hear from us, he needs to come looking for Charles Montgomery."

"I would never take you along if I thought there was any danger."

"Just give me Beau's number, Franklin."

He recited it from memory, and Elizabeth sent the text.

Once they left the main road, there wasn't much of anything except vast farm fields punctuated by the occasional crossroads cluster of modest homes. On the stretches of open road, Keane gave the Corvette some gas and let it run. Even Elizabeth seemed content to gaze out the windows at the passing scenery and listen to the big engine purr.

This remained one of the most rural, least populated areas in the sprawling metroplex that stretched in a broad swath from Richmond to Boston. The remote setting made property values affordable, and yet it was just a couple hours' drive to Washington, which made the Eastern Shore a favorite getaway for Washington's powerful and elite. Lately, momentum had been building for another bridge or even a tunnel that would link the Eastern Shore more directly to the Washington area. Keane felt it was a terrible idea in that it would destroy everything that was unique about the Eastern Shore.

Aside from farming and working the water, very little

industry existed. The Eastern Shore and Delmarva Peninsula were flat as a tabletop. Named for the three states that it overlapped, the peninsula was part of the coastal plain that had been underwater just a few thousand years ago. Much of the entire 183-mile-long peninsula was no more than a few feet above sea level. The soil tended to be sandy, and where it wasn't sandy, it was marshy.

Turning back the clock three centuries or more, this region had been punctuated by wealthy plantations, worked by indentured servants and slaves. Over time, the white indentured servants paid back the cost of their passage and were given land of their own. The enslaved population had no such escape from a life of drudgery. The sandy soil was ideal for growing tobacco, that colonial cash crop.

Montgomery's current home had been one of those plantations. They entered between two brick pillars that reminded Keane of the entrance to World's End. However, that was where the similarity ended. World's End had an almost quaint and forgotten feel, whereas there was no mistaking that the entrance to Tailwinds was a statement. A massive wrought iron gate blocked their way. Keane pressed a button and spoke into a speaker to announce himself. The gate opened silently to admit them, which was somehow eerier than if there had been a human sentinel at the gate.

He drove down the paved lane, lined with stately sycamores. Keane was impressed. He and Beau had run the numbers to see how much it would have cost to pave the lane at World's End, and decided that they could live with dirt and gravel. Montgomery must have deep pockets.

Keane parked the Corvette in a circular drive in front of the colonial-era brick home. Tailwinds had been built by the descendants of a soldier in the army of King James, who had fled to the Catholic colony of Maryland after the defeat of the king's forces in Ireland at the Battle of the Boyne in 1690.

They were shown inside by a clean-cut young man wearing a navy blue suit. "Come in, sir," he said, with a soldier's deference.

"Beautiful," Elizabeth murmured, taking in the ornate staircase, the cornflower blue walls hung with mirrors and oil paintings in gilt frames, and polished floors made of wide planks. More than two hundred years ago, this would have been a home fit for a lord. It was quite impressive for a retired Army colonel.

They were led to a new, modern wing at the back of the house, and shown into Charles Montgomery's private office. It was just as lavish, with Montgomery rising to greet them from behind a massive antique desk, but there were modern touches as well, such as the bachelor-sized television screen on the wall.

"Doctor Keane. And I understand that you are Miss Graham. How nice to meet you."

"The pleasure is mine, Colonel," Keane said.

Montgomery laughed. "I'm retired now, Doctor Keane. No need for military titles. Charles will do."

"And please, call me Franklin."

Montgomery was still gripping Keane's hand. "I can't tell you how excited I am to meet a descendant of Francis Scott Key. I come from a long line of soldiers, but none of them is quite so famous."

"Well, I would say that you are the one who is well known! I just saw your book at Barnes and Noble the other day."

"And I saw you on TV," Elizabeth added, having been temporarily forgotten by Montgomery.

Montgomery glanced at her, smiled vaguely, and turned his attention back to Keane.

"I understand that you came here today because of your interest in the history of Tailwinds," Montgomery said. "Why the sudden interest?"

"GAPS has been working to gather some information about

historic properties in Dorchester County because of the proposal for a new Chesapeake Bay crossing.

Montgomery sighed. "I suppose it's only a matter of time before that happens."

"Fortunately, it's not even a proposal yet. It's more in the fact-finding stage. I don't know how you feel about the possibility of a new crossing that would come ashore here in Dorchester County, and GAPS doesn't take a stand either way. What we are interested in is preserving historical sites."

Montgomery finally let go of Keane's hand. He looked startled. "You think my place is in the way?"

"Not directly, no. However, a new bay crossing would have a massive impact on the entire region."

"It would, indeed. Well, where should I start with today's tour?"

"How about where all history starts? At the beginning."

28

Montgomery led them into an elaborate formal parlor, just where guests would have been greeted by the lords of this tidewater manor two centuries before. The furniture was ornately carved and upholstered in rich brocade fabric. While elegant, the furnishings did not look particularly comfortable.

He pointed out a portrait of a man whose rugged face looked out of place above the soft lace collar that was fashionable well into the early eighteenth century.

"History runs deep here," Montgomery said. "Captain Fitzhugh was an officer in the army of King James II. James believed in religious freedom for all, so he was rather enlightened for the time. It turns out that William of Orange took exception to that policy as a good Protestant. After James's army was defeated at the Battle of the Boyne by William of Orange, the enlisted troops who had fought against the protestant king were pardoned, but not the leaders, most of whom were Catholic. Fitzhugh was forced to flee Ireland and wound up here. He probably built a modest dwelling on the property to keep the rain off."

"A vernacular structure," Keane said. "A lot of the earliest houses on the Eastern Shore were post and beam and daub, and they have not survived."

Montgomery nodded. "I'm sure that's exactly the case here. The brick house here came much later, when his family had become wealthy selling tobacco."

"Back then, the nickname for it was sot-weed. Europe couldn't get enough of it. Fortunes were indeed made," Keane said. "You have done a wonderful job of restoring the house to reflect that era."

"I really can't take credit for the restoration itself because I bought the place in 2008 during the Great Recession, from the owner of a media company that was a little too heavily invested in newspapers."

"His loss was your gain."

"I have to say that I see myself as a steward, Franklin. What do we really own in this world? Someday, this property will belong to someone else. I will take good care of it while it's mine."

Franklin smiled. "If only more owners of historical properties took the same view."

"I have to say, given your family history, that this seems like the perfect job for you."

"This is the part of the job that I enjoy." At last, Keane saw his chance to ask Montgomery the questions that had brought him to Tailwinds. "Earlier this week, though, I was involved in something more unpleasant. A man was murdered in the Cannonball House in St. Michaels, which GAPS was consulting on. You may have heard something about it?"

"I did. Homicides are rare enough on the Eastern Shore. It was terrible."

"Indeed it was. What made it worse was that the victim had been working on some project with an assistant curator at the Smithsonian, who was found dead the week before."

Montgomery took just an extra beat too long to respond. "How awful. Do you think there's some connection?"

Keane decided to gamble. He was not a police officer or skilled in any way with investigating murders. But he knew from a youth spent hunting with Beau that sometimes, to flush a rabbit or a pheasant, you had to beat a few bushes. "The murders may have had something to do with research they were doing about the Star-Spangled Banner at the Smithsonian."

"One of our most important national symbols," Montgomery said. He seemed to hesitate. "Do you know what they were researching?"

"As a matter of fact, I do. I don't know how much you know about the Star-Spangled Banner flag, but many years ago, one of the fifteen stars was cut away as a souvenir, never to be seen again. There is some speculation that the two of them had somehow come across this missing star."

If Montgomery made any attempt to hide his shock, he did not do a very good job of it. The retired colonel blanched. "Do you think there's any possibility that they did find this star?"

"Whoever killed Lindermann must have thought so. I heard from the police that his condo in Baltimore was ransacked."

"Someone must have known that he wouldn't be coming home, and decided to see if he had anything worth stealing."

"Maybe, but I doubt a Baltimore city librarian owned anything of real value. Just out of curiosity, the name of the Smithsonian assistant curator who was killed recently was Esteban Galarza. Did you know him?"

"No."

"Really? I would have thought that the name might ring a bell. Your new book was found in his office at the Smithsonian, inscribed to him. There was also something about him being a member of a group called Anacreon."

Montgomery was staring at him. "I haven't heard that anywhere. How did you know that?"

"It must have been reported in the media. Strange that you hadn't heard it. Tell me, what is this Anacreon about?"

Montgomery's eyes slid sideways for the briefest of moments. "Anacreon? Funny, the name means nothing to me."

"You didn't know Galarza?"

"I don't want to sound egotistical, but I've signed a lot of books. I don't remember him particularly. What's your interest in all of this, anyhow?"

Keane couldn't very well come out and admit that he knew the flag had been stolen, so he said, "The Smithsonian has asked me to look into whatever it was that Lindermann and Galazara were working on, in an unofficial capacity."

"I can see the Smithsonian's reasoning. Who better to research anything to do with the Star-Spangled Banner than Francis Scott Key's descendant?" Montgomery commented. He did not sound amused. "At the same time, perhaps it should not surprise us that there seems to be some bloodshed associated with the Star-Spangled Banner and the National Anthem."

"How so?"

"Come now, Doctor Keane. You of all people should know that our anthem demands violence and bloodshed in defense of our nation. No purple mountains majesties and amber waves of grain here, thank you very much. It is an anthem born of war."

"Indeed, it is." Keane had been thinking much the same thing recently. He was not reassured that he and Montgomery had been thinking along similar lines.

Their tour continued, but the tone of it had changed. It was too subtle to define, but Montgomery's demeanor was no longer so welcoming. Montgomery appeared preoccupied. Once or twice, he repeated something that he had said earlier. They passed another staircase going up, but he dismissed the entire third floor with a wave of his hand. "Storage and living space for some of the staff," he said.

By *staff*, Keane decided that Montgomery meant his paramilitary groupies. Distracted initially by the elegant surroundings of the house, Keane had not noticed the number of fit young men—and a woman or two—stationed in the hallways. Now, he noted them with a growing sense of discomfiture. It was almost as if they were on duty, like sentries. Clearly, these were ex-military men. He couldn't be sure, but he thought he saw the bulge of a weapon under one man's coat.

This was nothing short of a private security force. They seemed polite in a taciturn, professional manner, but Keane had no doubt that their attitude might turn on a dime—that is, at a command from Montgomery. He could sense a kind of fanaticism bubbling just beneath the surface like hot lava running under a skim of cooled stone.

Keane began to wonder if coming here had been such a good idea, after all. In particular, he did not like that he had managed to put Elizabeth in danger for the second time in as many days. First the protest, now the lion's den.

"Who are all of these men?" Keane finally blurted out.

After a moment's consideration, Montgomery said, "Society's detritus."

Keane was taken aback. "What do you mean?"

"These young men—and a few women, as you can see— have all served their country admirably in the military. Most of them served for ten or twelve years and then were dismissed based on the military's 'up or out' policy. They don't have many transferable skills, but they do make awfully good soldiers. So, I put them to work."

Keane laughed nervously. "It's almost as if you are building an army."

Montgomery smiled coldly. This new expression transformed his face, as if he had been wearing a mask that was beginning to slip. "And who's to say that I'm not? Doctor Keane, are you sure that your only interest is in the history of this house?"

"Certainly. Why else would I be here?"

"Why else, indeed?"

All pretense of this being a simple tour of the house had come to an end. Without coming out and saying it, both men sensed that the other was holding out. Montgomery brought them around again to the office wing, and they parted company politely enough, despite the retired colonel's cool manner.

"It has been a pleasure," Keane said. "I can't thank you enough for your time."

"Yes, thank you," was all that Elizabeth could manage. Montgomery had pointedly ignored her for much of the tour.

"One more thing," Montgomery said. He held up a finger. "I'll be right back."

He returned with two copies of his new book. He signed one copy of *Proudly We Hail* for Keane and one for Elizabeth, using an ornate wooden pen that he wielded with a well-practiced flourish.

Keane glanced at the inscription. "To Francis Scott Keane, Remember that the answer is always *yes*." The signature was a bold scrawl. It did not take a handwriting expert to deduce that the man had a large ego.

"Thank you," Keane said.

Despite the tension that both men felt, Montgomery smiled at him with amusement. "You know the question I'm referring to?"

"You might say that I'm acquainted with it. *Does that star-spangled banner yet wave over the land of the free and the home of the brave?*"

Liz glanced at her own inscription, which simply read, *With best wishes.*

A young aide escorted them back through the house. They

were almost to the front door when Keane noticed that the man coming the other way looked familiar to him. He was another military type, but older—and bigger—than the others. He had the look of a hardened campaigner about him, like a tough sergeant. The man caught Keane's eye, and there was a matching glimmer of recognition. The man slowed, as if he might say something, looking at Keane openly and quizzically as if trying to place him, but then he seemed to reach some decision. He stared straight ahead, ignoring Keane, but quickening his pace. He was headed in the direction of Montgomery's office.

Keane took Elizabeth by the elbow. "Walk faster," he muttered.

Outside, they wasted no time getting into the Corvette. Keane had the car rolling before Elizabeth had shut her door.

The big sycamores lining the lane flashed by.

"Franklin, what's wrong with you? Slow down."

He didn't answer but drove to the gate, which was closed. He stared at the gate, willing it to open, his hands gripping the steering wheel.

"Franklin?"

"I should not have brought you here and put you in danger," he said. "This was foolish."

"What are you talking about?"

The gate began to open, slowly, and he focused his attention on it instead of answering Elizabeth. As soon as a gap opened that was wide enough for the Corvette, he hit the gas and shot through. Only after they were a couple of miles down the road did he explain.

"I recognized that goon back there. The one we passed in the hallway. And I think he recognized me. I saw him keeping watch on Lindermann's place in Baltimore. He's the one who must have ransacked the condo, looking for the lost star."

"What does that mean?"

"It means I know Montgomery was lying. He must have had some interest in what Lindermann and Galarza were up to with their research. And if his goon remembers me from Linder- mann's condo, now Montgomery knows that I'm lying, too. The question is, what is he going to do about it?"

29

K eane let the Corvette fly down the open road. Under other circumstances, this would have been a carefree drive through a winsome autumn landscape. They passed marshes, vast fields of soybeans and corn ready for harvest, distant chicken barns and lonely farmhouses at the ends of long dirt lanes. However, he couldn't help but glance in the rear-view mirror from time to time, worried that one of Montgomery's thugs might have followed them. They were a long way from any sort of help.

As they drove toward Cambridge, another troubling realization was taking hold. Montgomery seemed to be interested in Bob Lindermann's research, considering that he appeared to have sent someone to keep an eye on his condo, and possibly to ransack it. Had Montgomery wanted the lost star that Keane now possessed? Could it be that Montgomery was involved in some way in Lindermann's murder? Or in Esteban Galarza's? The thought was chilling.

Elizabeth had been gazing out the window, seemingly lost in thought. Finally, she broke the silence.

"Have you had any insights about what the lost star might be a map of?" she asked.

Keane shook his head. "I'm not entirely sure that it even is a map. I'm honestly stumped. I was wondering which state the star might represent, hoping that it would offer some clue, but the stars aren't assigned to any particular state."

"Lindermann must have figured it out. Or maybe Galarza."

"Maybe. There's no evidence that they knew any more than we do, other than having possession of the star. Unfortunately, we are no longer able to ask them about it, either."

More disturbing thoughts came to mind. Keane realized that the visit to Tailwinds had raised more questions than it had answered. He now believed that Charles Montgomery was hiding something about having known Galarza. The colonel was being disingenuous about not remembering that he had signed a book for the Smithsonian assistant curator. Could it have been Montgomery who was responsible for the theft of the Star-Spangled Banner?

With his military background and paramilitary staff, the retired colonel seemed more than capable of pulling off such an operation.

But what would be his purpose for such a caper? The flag was priceless, and yet worthless at the same time—it could never be sold on the open market or openly displayed. There could be some private collectors who would pay a great deal for it. Montgomery didn't seem to need the money. Did Montgomery simply plan to decorate his home with the flag?

Keane dismissed the thought. Anyone, let alone Montgomery, would have to be insane to want to steal the Star-Spangled Banner. How could he ever hope to get away with it? And yet, Keane reminded himself, someone had indeed stolen the flag, and someone had gotten away with it, at least so far.

He shared his theory with Elizabeth.

"I agree that it's crazy," she replied, shouting to be heard over the wind roaring through the Corvette's open T-top. "I wouldn't have believed that Montgomery could be responsible. He's too much of a public figure. But having just spent time with the man, I have to admit that he's more than a little intense."

Keane had the same impression, but he wanted Elizabeth to expand on that. "How so?"

"Didn't we just both spend time with him? But let me see if I can put my finger on it. I would have said that Montgomery is creepy, but that's not quite right. No, the word *fanatical* would be the best way to describe him. He's like a modern-day John Brown or Guy Fawkes."

Keane nodded. That was a very apt description. "Both men attempted the impossible, but came very close to succeeding. Their actions were ultimately very symbolic and inspiring to many."

"Franklin, this is serious. What if Colonel Montgomery did have something to do with the theft of the Star-Spangled Banner? You need to call somebody!"

Keane agreed that it would be best to share his suspicions with authorities, but not then and there on the side of the road. They drove on to Cambridge, and parked on Main Street. The pleasant downtown area had brick sidewalks lined with shops and galleries. Small groups of tourists strolled the sidewalks.

"Why don't you see if you can find us something to eat while I make that call?" Keane asked.

"Agreed," Elizabeth said. She popped out of the Corvette, which was no easy feat, given that the car was so low to the pavement. "I don't know about you, but I could use a cup of coffee. I'm so wired right now that the caffeine is going to be soothing."

Keane declined a cup of coffee. The last thing his nerves needed right now was caffeine. If there wasn't a long drive ahead of him, he would have opted for a stiff drink. Or two.

He still had his calls to make, so he sat there in the car and made them as Elizabeth prowled the offerings of Cambridge's Main Street. Like a lot of small towns, Cambridge was still struggling to get beyond the Great Recession that had pulled the rug out from several already tenuous downtown businesses and employers. In fact, in could even be said that the town had never really recovered from the race riots that had rent it asunder in 1963 with gunfights between blacks and whites, and threats by rioters to burn down the town. That had been a long time ago, but racial tension cast a long shadow from one generation to the next.

On a brighter note, sharpshooter Annie Oakley had retired here in the early 1900s after traveling the world as part of Buffalo Bill's Wild West Show. Her home was now on the National Register of Historic Places.

His first call was to Roger Biesty at the Smithsonian. He was not quite ready to share his suspicions about Charles Montgomery or reveal his discovery of what might be the lost star, but he left a voicemail to reassure the director that he was still making inquiries. His call to Charlene Dearborn also went to voicemail.

With a sigh, he dug out the card that the FBI agents had given him during their visit to World's End. Again, his call went to voicemail. He was beginning to get the feeling that he must be unofficially persona non grata.

To his surprise, his phone jangled and he glanced at the screen. FBI.

"Doctor Keane, this is Agent Canfield. What can I do for you?"

As succinctly as possible, Keane summed up his theory that Charles Montgomery might be connected, in some way, with the theft of the Star-Spangled Banner. Keane had to admit that his explanation sounded thinner and thinner, even to his own ears.

The agent heard him out, but Keane's explanation was greeted by a long silence. "We told you to stay out of this."

"Which is exactly why I am passing this information on to you."

"Uh huh. So what you are saying is that Charles Montgomery, a retired Army colonel and accomplished public servant who is now a best-selling author and commentator on Fox News, murdered two people and stole the Star-Spangled Banner?"

"Well, when you put it like that—"

"Stick to your history books, Doctor Keane. Leave the detecting to us."

Keane might have tried to make his case yet again, but he was met by silence. The FBI agent had already ended the call.

He was more than happy to leave the criminal investigation to the FBI, but there were aspects of the historical investigation for which he still needed answers. The FBI would not be of much help there. However, Keane knew where he might find some of those answers. In the morning, he would point the classic Corvette south toward the Nabb Center at Salisbury University.

Elizabeth returned with her coffee, a couple of candy bars, and a bottle of water, which she handed to Keane.

"I'm afraid the offerings are somewhat limited," she said. "The only place open this late in the day was a pharmacy."

He uncapped the water and took a long drink. "Thank you."

"What now?"

"Let's get you back to St. Michaels. In the morning, I'm going to head into Salisbury to do some research at the Nabb Center."

It was a good hour's drive back to The Town that Fooled the British. By then, darkness was beginning to fall. The autumn days were not as long as they used to be.

Keane asked about the Cannonball House, which still had

not re-opened to the public. Elizabeth reported that the local ghost tour company was clamoring to add the house to its list of destinations in St. Michaels. The recent murder made it a hot property, considering that there had not been a homicide in St. Michaels in living memory, possibly not since the days of the Chesapeake Bay Oyster Wars, when squabbles over watermen's oystering grounds had turned deadly.

"What do you think about that?" she asked. "They want to make the house a stop on the ghost tour and come inside. It seems a little kitschy to me, if not in outright bad taste."

"Officially, I don't think much of ghost tours. The Great American Preservation Society promotes history and architecture, but not ghost stories." Keane smiled. "That said, I agree that they can be entertaining. And what's the harm if it gets a few more people in the door?"

"There is supposed to be a boy with a lantern who haunts the house," Elizabeth said. "But the recent murder is what people are really interested in."

Keane did not comment on the boy with the lantern. Although he had seen that apparition for himself, he wasn't about to share that with Elizabeth. As for Bob Lindermann, Keane certainly hoped that his spirit was not haunting the Cannonball House.

Keane was planning on just dropping Elizabeth off at her new place, but as she prepared to get out, she stopped short of opening the car door.

"Wait a minute. Are you going to drive all the way back to World's End and then to Salisbury University in the morning?"

"I thought I might book a hotel in Easton," Keane admitted. World's End was at least a 90-minute drive to the north. Heading there and back again in the morning would easily add three hours to his trip to the university.

"Listen, my new place has a very comfortable sofa," she said. "Why waste the money on a hotel room, even if you are a rich guy? Besides, I've been perfecting my crab cake recipe. I could use someone else to try my crab cakes out on." She paused. "Oh, I almost forgot that you don't eat seafood."

"I think I could make an exception in this case, but I hope that you are not one of those people who put green and red bell peppers in your crab cakes."

"No, I'm using a recipe for Crisfield crab cakes that I found in an old church cookbook at the St. Michaels library."

"Abomination avoided in that case, thank goodness. However, I really couldn't impose—"

"Franklin, it's already eight o'clock. If you head home, you've got nearly two hours of driving ahead of you and it's been a long day already. Besides, you're not going to be imposing on anything but the sofa cushions. Also, you can say hello to Star."

"Star?"

"The cat. Remember, the one you rescued from Lindermann's condo in Baltimore? The cat that you insisted I take so that your wolfhounds wouldn't eat him?"

"Star," he said, nodding.

"Well?" she asked.

Keane's instinct was to say no. He did feel that he would be imposing, no matter what Elizabeth said. Also, he felt that it would be awkward for the two of them to be alone together. He glanced at his vintage Timex. Elizabeth was right; it was almost eight o'clock. He felt exhaustion nagging at him and was not looking forward to the long drive, just to sleep in his own bed.

"All right," he said. "If you're sure I'm not imposing."

"Ha! I've got to tell you something, Franklin. You've been imposing on me for the last few days, ever since you sent that text message about there being an emergency at the Cannonball House. And I've also got to say that I've loved every minute of it. Who knew that history could be so exciting?"

30

E lizabeth's apartment appeared charmingly cluttered, with books stacked on every tabletop and pictures that she had not yet hung leaning against the walls. She was still in the process of moving in, but Keane had yet to meet a historian of any note whose home or office was neat and orderly. He supposed that this said a great deal about the average historian's state of mind.

There was indeed a couch, a brand-new Ikea model—cheap but long enough to accommodate his lanky frame. Star seemed to have claimed one end, curled up against the cushions and looking right at home.

Elizabeth warmed up two of her leftover crab cakes. No actual space presented itself for eating at the dining room table and there was a dearth of furniture in the tiny living room, so they both sat on the couch. Elizabeth connected her iPhone to a Bluetooth speaker, and jazz filled the space. She lit a candle on the coffee table. Keane began to feel that there was a little too much ambiance for what was just supposed to be sofa surfing. His misgivings increased when Elizabeth went back into the kitchen and reappeared with a chilled bottle of Pinot Grigio and two glasses.

Keane accepted a glass, but said, "Elizabeth, I don't want any misunderstandings."

"Don't flatter yourself too much, Keane," she said tersely. "Just because we have a glass of wine or two it doesn't mean that I'm going to let you jump my bones."

He set the glass down. "Maybe I should go."

"Listen, that came out wrong."

"I agree. Nobody says 'jump my bones' anymore."

Elizabeth took a big sip of wine as if fortifying herself. "Franklin, please don't take this the wrong way, and forgive me if I'm speaking out of turn, because I hardly know you, but it's like you have this pall of sadness hanging over you. It's Amanda's ghost, following you around."

Keane felt his jaw clench. "My wife is not a ghost."

Elizabeth winced. "I can't seem to get anything right tonight."

"Well, the crab cakes are good."

"That's something, at least." Elizabeth sighed. "You miss her terribly, don't you?"

"It's like a hole in my heart. You hear that spoken as a cliché all the time, but it's true."

"I'm so sorry, Franklin. She must have been really special. How did you two meet?"

"We were both grad students at Yale. Amanda was studying for her master of fine arts while I was earning my doctorate in history."

"Yale, huh? Gee, I won't be hanging up my freshly inked diploma from Towson State University anytime soon."

"Education is what you make of it, Elizabeth. A diploma is just a piece of paper."

They both sipped their wine, lost in their thoughts. Elizabeth poured herself a second glass. "What happened out there on the water that night?" Elizabeth asked.

Keane hesitated. Normally, he would not have opened up to someone he had known for only a few days about something so deeply personal and painful. However, Elizabeth seemed to exude a trustworthy quality. He had confided to her about the discovery of the lost star, after all, and even brought her along to Montgomery's lair. He had stopped short of explaining his unique gift for retrocognition, however.

"It's ... it's difficult to explain what happened, even though I've done so many times," he began. "We spent the day sailing and anchored in the Choptank. It was a wonderful spot, with no one else around. That evening, he saw some strange lights ... will o' wisps. We had never seen anything like them before, like something out of legend. The floating lights were beautiful and mysterious and more than a little spooky. We went below, and when I woke up in the morning, Amanda had disappeared. I can't help but think that the will o' wisps had something to do with it, or were a portent of some sort. You can probably imagine how far I got with the state police when I started talking about strange lights in the sky."

Elizabeth nodded. "Don't forget that I met Detective Crawford at the Cannonball House. He's not exactly a friendly guy."

She leaned toward him to pour wine so that scarcely a foot separated them, face to face. Her eyes flicked up and held his. In the movies, he was well aware that this was the scene where the two characters would have kissed.

But Keane wasn't looking for a Hollywood ending. He sat back against the cushions, out of reach. The moment passed.

Elizabeth turned business-like. She scooped up her wine. "Well, I am going into my bedroom, and I am going to leave you here on the couch." She nodded at Star and then said with the hint of a smile, "Just to be clear, that's the only company that you're getting tonight."

It turned out she was wrong about that. The cat slid off the sofa and followed Elizabeth into the bedroom. Elizabeth shut the door firmly behind her without looking back.

As he put his head down on the pillow, smelling the faintly chemical odor of the new fabric, a thousand thoughts and conflicting emotions threatened to sweep up Keane like a whirlwind. Part of what he felt, he realized, was regret. He had just soundly rejected the only woman who had interested him since Amanda.

Exhausted as he was, sleep now threatened to be elusive. However, he had become very good at emptying his mind through the practice of retrocognition. He shuttered off the detritus and the noise of his thoughts until there was only the vision of a will o' wisp moving across dark water toward a distant reed-covered shore. He followed it toward oblivion.

31

In the morning, Keane was up before Elizabeth—or the cat —made an appearance. He had learned a long time ago to keep a spare change of clothes and a toothbrush in the trunk of the Corvette for occasions when work kept him overnight unexpectedly, and this came in handy now. He left a note and was out the door before eight. He stopped for breakfast in Easton at a new place where the menu seemed filled with omelets made with egg whites and served not with hash browns, but with salad greens. What was the Eastern Shore coming to? Such a menu almost, but not quite, made him nostalgic for creamed chip beef, or scrapple and eggs.

His destination was the Nabb Center for Delmarva History at Salisbury University. Ostensibly, he would be researching Tidewinds on behalf of GAPS, just as he had told Charles Montgomery. In reality, he wanted to learn more about the changes that Montgomery had made in hopes that it would hint at what the man was up to at the historic property. He must be involved somehow in this Star-Spangled caper, but Keane still was not sure how or to what extent.

The Nabb Center was located in the impressive new library

at the Guerrieri Academic Commons. Keane loved libraries. It seemed to him that such places grew even grander in proportion to the waning need for physical libraries. Nonetheless, the library seemed popular with the students, who filled every available space by surrounding themselves with a host of electronic devices that included laptop computers, tablets, Kindles, and smartphones. A few read actual books and wrote notes on actual paper with actual pens, which gave Keane hope for the future. Keane was no Luddite, but libraries made him nostalgic for the days of ink and paper.

He climbed a staircase designed to resemble crabs stacked one atop the other with outstretched claws, and turned right on the third floor.

His old friend Eric Vaughn ran the Nabb Center.

"It's good to see you, Eric."

"O say, Franklin. It's good to see that your banner still waves."

Keane rolled his eyes, but couldn't help but grin. Eric never tired of making some allusion to Keane's family history.

"How's the 'Vette?" They both shared an affinity for old cars.

"I drove it down today, as a matter of fact. Still got that GTO?"

"I'd sell my firstborn before I'd sell that car!" Vaughn's vehicle was a 1968 GTO that had belonged to his father.

They shook hands, and Keane was pleased to see that his old friend was looking well. His hair was now mostly white, and the few extra pounds he carried hinted at the fact that he no longer sprinted up and down stairs with boxes of documents as he had done in the old days.

"I thought we might have seen you at the War of 1812 symposium," Keane said.

"My wife and I had a wedding out of town, or I would have been there. It sounds as if I missed all the excitement, what with Bob Lindermann being murdered at the Cannonball

House in St. Michaels. Bob could be about as pleasant as barb wire, and he sure as hell pissed off a lot of people over the years, but what happened to him was awful."

Keane nodded. The historical community was a small one, and Lindermann's death had shaken everyone in it.

They stood there a moment, considering that, and before their thoughts turned maudlin, Keane said, "This new home is amazing."

Vaughn nodded, proud to show it off.

When Vaughn had taken over as director, the center consisted of a few rows of filing cabinets in a dark corner of a basement in the previous library building. That had been in the era before the internet, when only a few dedicated scholars were even aware of the center's existence. Quietly and with patience, Vaughn had continued to amass records pertaining to Delmarva history long into the digital era. Finally, the research center had surroundings that matched its reputation.

"When you told me that you were coming down, I pulled some files about Tailwinds."

"Files?"

"Believe it or not, we haven't digitized everything." Vaughn paused, his curiosity shining through. "Charles Montgomery owns that place now. I understand that he's done quite a bit of restoration work."

"What's your take on Montgomery?" Keane asked.

Vaughn shrugged. "A lot of people believe his nonsense, this idea that the Constitution was handed down from on high like the Ten Commandments and should never be deviated from. He's on TV often enough, and people sure buy his books. But he can't be all bad if he's poured so much money into Tailwinds. He clearly has an affinity for history."

Keane nodded, not wanting to show his hand too much, even with Vaughn. He had no idea what he might learn from looking over the Nabb Center's files on Tailwinds. Montgomery had invested a great deal of time and money there, and many preservationists might be happy to look the other way in terms of Montgomery's politics as a result.

Taking the files to an empty worktable, Keane got busy reading. He found estate inventories from the late 1700s, hand-written surveys, even handbills describing runaway slaves from the plantation. It was a treasure trove. However, nothing in the historical records hinted at Montgomery's true interest in the property or what he ultimately planned to do there—such as start his own republic in the remote marshes of Dorchester County.

Vaughn stopped by to check on him, carrying a fresh stack of documents. "Of course, I know your primary area of interest is the War of 1812. I have some interesting information here about the construction of the star fort that you should take a look at sometime."

Keane was only half-listening, his attention taken up by the documents spread before him. Suddenly, he froze. "Wait, what did you just say?"

"Just that I've come across an interesting letter from the War of 1812 era."

"Yes, but what about it? You mentioned something about a fort?"

"Right, the man was working on the construction of what he called the Star Fort. At least, that's how he identified the fort in his letter. He was referring to Fort McHenry, of course."

"The Star Fort!" For strategic purposes, Fort McHenry had been designed as a five-sided fort. Seen from above, its elaborate redoubts added to the overall appearance of a star. Keane walked over and gripped Vaughn by the shoulders and grinned broadly. "You have just made my day."

Without further explanation, Keane hurried out of the library toward the parking lot, leaving his mystified colleague behind.

There was no doubt that the star taken from the Star-Spangled Banner was a map of some sort. But a map of what? Until that moment, Keane had been stumped. Now, it seemed so obvious that he was not sure how he could have missed it. The star represented Fort McHenry itself.

Now, an even greater question remained. What had Francis Scott Key felt compelled to secret away at Fort McHenry?

Keane planned to find out, but he was going to need a little help.

32

B ack in his car, Keane took a moment to decide upon his next course of action. The research into Charles Montgomery and Tidewinds seemed to be a dead end. It might prove useful if GAPS ever called upon to mitigate any damage to historical sites caused by the construction of a new Chesapeake Bay bridge in the near future, but it did not give him many insights into Montgomery. For such an outspoken public figure, he still managed to remain something of an enigma. Whatever his plans were for Tidewinds and his small army of militant followers, Montgomery had managed to keep that under wraps.

Where one door closed, another opened. The realization that the lost star was actually a map of Fort McHenry was an unexpected windfall of his visit to the Nabb Center, and wholly thanks to his old friend, the curator. Keane thumped the steering wheel in frustration at his own obtuseness. How could he have missed that connection? The association with Baltimore's so-called Star Fort now seemed obvious.

He pulled back out onto Route 13 and headed north, keeping an eye on the speedometer. His right foot seemed to have a mind of its own. The route was infamous for its speed traps, with each small town along the way fattening its coffers by dropping the speed limit to thirty or thirty-five in town limits, thus ensnaring motorists. The Corvette was far from inconspicuous to the small-town cops armed with their radar guns. Only when he approached Dover and the seventy mph Route 1 could he let the big engine run.

He needed to get back to World's End to think this through. He needed to examine the lost star again. And he needed time to plan.

It was still daylight when he turned into the long lane at World's End. The gloom of the overhanging Osage orange trees, however, made it seem much later. He spotted deer, rabbits, and a blur of red that could only be the resident fox. The sight gladdened his heart.

Boru and Danu heard the car and came bounding down the lane to greet him. Both dogs were so big that from the low-slung driver's seat of the 'Vette, Keane had to look up at them.

He parked the car and gave the dogs a good scratching around the ears, praising them in Irish as he did so, just like Jack Keane had done with his dogs.

He entered the house through the side door, into his rooms. Immediately, he saw that the pizza box containing the lost star was nowhere in sight.

Keane froze. He felt his stomach drop toward the floor. He looked around anxiously. He was positive that he had left the pizza box on the big dining room table. His theory was that hiding it in plain sight might be most effective, just as it had been for Lindermann.

Now, he seemed to have been wrong about that.

He considered a couple of possibilities. One was that either the FBI or one of Montgomery's thugs had entered the house and taken the star. With Boru and Danu on duty, however, that possibility seemed unlikely.

Which left a second possibility.

"Ed!" he shouted, sounding a bit more hysterical than he would have liked.

English Ed came shuffling in, wearing stylish Nike sweat-pants, slippers, and a T-shirt that urged, *KEEP CALM AND CARRY ON.*

"What's all the shouting about? Was someone murdered?"

"Did you throw out a pizza box that was on the worktable?"

"I might have. I can't remember."

"Ed, I've asked you a million times to leave my things alone." He regretted that he sounded like the petulant teenage boy that he had once been.

"Oh, bollocks to that. I'm just clearing things away. Trying to do my job."

"Ed, you haven't done any work around here since the nineteen-eighties."

"I don't see what all the fuss over a pizza box is about," the old man huffed, and shuffled back into the main house.

Keane hurried around to the back door leading to the kitchen. There, buried under a couple of trash bags, was the pizza box with the star inside. Keane sighed with an enormous sense of relief.

He brushed off the box, which was a little worse for wear and now had some new stains, but was still usable. He brought it back inside and put the box on the table. He flipped open the lid to gaze at the star inside. He could just see the hand-drawn star and the *three paces* written just above it, between the mark and the point of the cloth star, the ink faded by time.

What could be so important that Francis Scott Key had used an actual star from the Star-Spangled Banner to make a map? He certainly hadn't wanted the map to be deemed unimportant, and yet the use of the star was a code in itself. Only someone familiar with Fort McHenry could have any hope of deciphering what the map meant. Even Keane had only just figured it out.

There was only one way to find out where the map led. He needed to take a trip to Fort McHenry.

However, it wouldn't hurt to have a little help.

Immediately, Elizabeth Graham came to mind.

He took out his phone and gave her a call.

"Aren't you the early riser," she said. "You were up before the chickens this morning. I thought that you would at least buy me breakfast."

"I certainly owe you breakfast, at the very least," he said, and thanked her again for the use of her sofa. "Let me buy you breakfast tomorrow morning. Or maybe lunch. Can you meet me here at World's End?"

"Sure. What's up?"

Keane hesitated. Dealing with Charles Montgomery, and the potential stakes, had made him cautious about stating anything important over a mobile phone. "This involves the planetary object that we've been discussing?"

"OK," she said slowly, her tone indicating that she thought Keane had lost his mind.

"I have determined what it represents," he said.

"We already know it's a map," she said.

"Not over the phone," Keane cautioned. "Anyhow, you are correct that we knew the what, but not the where. I've figured out the where."

"I'll be there by ten," Elizabeth said.

After he got off the phone, Keane called the dogs for a walk in the gathering twilight. The evenings were much cooler now. Keane could smell autumn in the air, even if the leaves had weeks to go before they turned. A hint of wood smoke drifted on the faint breeze, indicating that one of their distant neighbors had a fire going.

Beau was driving back from the wharf after a day of fishing and slowed when he saw Keane strolling under the massive sycamores lining the road.

"How's things, Cuz?" Beau asked.

"A little crazy right now, to tell you the truth. How about you? Catch anything?"

"Remind me not to take charters again with bankers," Beau said. "They drink too much, and don't fish enough. I felt more like a taxi driver after last call than a boat captain."

"Beau, what did we used to tell each other when we were about to do something stupid?"

Beau grinned. "That's easy. 'Don't do it.' If I recall, it was usually you saying it to me. You want some help?"

"It's probably best if just one of us ends up in prison. Someone needs to stay here and take care of World's End when old English Ed goes completely senile."

"That serious, huh? Are you sure you want to go through with this?"

Keane grinned. "Hell, yeah."

"That's my boy. Don't worry. I'll have the bail money ready. Does this by any chance involve that nutjob Charles Montgomery? I'd steer clear of him, if I were you."

"This doesn't involve Montgomery, at least not directly."

"That much is good to know."

Beau had been kidding about the bail money, but Keane suspected that his cousin would need quite a pile of cash if he got caught doing what he planned to do tomorrow.

33

K eane went to bed exhausted, but found that he tossed and turned. Around midnight, Keane gave up trying to sleep. Tired though he was, he had too much on his mind, not the least of which concerned his plan to visit Fort McHenry. Something else nagged at him, although he couldn't quite put his finger on it.

He went downstairs and clicked on one small lamp, leaving deep shadows in the room. The dogs stirred and went right on sleeping. Keane stepped around them. He opened a couple of windows to let in some fresh air. The chorus of crickets went up a few decibels, but the night was quiet otherwise. He looked in the direction of Beau's compound, but no lights were visible through the trees. Professional hunting and fishing guides tended be early risers. Beau had gotten into the habit of early mornings in the military.

He still wasn't sure what was bothering him. He found himself sitting in front of his MacBook Pro at the big farm table. He flipped it open and without really thinking about what he was doing, he typed a name into the search engine.

Charles Montgomery.

That was it. The something that had been nagging at him was actually a *someone*.

Earlier that day, he had called an old friend in the Maryland State Police. A.J. Heaps had been one of the local kids that he and Beau had hung out with as teenagers. Heaps had been one of Beau's friends more so than Franklin's, but over the years, Heaps had stayed in touch with them both and visited World's End every fall to do some dove hunting. Heaps had not been involved in the investigation into Amanda's death, but he was one of the few who had never doubted Keane. Heaps had kept him updated on what he knew or heard through the state police grapevine.

After they'd caught up, Keane asked, "I've been looking into something, and I was just curious as to whether a man named Charles Montgomery was on the state police radar at all."

"Charles Montgomery? Doesn't ring a bell," Heaps said. "What is he, some kind of drug dealer down in Cecilton?"

Keane laughed. Heaps was referring to the nearest town to World's End, a country crossroads that consisted of a traffic light, a gas station, and a post office. "I doubt very much that Montgomery is into drugs. He's down in Dorchester County, where he has quite a beautiful old place on the Choptank River. You may have seen him on television—"

"You mean *that* Charles Montgomery? What does this have to do with historic preservation, might I ask?"

"Quite a lot, I'm afraid, or so I think," Keane said.

"There's nothing specific that I've heard about him, Franklin." Heaps was quiet a moment. "However, you don't have to be in the state police to know that he may be a good person to stay away from."

"How do you mean?"

"Just be careful, Franklin," Heaps said. "A guy like that has a lot of powerful friends and attracts a lot of wing nuts. Stick with your old houses and history, buddy."

Beau had given him much the same warning just that evening.

Thinking about it now, Keane realized that he had been naive in hoping that he could learn anything about Montgomery from his visit to Tailwinds. While Montgomery had seemed willing enough at first to share the history of his historic home, he and his operators were far too sophisticated to reveal any of the cards that they held concerning the Star-Spangled Banner. It was Keane who had accidentally given away more than he gained, when Montgomery's thug had recognized him from Lindermann's condo in Baltimore.

The question remained, what did Montgomery plan to do with the information that Keane had been in Baltimore? A man with Montgomery's resources would have no trouble tracking him down. Could he be in trouble, even now? Worse yet, Keane had unwittingly implicated Elizabeth. The thought that he may have put Elizabeth in danger troubled him.

He fought the urge to text her, considering that it was after midnight.

He could see now that he should have dug deeper and done some research before his visit to Tailwinds. Had he been more aware of the sinister side of Montgomery, he might have stayed away.

Once Keane pressed the Enter key, the search returned dozens of hits. Charles Montgomery was quite the newsmaker.

Keane knew the basics, of course. But he was not much of a TV watcher. He didn't even have a cable hookup at World's End, or even a Netflix account. The two big screens—one upstairs, one downstairs—were mainly for watching movies from his DVD collection on the rare occasions that Keane took an evening off. If something was going on in the world, he depended on English Ed to tell him about it.

Many of the search items were links to video clips from Montgomery's television appearances. He had also been on dozens of podcasts and YouTube channel interviews, both of which were increasingly important media outlets.

Keane clicked on a link to a video clip of the retired colonel being interviewed about current immigration policy as a guest on a political commentary show.

"Nations have a responsibility to safeguard their borders and preserve their heritage," he said. "These ideas are nothing new in the United States, of course. We could go all the way back to the Chinese Exclusion Act of 1882."

"But it sounds as if what you're talking about is returning to nativist policies," the TV host said.

"You make nativist sound like a dirty word," Montgomery scoffed. "Since when is nativism a bad policy? It worked for America more than a hundred years ago, and it can work for us now."

The clip had been posted on YouTube, and it had more than two hundred thousand likes. Judging from the hundreds of comments, Montgomery had succinctly summed up the way that many of the people watching the video felt.

Some of the clips were posted by the media outlets themselves, but many others were posted by Anacreon. The name sent a chill through him. He clicked on the name, but it was only a screen handle without any explanation, although the only posts Anacreon had made were Charles Montgomery videos.

Politics was not Keane's realm, but he was familiar enough with history. The Chinese Exclusion Act had not only limited Asian immigrants to the United States—although construction of the Intercontinental Railroad had depended heavily on the cheap labor they provided—but had denied Asian immigrants any chance of citizenship.

Beyond the open window, from far across the dark fields, came the cry of some animal. To Keane's ears, it sounded like the dying scream of a rabbit or even a young deer pulled down by coyotes. He listened uneasily as the scream faded to a whimper. Boru, ever vigilant, lifted his great head and growled from deep in his chest.

"Easy boy," Keane said softy, although he was unnerved by the sound.

When she had visited World's End, Elizabeth had noted how peaceful it seemed. She was right about that, but the sound reminded Keane that an entire cycle of life and death was happening, just as it always had before the first footings of the original house were set in the late sixteen hundreds.

Keane turned back to the MacBook. He clicked on another link, and another. The more clips that Keane watched, the more disconcerting they became, because this was too much like having Montgomery in the room. There was also a sameness about Montgomery. He always wore a suit and tie, his silver hair remained cut in military fashion. His voice and mannerism were alternately gruff and avuncular. Keane grew tired of the sight of him.

Keane was more inclined to research history, particularly the history of old houses for preservation efforts. Researching a living person to any extent was new territory. When he delved into history, he felt like an explorer. Watching these seemingly endless videos of Montgomery, he felt exhausted by the constant rhetoric.

From outside the window came another scream, this time much closer. Keane jolted in his chair. The ungodly sound chilled him to the bone and he sat listening, unable to move. Then the banshee wail stopped as suddenly as it had started. Keane found that he had been holding his breath, and he remembered to breathe again. He reminded himself that it was only an animal.

The noise brought both Boru and Danu to their feet, and the big dogs surged toward the window, barking savagely.

Keane got up and closed the windows, momentarily

nervous about being framed in the rectangles of light. He pulled down the blinds.

He returned to the computer, but he'd had enough of listening to Montgomery videos. He searched for Anacreon, but other than the historical background about the Greek poet, that led to a dead end. Anacreon remained a mystery, its purpose and meaning known only to Montgomery and his followers—such as Esteban Galarza, or "Steve," as the inscription in the copy of Montgomery's book had called him.

Keane closed the laptop and picked up the copy of *Proudly We Hail* inscribed to Galarza. He flipped through a few chapters, dipping into the text here and there. He skimmed over a lot of what seemed to be an allegorical history filled with stories of the "George Washington cut down the cherry tree" and "Honest Abe" variety without any room for nuance. It was American history as dogma. Montgomery had included his agenda for preserving those values. Helpfully, the book included an index, where Keane found the Star-Spangled Banner listed on page eighty-three. He turned to that page and began to read.

ONE OF THE key foundations of our common bond as Americans comes from our shared national symbols. There is Uncle Sam, of course, and the bald eagle. But one of our most important national symbols as a people is our flag. Born of fire and blood and sacrifice, it represents our shared sacrifices from the War for Independence to the Civil War to World War II and beyond. If there is one flag that waves above all the others, it is the Star-Spangled Banner that flew above Fort McHenry during the Battle of Baltimore in the War of 1812. We sometimes overlook this Second War of Independence or dismiss it as a minor conflict, but that would be a mistake. The Star-Spangled Banner represents resilience and unity as Americans. *When freemen shall stand.* It is our greatest symbol of liberty.

When the flag is threatened, we must rally around it. Those who threaten to destroy the flag aren't attacking a scrap of fabric, they are attacking a cloth soaked in history and blood, a representation of America itself.

KEANE FELT that he was as patriotic as any American. For him, it wasn't just about history, it was also about his own family—chief among that family being the man who had written the words to the National Anthem.

He was uneasy about that mention of the Star-Spangled Banner, but Keane was unable to read between the lines. He still didn't know what Montgomery was up to, or what his motivations were.

Finally, sleep tugged at Keane. He turned off the lights and climbed the stairs, leaving the dogs to keep watch for whatever had prowled beyond the windows tonight.

34

K eane awoke early the next morning and spent some time taking high-resolution photographs of the star using his Nikon camera. For what he had in mind, he had decided that taking along the artifact itself wasn't a good idea. He certainly was not going to stuff a piece of the Star-Spangled Banner into his coat pocket, if it could be avoided.

He was not sure where to secure the star when he was done, then settled on returning it to the stained pizza box on his work table. Hiding the star in plain sight had worked so far, just as long as English Ed didn't go on another cleaning binge.

Elizabeth arrived at World's End by ten. They drove into the nearby town of Chesapeake City and he bought her breakfast at a little place he knew on Bohemia Avenue before they got on the road to Baltimore.

Neither of them talked much on the way down, so Keane focused on his driving. The Lincoln MKX SUV felt right at home on the interstate. At the tunnel, he got into the right-hand lanes in order to exit onto Key Highway—named, of course, for his famous ancestor.

Across the state of Maryland, dozens of public buildings and places were named after Francis Scott Key. The Key Bridge carried I-695 over the harbor. There was a Francis Scott Key high school and not one, but two, elementary schools. Dozens and dozens of small businesses in the Baltimore area had adopted the name to impart an element of tradition and trust, right down to Key Insurance and Key Hardware and Key Liquors. A shopping mall in Frederick County was named after Francis Scott Key, and even a minor league baseball team: the Frederick Keys.

It never ceased to amaze Keane how one inspired act of creation—in this case, jotting down a few lines of poetry on the back of an envelope—could reverberate down the centuries that followed. It was likely that countless people had been inspired to write a poem or song to commemorate history. A few might even have witnessed the event. Out of all those poems and songs, however, only one had become the National Anthem. Key had simply been in the right place at the right time. He had written from his heart. In the end, it wasn't the poem, but the song that caught fire. The popularity of his poem was purely organic—he had not been a self-promoter in any way, and he had not tried whatsoever to profit from his poem.

Still musing, Keane turned off Key Highway onto Fort Avenue.

Fort McHenry National Monument and Historic Shrine was located on a point of land that bumped out into the entrance to Baltimore Harbor. Two hundred years ago, the fort was removed from the city itself, separated by pasture land and marshy areas. A visitor approaching along the muddy lane from the city was more likely to be chased by a bull or a mean hog than a redcoat.

Today, the fort was just beyond the fringes of the sprawling city. Fort Avenue leading to the fort was lined with row homes, with a more recent edition being condos where the Baltimore grain port had once been located. Huge ocean-going vessels occupied the docks and piers across the harbor from the fort, where two centuries ago there had been nothing more than a marshy expanse.

"How do you propose finding anything at Fort McHenry? Without any equipment, I mean."

"I have the map. A flashlight. And a shovel."

"Is that enough? What about a GPS? I don't know. What else? Maybe a compass?"

Keane hesitated. Of course, the map and the shove and the flashlight would be useful, but he was also relying on his retrocognition abilities to help him find whatever Key had left at the fort. He had not explained his talent for retrocognition to Elizabeth. It was not something that he normally shared with anyone—beyond those that Keane had studied with to improve his skills, Beau was just about the only person who knew. "I have a few tricks up my sleeve," he said vaguely.

"Would one of those tricks be a metal detector?"

He shook his head. "It's a little more complicated than that."

"Complicated? What, do you own a pocket-sized ground-penetrating radar unit?"

"Nothing like that, I'm afraid." He hesitated, wondering how much he should tell her. He felt that he could trust Elizabeth, but at the same time, he didn't want to scare her off and have her think that he was some kind of devotee of reading tea leaves and UFO blogs. He cast about for a way to explain himself. "Are you familiar with divining rods?" he asked.

"Sure. Old-timers used them to locate water sources. There's something about having to use a forked branch from a willow tree for it to work."

"We have more modern tools, of course, but a divining rod does work. It seems like magic, but there is some science behind it. The water underground generates its own magnetic field, and someone with the right knowledge can feel the difference in the magnetic field above ground, using that willow branch."

She looked at him skeptically. "You're telling me that you're going to use a divining rod to find whatever is hidden at that fort?"

"Not exactly. What if I told you that people could be like divining rods, only instead of locating water, they can tap into past events?"

Elizabeth seemed to think that over. "Wait a minute. You're serious, aren't you?"

"I'm afraid so. I have certain, uh, *abilities* to see into the past." He tapped his head. "This is my divining rod."

Elizabeth laughed, which felt like an ice pick jabbing into Keane's heart. *She thinks that I'm a fool.* "Franklin, I hate to tell you this, but all historians see into the past. It's what we do."

"It's more than that. I'm not talking about what's in books or archives. I can witness events that took place in the past. It's something that I call retrocognition."

"I'm sorry, but this is one of the craziest things I've heard," she said. "I didn't think you went in for that sort of mumbo jumbo."

"Look, what if I could prove it to you?"

"What are you talking about?" She waved her arms at the parking lot around them. "Are you going to reveal the past to me? Hello, we are at Fort McHenry, one of the most historic locations in the United States. You know the history of this place inside out. You could make up any old story you want."

"Then forget about Fort McHenry for now," Keane said. "What if I could look into your past and see something about you? That only you could know?"

Elizabeth stopped waving her arms and stood stock-still. She'd had a smirk on her face when she had been making fun of Keane's self-proclaimed talent. Now, the look on her face was slightly nervous. "You can do that?"

"It's not something I normally do. Look into the past of a single person, I mean. But I'll do it if it helps you to believe me."

She crossed her arms and said, "OK, I'm waiting. Knock yourself out."

"It's not quite that simple. There's no on and off switch. And the parking lot probably isn't the best place to be doing this. Too many people are coming and going."

"This is your show," she said. "Tell me what you want to do."

"Come with me."

Keane led the way to a bench along the waterfront and gestured for her to sit beside him. They were quite alone, which was perfect for exercising Keane's talent.

The fort grounds occupied a sort of peninsula, with sprawling green lawns surrounded on three sides by water. A gentle breeze blew in from the bay, carrying the fresh smell of salt. Out on the water, the breeze filling the sails of several vessels plying their way up or down the harbor, which was technically the Patapsco River. Sunlight glittered on the waves. The setting was both beautiful and peaceful, so much so that Keane was tempted to call it a day and just sit here with Elizabeth, enjoying the view.

"Franklin?" Elizabeth asked, pulling him back to the present. "How does it work?"

"Basically, you have to open your mind to it. Of course, it's hard to focus on any one event or time period. It's rather unpredictable. You've heard that some people have a kind of sixth sense. Over time, I have trained mine to be receptive to retrocognition."

"When I think of training, I think of someone up before the sun, getting in their morning run."

"The kind of training that I did didn't involve much running. I studied with Appalachian folk seers and Native

American shamans. These people are quite amazing, with a
tradition going back hundreds of years. The Appalachian seers
have a Scotch-Irish heritage, so their roots are in Irish and Scottish traditions. If you go back far enough, some might even call
it magic or witchcraft, I suppose. The Native American traditions have their own origins. It's an oral tradition, of course,
passed down from one generation to the next, which makes
sense, because these abilities generally run in families."

"Now you sound like a folklorist!"

"You might call it cryptofolklore," Keane said. "Studying the
kinds of things that can't normally be explained. It's not main-
stream, but there's quite a folk tradition of things like this. Of
course, most seers want to get a glimpse of the future and
predict things to come. I took my abilities in a slightly different
direction."

"Franklin, if anyone else had told me this, I'd think that they
were nuts. But because it's you, I'm willing to give you the
benefit of the doubt."

Keane felt the jab in his heart fade. "You believe me?"

"Let's just say that I'm an agnostic on the matter. I believe
that it's possible."

"Let me see if I can prove it to you. Will you take my hand?
It would be best to have some kind of bodily contact, although,
honestly, I have to say that it's a bit distracting."

"I'm glad to hear that."

Keane held Elizabeth's hand gently in his own. He breathed
deeply of the salty air, gazed out at the water, and worked to
clear his mind. It wasn't easy—he was worried about the night
ahead of him, and he had meant what he'd said about Elizabeth's touch being distracting. He took another deep breath
and tried to concentrate.

Time passed, and Keane's mind began to drift. Unbidden,
an image came to his mind of another body of water—a swimming hole on a sleepy river—and he became aware that this

memory was not his own, but Elizabeth's. Water was good—it held power of its own, much like that force he had mentioned could be detected with a diving rod. It seemed to be a late summer day, judging by the few leaves that drifted on the gentle current. A man was swimming, doing a lazy backstroke, and Keane knew this was Elizabeth's father.

Through Elizabeth's eyes, he watched the man swim. He sensed that the little girl wanted to join him, but was afraid. They had been taking a drive, bound for a day at a community swimming pool, when on an impulse her father recalled how as a boy he had enjoyed swimming at this place.

"I know it's here somewhere," he had muttered, turning the car first down one dead end, and then another. Finally, he found the wide place in the road where the local kids would leave their bikes. He parked the car and brought Elizabeth down a well-worn path to the swimming hole.

They already had their suits on. The man had plunged right in, but Elizabeth had found the sight of the shaded water unsettling. She was used to swimming pools.

The man in the water went under. One moment he had been there on the surface, and then suddenly he was gone. Not so much as a ripple broke the smooth surface of the water. A minute passed. The girl on the bank sensed that something was wrong, yet there was nothing she could do, no one to call for help. She got to her feet and called, "Daddy?"

Still, her father did not appear.

Keane sensed the girl's panic, torn between plunging into the water after her father or running back to the road for help.

Just then, her father broke the surface. He was gasping for air, and reached the shore in a few strokes.

"There was a snag under the water," he explained. "I caught my foot and got dragged under. It's all right; I'm fine. But if we do any more swimming today, let's do it at the pool."

Together, the girl and her father made their way up the

path and back to the car. They held hands, which she hadn't done in a long time because she thought she was too big now for that. Today was different—her father hadn't made a big deal of it, probably not wanting to scare her, but the girl sensed how close she had come to losing him at the bottom of that swimming hole.

Keane let go of Elizabeth's hand and turned toward her on the bench, very much back in the present. That was the thing about retrocognition—when a vision was gone, it was gone. It was a little like trying to go back to sleep and re-enter a good dream. Nice as that would be, it just wasn't possible.

"Looking out at the harbor triggered a memory for you," he began. "Your father took you to a swimming hole when you were a little girl, and he almost drowned."

Briefly, Keane summed up some of the details that he had seen. When he finished, Elizabeth was just staring at him.

"Oh my God," she said. "You were serious. You can see into the past."

"Mostly I'm trying to see past events, not memories, but that's essentially how it works."

"Have you always been able to do this?"

"It's probably true that I always had some talent for this, but I didn't recognize it for what it was or harness it until Amanda drowned. I thought, just maybe, that it would help me to understand what took place that night."

Elizabeth was staring at him. "You are full of surprises, aren't you, Franklin Scott Keane? I'm still trying to wrap my head around what just happened."

"I wasn't sure that I should tell you at all. But because you agreed to get mixed up in all this and help me get into Fort McHenry after hours, I felt that you deserved to know a little something about my methods."

"Thank you for trusting me," Elizabeth said. "Maybe this

retrocognition ability of yours will work, but I've got to say, I'd put a whole lot more faith in a metal detector."

The sun was starting to go down, which meant that the fort would soon be closing for the night. Keane reached out again for her hand, and squeezed it. "Ready?" he asked.

35

B ack in the visitor center parking lot, Keane sat behind the wheel of the SUV, waiting for the fort's closing time to approach and working up the nerve for what he planned to do. Elizabeth occupied the passenger seat.

"I'm not sure that it's technically a felony," Elizabeth said. "You could probably plea bargain it down to a misdemeanor, or possibly temporary insanity."

"That wouldn't be so bad," Keane agreed. "In that case, I would only lose my job, suffer public embarrassment, do a few hundred hours of community service, and pay an enormous fine."

"Not so bad," Elizabeth agreed. "Of course, there is a third option."

"What's that?"

"Don't get caught."

"Believe me, I don't plan to."

Keane saw no alternative but to investigate the fort himself, using Francis Scott Key's map as a guide. If he'd had a better relationship with the chief ranger, Ted Shelmire, it was just possible that he might have approached him about the map.

Disturbing the ground at a place like Fort McHenry required a myriad of permits and consultations. But if Keane had at least had Shelmire's blessing, some unofficial investigation might have been arranged. Alas, that was not the case. His only option seemed to be a shovel and a flashlight.

The shovel was a folding model favored by the military; the flashlight was a Maglite favored by security guards because it made a good nightstick in a pinch. Keane had hidden them both inside a backpack, along with two bottles of water, two granola bars, and a wire coat hanger.

While security was strict at many indoor public attractions, the standards were still fairly relaxed at most outdoor national parks. This was certainly the case at Fort McHenry, where visitors could bring in food for picnics and even walk dogs on a leash. Keane would not have gotten very far with a shovel and pick, but nobody paid any attention to a tourist with a backpack. Besides, Keane had no plans to enter the visitor center or museum store, where he was more likely to be recognized. He would stay outside.

One issue that he had not considered was the fact that he was well-known to most of the rangers. After all, the descendant of Francis Scott Key himself was no stranger to Fort McHenry and he was instantly recognizable to most of the national park staff. Keane had driven back out to a convenience store and bought a baseball cap embroidered with the word "Hon" and large Ray Ban-style sunglasses, hoping that it would do something to disguise him. Being spotted at the fort might lead to complications or raise questions later that he didn't need.

"Are you sure that you are all set?" Keane asked.

"I'll head to the hotel after this," she said. "I'll be back first thing in the morning. You do know that this whole scheme is crazy, right?"

"It's not too late for you to bail out," Keane said. "I'm going through with this no matter what, but you don't need to."

"No way," Elizabeth said. "Like it or not, we're partners in crime now."

Keane winced. "I wish you wouldn't put it quite like that."

She patted his arm. "Don't worry, Franklin. Like you said, just don't get caught, OK? Call me if you need me. Otherwise, I'll see you in the morning."

Keane watched her drive off in the SUV. Elizabeth was a remarkably good sport. He began to regret that nothing had happened between them the other night in St. Michaels. He thought that it might have, if only he had let it.

Pushing those thoughts from his mind, he started down the path toward the visitor's center and the sally port beyond. His backpack was slung casually over one shoulder, as if he had no more in mind than a stroll along the ramparts.

Now that summer hours had ended, the fort closed to the public at 4:45 pm. It wasn't all that unusual for harried visitors to pay the fifteen-dollar entrance fee with just an hour or so before closing time, which was just what Keane did now. He made sure that he paid cash.

"You only have about thirty minutes until the fort closes, but your ticket is good for re-entry for a seven-day period, so hang onto your receipt," the uniformed ticket seller said helpfully.

"Good to know," Keane replied, and forced a smile.

Leaving the visitor center, he entered the fort itself through the sally port. This was the gateway into the fort that could be barred against attackers. In this sense, Fort McHenry was not all that different in design from a medieval castle.

Inside the fort, to one side of the sally port, were cells with iron bars, designed to hold important prisoners. It was where Francis Scott Key's nephew had been held during the Civil War,

locked up with other prominent Marylanders for his seces-
sionist views.

In that sense, the United States Government had become
the despot it had fought against in the War of 1812. Keane was
reminded that history had a strange way of coming full circle,
with idealists often becoming the very thing that they had
despised.

This late in the day, activity in the fort was winding to a
close. The fort was popular for school field trips, but any children had long since gone home. A few middle-aged couples
wandered about, pausing now and then to take photographs of
the cannons scattered around the parade grounds, or reading
the interpretive signs. Nonchalantly, Keane followed the same
routine.

A park ranger passed by. Keane didn't know her name, but
she looked vaguely familiar. He tugged the hat down more
tightly and turned his face away.

From previous visits, Keane knew that the security was
surprisingly low tech. The fort itself had no motion-sensing
alarms of any kind, although the two-story barracks were all
equipped with smoke alarms wired directly to the Baltimore
City Fire Department dispatcher. The only real security was in
the visitor center, which was a separate building constructed in
2011 outside the fort. The visitor center contained actual arti-
facts of value, unlike the fort grounds.

Keane ducked into the dark interior of a re-created barrack,
complete with uncomfortable-looking bunks with wool blankets. A not-very realistic mannequin lay stretched out under
one of the wool blankets. Keane remembered the mannequin
from a previous visit, and that it was what had inspired his idea
for a hiding place. He glanced at his watch. Just another 15
minutes to go until closing. He heard an announcement over
the loudspeaker system that the fort would be closing soon.

A couple came into the room to look around.

"Huh," the man said, taking in the rudimentary furniture and hard wooden bunks. "And I thought I had it bad at Fort Dix."

Keane chuckled politely, but did not speak, not wanting to get engaged in conversation, with minutes to go before the fort closed. He pretended to be fascinated by a rough table set with a pewter dish, a spoon, and a two-tined fork.

"Where's the dishwasher?" the man's wife said.

"Never mind that," the man said. "Where's the TV?"

Again, Keane chuckled. He was contemplating prodding them with the fork if they didn't leave soon. Fortunately, they shuffled out.

Sighing with relief, Keane slipped off his backpack and slung it under the bunk. The hat and sunglasses followed. Originally, he planned to hide under the bunk himself. But there was scarcely a foot or so of clearance, and he wasn't eager to crawl under there with decades of cobwebs and possibly a harbor rat or two for company. Instead, he pulled the mannequin out from under the blanket and slid it out of sight under the bunk. He climbed into the bunk and pulled the blanket up to his nose.

Another fifteen minutes went by before Keane heard shoes scrape in the doorway. A park ranger, wearing a telltale flat-brimmed hat, poked his head into the dim room, checking to make sure that all of the barracks exhibits were empty. He shouted, "Good night, John Boy!"

Keane nearly sat up with a jolt, until he realized that the ranger was not talking to *him*, but to what the ranger must have thought was the mannequin.

Once Keane's heart stopped pounding, he appreciated the park ranger's sense of humor.

Then the door slammed shut and Keane settled down to wait.

36

K eane waited until darkness fell and the fort grew still. He pulled off the blanket and reached under the bunk to retrieve his backpack. He dragged out the mannequin and tucked him under the blanket once again.

"Good night, John Boy," he said.

He replaced the mannequin because if someone did become suspicious later about what had happened at the fort, he saw no point in giving them any more clues than necessary.

He tried the door, praying that it had not been locked, after all. If the rangers had suddenly begun locking all the doors, his night of misadventure was going to end very quickly. He gave the door a firm shove, but it barely moved. Either the edge of the door was sticking or the door was, in fact, locked. He felt a sinking feeling, but wasn't about to give up. He braced his feet and shoved again; this time, the door practically burst open.

Keane poked his head out. A few security lights played over the parade ground, but the interior of the fort was otherwise dark. The stars had come out in a moonless sky, although it was hard to make out any constellations due to all the light pollution from Baltimore. Directly across from the fort, the waterfront docks and piers in the distance blazed with light as the stevedores worked around the clock to unload ships. Keane stood for a moment to get his bearings. He was utterly and completely alone within Fort McHenry.

Or was he? His talent for retrocognition sometimes came unbidden. All around him, in the darkness, he could feel the energy of those who had gone before, passing through the fort over the years. Some had lived here, some had fought here, and some had died here, all leaving behind an echo of themselves.

Keane cocked his head and listened, but the presence of so many others was like whispering just beyond his ken. He knew they were there, like voices in another room, but he could make no sense of it.

He moved on.

The star map had no reference point, but Keane assumed that as with most maps, it was oriented to the north. That hadn't always been the case with maps, of course; Augustine Herman's famous first map of the Chesapeake Bay had been drawn horizontally so that north was held in one's right hand, rather than at the top of the map. The familiar Compass Rose was more than decorative back then; it was a necessary key to reading a map. However, by Francis Scott Key's time, orienting maps with north at the top was the accepted practice. It stood to reason that Francis Scott Key would have followed that convention. Keane had no doubt that the point of the star marked on the map indicated the northernmost point of the star fort. Also, the point aimed more or less directly at the city of Baltimore.

Keane crossed the parade ground and passed the massive flagpole, now empty. The flag was struck each evening before dark. On his left stood another two-story barrack, this one with a second-floor porch or gallery. He strolled right out into the earthworks. The enclosed space was roughly diamond-shaped, about thirty feet long and twenty-five feet wide. The actual point was made of the earthworks and a brick wall, taking up perhaps ten feet.

Keane considered what to do next. It stood to reason that Francis Scott Key had paced off a distance across the actual walkable ground inside the earthworks, rather than starting at the point and having to jump down to continue pacing across level ground. There was no way to be certain, but that was Keane's best guess.

Keane pressed his back to the earthen wall and took three even steps, in keeping with the measurement on Key's star map. If each step covered roughly three feet, then this was a distance of nine feet. He slipped the day pack off his shoulder, took out the wire coat hanger, and quickly untwisted it until he had a serviceable length of wire. As a precaution, he wrapped a bit of black electrical tape over the end to prevent any friction or static electricity if he struck a buried live shell. No sense joining his ancestors any sooner than necessary.

He inserted this probe into the earth at his feet. The ground was hard-packed, but it had rained recently enough that his makeshift probe sank easily into the ground, first six inches, then ten inches, then more than a foot.

The probe encountered nothing but soil beneath his feet. Keane was hoping for some solid object.

Keane pulled out the probe, straightened up, and tried a spot a foot closer to the center of the enclosed space. Still nothing. Methodically, he worked a few feet forward and then a few feet back. Still nothing.

Keane was nonplussed. In his mind, in planning all of this, he had pictured how the probe would strike the hidden object, whatever it might be.

Not ready to give up so quickly, he took the folding shovel out of the rucksack and plunged it into the turf. He cut out a neat patch of turf, almost like a section of carpet, and set it aside. He dug frantically, well below a foot deep, thinking that perhaps the wire of his probe simply hadn't reached deep enough. Soon, he had a good-sized pile of rich, dark earth to show for his efforts, but nothing else. He jammed the probe into the bottom of the pit in all directions, but still found nothing.

With a sigh, Keane began to refill the hole. Once he replaced the square of turf, it was almost impossible to tell that the ground had been disturbed. He felt better about that; digging holes at a national monument was desecration of a sort. He stood there, uncertain of what to do next. He couldn't go around digging up all of Fort McHenry. Maybe he should have brought along a metal detector, but that wouldn't exactly have fit inconspicuously into his rucksack.

Keane folded the shovel, put it back into the rucksack, and stuffed the wire after it. He stood there, trying to determine his next course of action.

His phone vibrated with a text message from Elizabeth.

Find anything?

Nothing yet.

So now what?

I'm going to keep looking.

Good luck. It's late. I'm going to bed.

Keane felt reluctant to end the conversation. He felt a sense of loneliness that couldn't even be explained by the fact that he was the sole occupant of the historic fort. It was a sense of ennui that spoke of an emptiness in his very soul. He tapped out another message.

Did you get some dinner?

Crab cake at a pub. Not as good as mine!

Peppers in the crab cake?

Yes! Gag, right?

Cretins.

See you in the morning.

Her description of the crab cake reminded Keane about the

snack that he had brought. He dug out a granola bar and a bottle of lemon-flavored tea. The granola bar was no crab cake, but munching it gave him time to think.

He must be interpreting something incorrectly. He was sure that the map itself represented the fort. It could be nothing else. What did he not get? There was another possibility, which he hated to consider. At some point in the past, it was possible that whatever Francis Scott Key had hidden had been dug up or otherwise disturbed.

Keane finished the tea and put the empty bottle into the rucksack. A glance at the old Timex on his wrist told him that it was now one a.m. He had not needed the caffeine to stay awake. His mind was racing.

And that, he thought, might be the problem.

A breeze blew across the harbor, smelling salty and cool, and Keane turned up the collar of the jacket he wore. Keane closed his eyes and took a deep breath. He exhaled. Then he listened. Across the water, he could hear faintly the clank and clang of a ship being unloaded. A tug churned past, pushing a barge down the bay. He heard the deep rumble of a jet passing overhead. Vaguely, he could hear traffic noises. He focused on these sounds, one at a time, using them as a way to focus his thoughts and empty his mind. This was a technique he had learned in developing mindfulness or meditation, which was the doorway to his power of retrocognition.

When he opened his eyes again, he was not alone.

37

W hen Francis Scott Key wrote the lines about bombs bursting in air, he had not been exaggerating about what he saw that night in Baltimore harbor. The Royal Navy vessels under Rear Admiral Cockburn had hurled hundreds of shells and rockets at the star fort. By all accounts, the bombardment created an impressive fireworks show, but it had not been all that deadly.

Keane knew that the real fight had taken place at North Point, just across the harbor from the fort. Many people today did not realize that the British had made a two-pronged attack on Baltimore. The bombardment of the fort had been one prong. Meanwhile, British troops under Sir Robert Ross had made a land attack with the intent of capturing Baltimore.

The attack had been no parade ground stroll. Heat and humidity weighed on the British as they advanced in their heavy wool uniforms, damp from a late summer downpour. The path was snarled with weeds and briers. But still, the British pressed on.

This attack was foiled when two eighteen-year-old Baltimore lads named Harry McComas and Daniel Wells had fired on Ross, wounding him mortally. In turn, the Redcoats ran down the two young men and gutted them with bayonets. The death of Ross had deflated the attack and very likely, saved the city from being sacked. Altogether, more than fifty men on both sides lost their lives at the Battle of North Point.

Later, the Royal Navy vessels in Baltimore Harbor unleashed their guns to fill the sky with bombs. Having used his abilities to revisit that night, Keane saw these bombs now, hissing through the night. The Congreve rockets looked much like modern fireworks, oversized bottle rockets, arcing upwards in a whooshing stream of sparks, then exploding over the fort. The rockets were inaccurate, but they were terrifying to behold. The British ships also kept up a steady volley of solid shot and explosive shells that burst over the fort, raining chunks of red-hot iron shrapnel upon the defenders. A single piece could easily decapitate a man or lop off a limb. Fort McHenry was a terrifying place to be.

And yet, the earthen bulwarks of the fort did their job, absorbing the body blows from the solid shot. The fort's massive guns could easily destroy even a Royal Navy frigate, but their range was limited. The British ships lay at anchor just beyond reach of the fort's defenses and fired away with their own longer-range weapons.

All at once, Keane seemed to be there. He felt the concussion of the explosions and the hot wind as shrapnel whirred overhead. It was a scene of destruction both terrible and lovely. In the flickering light, the storm flag was visible. On the point of the star fort closest to the British fleet, a gun crew worked to load and fire the cannon that seemed to have the best hope of reaching the enemy.

Peering through the swirling gunpowder smoke, Keane watched the gun crew at work. They wore naval uniforms because the best gunners had come from Commodore Joshua Barney's flotilla. Some of these same men had seen hot action against the Barbary Pirates and British ships of the line, so they were unfazed by the shot and shell bursting overhead.

Stripped to the waist in the September heat, a man wielding a long wood-handled swab dipped one end in a bucket and ran it down the barrel to quench any sparks remaining from the last round fired. Another man ran up and stuffed in a white bag, big as a modern sack of flour, into the muzzle of the gun. The sailor with the swab reversed it and rammed home the powder charge. Another sailor standing at the foot of the gun stuck in a wire through a hole in the barrel to puncture the sack and expose the gunpowder.

A tall officer strode toward the gun, seeming not to notice the bombardment all around him. He wore a cockade hat and a blue uniform. Surely, this was none other than Major Armistead.

"Make this one count, lads!" he shouted. "Some extra powder will increase the range."

"More powder might breach the barrel, sir."

"I don't give a damn!" Armistead shouted. "Let's teach *Cock-burn* a lesson."

Another sack of powder went into the gun.

Two men wearing white canvas breeches, stained with mud and gunpowder, and blue striped shirts and stocking caps, carried an enormous iron ball between them using a device that resembled massive ice tongs. Even at this distance, Keane could see them straining with the effort. Someone had scrawled *A present for King George* on the cannonball with white paint. The cannonball disappeared into the barrel.

Another sailor stood by the end of the barrel, holding a short lanyard that led to the firing mechanism. At his command, the other men turned their faces away from the gun and covered their ears. He tugged the lanyard and the gun fired. The air quivered with the concussion.

In the haze over the harbor, Keane could see the gigantic

splash the cannonball made, just short of the fleet. No other shot had reached that far, and the near-miss seemed to cause consternation aboard the flagship. The message was clear that the guns of Fort McHenry were not to be trifled with. With a shock, Keane realized that this was likely the ship that Key was watching from. Had the ball struck its target, the course of history might have been changed and Americans would be singing an altogether different anthem.

Keane watched the battle, captivated, acrid smoke burning his nose and eyes. He did not know how long he stood there, suspended in time. Amazed, he looked on as the United States flag over the star fort was struck. But this was no sign of surrender. In its place, a far larger flag was raised. The salty breeze stirred the flag, causing the broad red and white stripes to roll and snap above the smoke. Keane realized he was witnessing the Star-Spangled Banner being raised above Fort McHenry.

And then the vision began to fade. The soldiers and sailors dissolved into the night air and blew away like the smoke from the guns. Keane found himself back in the present, quite alone, staring at the star point of Fort McHenry where that life-and-death struggle had taken place.

Witnessing the battle had given him a revelation. *Of course,* he thought. Key had not marked the *northernmost* point of the fort on his map. He had marked the *star point* that he must have seen from his viewpoint aboard *HMS Tonnant*. To Key, and others who had witnessed the battle, it must have been obvious that this was the most important part of the star fort. For Key and his compatriots, it would be the equivalent of sacred ground.

This is what Key had marked on his map. This was where Key had hidden something. Eagerly, Keane crossed the parade ground, headed for the point where most of the action in the fort had taken place that night.

38

K eane reached the point of the star fort that was closest to the harbor and stood within the diamond created by the earthworks. It felt somewhat surreal to be occupying the ground where, just minutes before, he had witnessed a battle taking place. The neatly groomed grass and tidy brickwork hardly seemed like a battleground. *A battle that took place more than two centuries ago*, he reminded himself.

He walked down to the interior corner of the star, gulped down a deep breath of anticipation, and took three steps as indicated by Key's map. He took out the wire and probed the ground.

Nothing.

He tried a different spot, pressing the wire in as deep as he could manage. He tried again and again. Still nothing. Puzzled, he straightened up and tried to think things through.

He felt so frustrated that he was tempted to get out the shovel and just start digging on the spot. Whatever Key had hidden was here—it had to be. The ghosts of the fort had indicated that much.

With a growing feeling of despair, he reviewed the facts.

Three paces, the map stated. And Keane had taken three paces. It was only natural that his steps might vary a little from his ancestor's, but the steps should have brought him to the right general location. What was he doing wrong?

Again, he had the nagging thought that someone had beaten him to it and already found Key's secret.

He returned to his starting point and took the three steps once more. He couldn't help but imagine that he was some old duelist, counting off ten paces before turning and firing his dueling pistol.

He ended up in the same place. He took out his phone again and studied the photograph of the star map, with its elegant handwriting in brown ink, but there was no mistake. The note indicated *three* paces. Not one less; not one more.

Keane put away his phone and looked around in frustration.

That was when Keane realized his mistake.

It was the random thought about dueling that had triggered the realization. According to the Code Duello, the standard practice was for the adversaries to stand ten paces apart. These paces were not to be confused with *steps*. At ten steps apart, a distance of roughly thirty feet, two duelists could hardly miss. In most cases, however, the whole point of a duel *was* to miss one another honorably. At ten *paces*, a distance closer to sixty feet, a modicum of marksmanship was required to hit a target. This made ten paces a much safer distance for two gentlemen to go through the motions of honor when they were not intent on bloodshed.

The difference was that a step was just that—one step, or a distance of roughly three feet. He knew that *pace* was a Latin word. A pace was measured according to the distance covered when the same foot touched the ground again. Thus, a pace was equal to not one, but *two* steps. In his haste to uncover the anthem author's secret, Keane had misinterpreted the map.

Momentarily, he felt like a fool. But then a sense of relief and excitement nearly overwhelmed him. Maybe whatever Key had buried was still waiting to be found, after all.

He trotted to the wall and counted off three paces, to where his right foot touched the ground for the third time. He bent down and pushed the wire into the soil.

Nothing.

Quivering now with anticipation, Keane tried a spot just a little to the right of his foot. He probed. About twelve inches down, the tip of the wire struck something immobile. He probed again and again, trying to get a sense of the outline of the object. It seemed to be about two feet long, and narrow—certainly no more than eight inches wide. What could it be?

He retrieved the folding shovel from the rucksack and repeated the process of cutting through the sod. Then he began to dig down. His shovel struck an object. Carefully, he worked the shovel around the edges, exposing more of the object as he went. What in the world could it be? The object was not a chest or box, but seemed to be long and narrow. Cylindrical, he decided. Pausing from time to time to clear away the dirt, he kept digging until the entire object was exposed. It was about one foot long and perhaps three inches in diameter. He pulled it from the soil much like he had once helped his grandfather dig potatoes out of the garden.

He wiped away as much of the dirt as he could. He seemed to have found a cylindrical wooden case, similar to a gift box for an expensive bottle of liquor.

What was in that cylinder? He couldn't wait to find out, but prying it open out here on the bastion did not seem like a good approach.

He put the object in his rucksack and refilled the hole, replacing the flap of turf so that, again, it was hard to tell by the light of day that the area had been disturbed.

He straightened up and stepped on the soil area where he

had been digging to flatten it out. He then held himself very still and listened, but all he could hear were the distant noises of the port and Baltimore itself. The other presences that he had seen earlier seemed to have faded into the night, and he was alone once more.

Keane retraced his steps and returned to the barracks room where he had initially hidden. It seemed as good a place as any to spend the night. He was, after all, locked inside the fort until it reopened for visitors in the morning.

He paused to send a text to Elizabeth. *Found something. Call me.*

When there was no immediate response, he guessed that Elizabeth must be asleep. He shut the door and turned on his powerful flashlight to illuminate the room. Then he cleared off the table that was set with the pewter plates and two-tined fork. He replaced them with the cylinder he had dug out of the earthworks.

Studying it from all angles, he tried to determine what it might be. This was a utilitarian case of some kind, meant to protect whatever might be contained within. But what could it be? Only one way to tell.

Taking a two-bladed Victorinox Swiss Army knife from his pocket, Keane snagged out the larger blade and went to work on the wooden cylinder. Dampness and time had weakened the cylinder, opening a seam in the fitted joints of the wood. Keane worked in the knife blade, and twisted the bright blade, widening the seam in the wood. He took his time, not wanting to damage whatever the cylinder contained. The wood was not waterproofed; in places, it was even soft and punky with decay. He despaired of whatever might be inside having survived being buried for something like eighteen decades.

Finally, his blade encountered some material that was not wood. He used his fingers now to widen the gap. Eventually, he was able to pull the wood apart. Encased within the wood was a cylindrical glass jar, and inside the jar were two rolled-up sheets of foolscap paper.

What in the world?

The glass itself was thick and of a greenish-blue cast, like an old Mason jar, and also like an antique mason jar, a hinged clasp held the cap in place. The cap was also carefully sealed in what appeared to be wax, which Keane pared away with his knife.

The jar had effectively kept any moisture at bay, leaving the paper inside perfectly preserved. It was like finding a message in a bottle that had washed up not on a beach, but within the walls of the historic fort. What could Francis Scott Key have felt compelled to go to so much trouble to hide?

Keane reached inside and gingerly pulled out the two sheets of paper.

The outer sheet, which was smaller, was a note in handwriting that Keane recognized. He had studied his famous ancestor assiduously. Even before he glanced at the signature, there was no doubt in his mind that this had been written by Francis Scott Key. Although he recognized the handwriting, Keane could see that the author's penmanship had grown shaky with old age, no longer the elegant strokes of the pen evident in original copies of *The Star-Spangled Banner*.

On his phone, he pulled up a copy of the original "Star-Spangled Banner," to double-check the handwriting. The handwriting matched.

The second document was written on heavy parchment, giving it an official feel. Hunched over the table, straining to see in the harsh battery-powered light, Keane began to read.

39

T*aken from* HMS Tonnant *on September 14, 1814, from the possession of Admiral Cockburn, RN, and until this moment, kept from sight.*
  Francis Scott Key

KEANE STUDIED THE NOTE AGAIN. Considering that Key had died in 1843, the note must have been written close to that date. He turned his attention to the second document, the one that Key had gone to such lengths to preserve. He knew that the ornate handwriting was typical of official documents from the time period. Fortunately, he'd had more than a little experience deciphering these old handwriting styles.

AUGUST THE 24TH, **Year of Our Lord Eighteen Hundred and Fourteen**
  To the Right Honorable George Cockburn, Rear Admiral in His Royal Majesty's Navy

· · ·

DEAR SIR,

If you are reading this letter, then it goes without saying that you have occupied our White House. I offer you my respect upon this achievement, if not my congratulations, a differentiation which I am sure that you can understand, given my position as elected executive of government. The letter which follows is an appeal to you as the senior military commander in the Mid-Atlantic, and as a gentleman, to halt this devastation and suffering in our current conflict. This war between our two nations has been long and arduous, with much loss of life and treasure. The field of action has been extensive, from Canada in the north to our Southern-most states to the High Seas as far as the coasts of France and England herself. Now, it appears that war has come to the very doorstep of our American capitol. You can imagine our great sorrow and consternation, almost as if Napoleon Bona-parte had marched upon London. Be assured that while you have conquered our capital city, British might has not conquered our hearts and minds as Americans.

It is hard to say how this conflict shall end or what the ultimate outcome shall be of this war. Our government shall persevere in the way that ideals always transcend time and place. However, as the duly elected president of these United States, I wish to extend an offer to cease hostilities between our nations. The time has perhaps come for us to discuss our differences in diplomatic fashion rather than settle them on the battlefield.

Please understand that this missive is in no way a capitu-lation or an admission of defeat, but rather an appeal to common sense and decency. As the military commander of British forces in the field, you have the authority to cease the current hostilities. As the Commander in Chief of United States forces, the president has the authority to direct our own troops in the field to stand down. At your convenience, please send a messenger into the American lines to the west of the city in the village of Brookville. Our government shall respond accordingly, so that these initial steps toward a cessation of hostilities may begin.

I AM YOUR OBEDIENT SERVANT,
    James Madison, Esq.
    President of the United States

KEANE READ THE LETTER AGAIN, allowing his stunned mind to absorb it. President James Madison had offered to end the war in August 1814 when British troops marched into the United States capital city. Key had not explained, but the implication was clear. If Cockburn had possession of this letter, then he had chosen not to act upon it. Madison had been like a beaten dog with his tail between his legs. Rather than agreeing to halt the war, Cockburn had opted to let the war continue. As a prisoner aboard *HMS Tonnant*, Key had discovered the truth. He had stolen the letter and kept it quiet, knowing that the triumph at Baltimore two weeks after the president's capitulation would seem like a hollow afterthought just when the United States needed a real victory.

This letter undermined everything that Keane knew about the Battle of Baltimore, the "Star-Spangled Banner" poem, and the Star-Spangled Banner flag. If this letter came to light, even the National Anthem would seem to celebrate a sham victory. America would become a laughingstock among nations.

Keane stared at the letter in his hand. It did not seem like a document at all, but more like he was holding a huge sizzling cannonball with a lighted fuse. Hands shaking now, he set the letter down on the table and wondered what to do with it.

Elizabeth still had not texted back or called. Keane was

frustrated that he had just made the find of a lifetime, but wasn't able to share the news with anyone.

Suddenly, he felt quite exhausted. Instead of energizing Keane, the discovery of the letter had left him drained. Dawn was not far off. Too tired to move the mannequin off the bunk, he crawled into the bunk with John Boy for company, and despite a thousand thoughts racing through his mind, he managed to sleep.

40

K eane slept so deeply and for so long that he did not even hear the ranger going around opening up the barracks. The sound of the sticking door being shoved open jolted Keane awake.

The ranger called, "Rise and shine, John Boy." Fortunately, he did not bother to poke his head inside the room, where he would have been greeted by the sight of Keane sharing the bunk with the War of 1812 mannequin. Spread out on the table were two original documents, one signed by Francis Scott Key and the other by President James Madison, a letter in which, contrary to the known historical record, the United States president capitulated to British forces in August 1814.

Quickly, Keane gathered up his things, his heart hammering. How in the world had he overslept? It didn't help that the tiny barracks room was so dark. Also, he had been counting on hearing from Elizabeth. He checked his phone. Still no messages, which was a little strange.

He rolled up the letters and returned them to the glass cylinder, which he tucked into the rucksack. He tossed the crumbling pieces of the wooden case far under the cot. Judging by all the cobwebs and assorted bits of trash under there, someone might find them by 2114, just in time for the tricentennial of the Battle of Baltimore.

Keane ran his fingers through his hair, trying to get rid of his bedhead, then remembered his hat. He jammed it down on his head. He looked exactly like someone who had just woken up. He had also neglected to bring a toothbrush, so that his mouth felt and tasted like the moth-eaten blanket that he had lain upon. He grabbed his water bottle and drained the last of it, then popped a stick of gum, which helped.

He sat on the bunk until exactly ten a.m., when the fort opened to visitors. He strolled out into the morning sunshine, blinking in the light, and made his way toward the exit at the sally port. Already, a few tourists were wandering in.

He was almost to the sally port entrance when he heard someone shout his name.

"Keane!"

He turned. His right hand gripped the strap of the rucksack over his shoulder, ready to make a run for it. He just hoped that Elizabeth was out in the parking lot so that they could make a quick getaway.

Steaming toward him was Ted Shelmire, the chief ranger at Fort McHenry. The September day promised to be warm, and Shelmire smelled strongly of aftershave and Right Guard. Shelmire was not Keane's favorite person, based on various professional disagreements that they'd had over the years. The biggest one had been over the new visitor center that Shelmire had advocated building within the fort's walls. Wiser heads had prevailed thanks to Keane's influence—when the descendant of Francis Scott Key spoke up about Fort McHenry, people tended to listen. Shelmire had felt slighted both personally and professionally.

Shelmire now avoided Keane, although he hadn't missed

the opportunity to sit through Keane's lecture at the War of 1812 symposium in Easton and shoot daggers at him with his glare.

"Well, if it isn't Ranger Shelmire," Keane said. He took a deep breath, trying to appear normal.

"You're here early, Keane. What did you do, sleep here?"

Keane blanched. "You know me. By dawn's early light and all that."

"Very funny," Shelmire said flatly. "I'd appreciate some notice if you plan on doing research here."

Keane forgot the urge to get away as quickly as possible, suddenly annoyed by the ranger's attitude. "The last time I checked, this was a public institution. No one needs to make an appointment to visit Fort McHenry."

"Take it easy, Keane. You can get off your high horse. You know what I mean. You're not a tourist from Indiana. You're the great-great-grand whatever of Francis Scott Key. If you're here, it's for a reason. Care to share?"

"Not particularly."

Shelmire didn't say anything. "Say, how *did* you get in here so early? There was a line waiting to get in this morning, and you weren't in it. Our first visitors are just walking in."

"I'm afraid I haven't been entirely honest with you, Ted."

"Oh? This ought to be good." He crossed his arms on his chest and waited for Keane's explanation.

"I'm afraid that I was not in line until the very last minute, and I misled those people to let me jump the line because I told them I had official business."

"Official business?" The ranger harrumphed. "Last time I checked, the Great American Preservation Society was not part of the United States Park Service."

"I know that, Ted. I have to admit, I'm a little ashamed of myself. But you see, I needed some photos for a talk I'm giving later today and I just couldn't wait around."

"Why am I not surprised? There's always a special exception when you're involved."

Keane hefted the rucksack. "I need to get going."

The chief ranger threw up his hands. "Then go! Just don't let the door hit you in your star-spangled ass on your way out."

Keane turned and left, forcing himself not to run.

Shelmire had gotten hot under the collar when Keane had said that he had jumped the line. Imagine how he would react if he found out that Keane had spent the night digging up the earthworks?

He was sure that Shelmire would like to do nothing less than prosecute him for relic hunting in a national park, which was a federal crime and a felony. Shelmire might discover in the next five minutes that someone had been inside the fort the night before.

Keane walked faster. At this early hour, not many vehicles were in the parking lot and he spotted his SUV quickly and walked toward it.

To his surprise, Elizabeth was not at the wheel. In fact, she was nowhere in sight. He looked around, wondering if they had somehow passed each other if Elizabeth had decided to enter the fort just as Keane was walking out. But that seemed unlikely. Keane had seen the first visitors walking in, and he and Chief Ranger Shelmire had practically stood in the sally port.

He tried the door of the SUV. It was locked. With a growing sense of unease, Keane wondered, *where was Elizabeth?*

Only then did he notice the piece of paper tucked under the windshield wiper. It was handwritten, with a phone number jotted at the bottom. The note contained two words.

Trade you.

41

K eane was puzzled at first by the note, and then everything clicked into place with such devastating certainly that he reeled as if struck by a blow. This was not a note from Elizabeth, but from whoever had taken her. It could only have been left by Charles Montgomery or his henchmen. Somehow, Montgomery had figured out that he and Elizabeth were at Fort McHenry.

Keane realized that he shouldn't be surprised at that. Montgomery was ex-military, a high-ranking retired officer with resources and connections. He just may have managed to steal the Star-Spangled Banner from the Smithsonian Institution, after all. It was not out of the question that he'd had Keane followed or had somehow tracked his phone. Was he being watched, even now? The parking lot was slowly beginning to fill up. He looked around but saw no one suspicious.

Keane called the phone number.

Keane recognized Montgomery's voice. "Is that you, Keane?"

"Let her go."

"Are you willing to trade?"

"Of course I am."

"Then bring the object in question to Tidewinds. I'll let the young lady go. No police."

"Let me talk to her to make sure she's all right."

Keane heard the phone being passed off, and then Elizabeth came on. She sounded frightened. "Hello?"

"Elizabeth, are you—"

Montgomery came back on. "I'm on a tight schedule, Keane. Be here by midnight if you want to see her again." He ended the call.

Keane stood there staring at the phone in disbelief. *Elizabeth had been kidnapped.* As the seconds ticked past, the enormity of it began to sink in. In so many words, Montgomery had threatened to kill her. His meaning was clear: he wanted Keane to trade Elizabeth's life for the lost star.

Keane had to wonder if there was something wrong with him, because he kept losing the women in his life. He had known Elizabeth for only a few days, but it seemed longer. He vowed that he would get her back, if it was the last thing that he did. He had no compunctions about giving up the lost star if it would save Elizabeth, but he was doubtful that Montgomery would keep his word. Both Elizabeth and Keane knew too much about his plans. It was going to take more than a simple trade to protect Elizabeth's life—and his own.

As for the letter from James Madison to Rear Admiral Cockburn, well, Montgomery didn't know about that, did he?

He thought about Montgomery and his small army. This wasn't going to be easy. He was going to need some help.

Calling the police, or even the FBI, was out of the question. First of all, Montgomery had clearly expressed what would happen to Elizabeth if Keane did that. Then there was the more practical matter of trying to get the police to believe him. Montgomery was rich and famous. He did not seem like a likely kidnapper.

It didn't help that Keane might have some explaining to do

about the lost star. He had taken it from a murder victim's condo. He had gained possession of a national artifact under questionable circumstances. He would have to describe where and how Elizabeth had been kidnapped. He did not look forward to explaining to anyone that she had been his accomplice in digging up the earthworks at Fort McHenry.

Chief Ranger Shelmire would love that one, once he got wind of it.

He made another call.

"Yeah?" the voice on the other end was gruff. In the background, Keane could hear the rumble of a marine diesel engine, which meant that Beau was out fishing on *Rascal*.

"I need some help," he said. "That individual you warned me about? He's taken Elizabeth."

It seemed to take Beau a moment to process that information. "Where are you?"

"I'm stuck at Fort McHenry. My car keys disappeared along with Elizabeth."

"I'm about halfway between you and Rock Hall," Beau said. "You know that pier at the fort? Meet you there in thirty minutes."

Keane walked toward the pier, located just a couple hundred feet from the parking lot. The pier was where the *Pride of Baltimore II* and other tall ships docked when visiting Fort McHenry. A wrought iron fence roughly three feet high kept the public off the pier after hours, for safety's sake. The gate was closed now, and Keane did not want to attract any more attention to himself than necessary, so he sat down on one of the benches there and glanced at his watch. He took a deep breath of the salty air and gathered his thoughts.

Twenty-five minutes later, out on the Patapsco River, he heard a powerful diesel engine approaching. Sound carried farther over water, and the approaching vessel was still a long

way off, hardly more than a speck. Keane had no doubt that it
was Beau's boat.

He scrambled over the wrought iron fence and out onto the
pier.

"Hey!"

Keane turned. Out of nowhere, a National Park ranger had
appeared. He was a young ranger whom Keane didn't recognize. "Is there a problem, Ranger?"

"That gate is there for a reason, sir. The pier is off limits."

He felt exasperated. He had dug up what seemed like half
the fort during the night and Elizabeth had been kidnapped
from the parking lot. Where had the park rangers been for
that?

Out of the corner of his eye, Keane could see that the
approaching boat was no longer just a speck. *Rascal* was headed
right for the pier with no sign of slowing down. Beau was
bringing the boat around in a wide arc so that when they left
the pier, the bow would be pointed back toward the Patapsco.

Keane waved at the ranger. "Sorry, but I have a boat to
catch."

At that, he turned and walked out onto the pier. Behind
him, he could hear the sounds of the ranger trying to scramble
over the fence. The ranger, being shorter than the long-legged
Keane, had found that the four-foot height was just a little too
high to step over without the spiked top of the fence coming
into contact with certain soft areas of the male anatomy. The
ranger's shout ended in a high-pitched yelp, but he kept
coming.

Rascal approached, slower now, but still pushing up a bow
wave. In a photograph, the saltwater would have appeared blue,
but in reality it was more of a bottle-green color. A man Keane
didn't recognize stood in the bow, ready with a line. One of
Beau's fishing clients, perhaps?

Behind Keane, the ranger had extricated himself from the

fence. The man looked none too happy. He walked stiffly but quickly toward Keane, something held in his extended hand. Keane realized that it was a Taser.

"Seriously?" Keane asked, hands on hips. Then he turned and ran down the pier.

At the helm, Beau saw what was happening and brought the bow in close, expertly skimming along the pier without any intention of stopping.

Keane ran for the boat, and leaped.

He landed in a heap on the bow, his fall broken in part by the man who had been standing there ready to cast the bow line. As soon as Keane was aboard, Beau gunned the big diesel engine. The park ranger was left on the pier, quickly becoming smaller and smaller as *Rascal* headed out to the bay.

Keane helped the man up who had softened his landing, and patted him on the shoulder. "Thank you for that. I'm sorry if you had to cut your fishing trip short."

"Are you kiddin' me? This is a helluva lot more fun than fishing. When Captain Beau said we had to run into Baltimore to pick up his cousin, he didn't say mention anything about helping him escape." The man frowned. "Hold on. You didn't just rob a bank or something, did you?"

"Does breaking into Fort McHenry and stealing a letter written by James Madison count?"

"Ha! That's a fish story if I ever heard one." The man clapped Keane on the shoulder. "And here Captain Beau said you were the serious one in the family."

Keane made his way to the helm, where Beau was busy guiding *Rascal* under the soaring height of the Francis Scott Key Bridge.

"Thanks for the ride."

"You know me," Beau said. "I'm practically the Uber of the Chesapeake."

Beau wasn't one to ask a lot of questions, but Keane felt that he owed his cousin a more detailed explanation.

"I still haven't told you what this is all about," Keane said. "You're probably wondering why I was at Fort McHenry."

"You've never done anything without a good reason, Cuz," Beau said, as if that was explanation enough.

"This is a little out of the ordinary."

Beau grinned. "It wouldn't be the first time."

Keane started at the beginning, with the murder at the Cannonball House in St. Michaels and the killing at Rock Creek Park of the Smithsonian assistant curator. He explained how he had been asked by the Smithsonian to conduct a shadow investigation of the disappearance of the Star-Spangled Banner. He explained how he had come across what appeared to be the fifteenth star from the Star-Spangled Banner flag, cut from the flag itself by none other than Francis Scott Key. He described how his suspicions had led him to Charles Montgomery as a prime suspect in the flag theft and the murders.

Finally, Keane explained how the star had been a *de facto* map that he had used to locate a letter buried at Fort McHenry by Key.

"A letter?" Beau snorted. "After all that trouble you went to, it's a goddamn shame ol' Francis Scott Key didn't bury something useful, like Spanish doubloons."

"The letter might shake things up quite a bit," Keane said. "Key took it from the Admiral Cockburn's flagship during the Battle of Baltimore."

"You mean took, as in stole?"

"Well, technically, I suppose that he did steal it."

Beau laughed. "The apple doesn't fall far from the tree. You stole that letter from Fort McHenry. Gramps stole silver to get his company started, and Francis Scott Key stole secret documents from the British. Does that make him a spy?"

Keane thought about that. "Not a spy. More like a protector. He knew that if the letter was made public, it would strike a terrible blow to American morale just at a time when we needed it most. The British had just burned the White House and our Capitol. The Royal Navy ruled the Chesapeake Bay. Baltimore was under attack."

Beau nodded and processed what he had just heard, without taking his eyes off the expanse of the Chesapeake ahead. "I think I like it better when history stays in the past, where it's supposed to be."

"Listen, Beau, all I care about right now is that Montgomery and his thugs took Elizabeth." Keane's voice caught in his throat. "I've already lost one woman in my life. I can't lose another. I couldn't stand it."

"Don't worry about that," Beau said. "We'll get her back. Now, just for the record, you look like hell, Cuz."

"Being up half the night tends to do that."

"Go down and pour yourself some coffee. Get something to eat. We need you on your toes for that rendezvous."

"The Lincoln is back at Fort McHenry. I'll have to get back to World's End and get the Corvette—"

"Who said anything about driving? Listen, Montgomery *expects* you to arrive by car. What if you come by boat instead? We'll have the element of surprise. You can get the lay of the land before you go knocking on the front door."

Keane nodded. They would need every advantage they could get.

42

Liz came to slowly, her mind piecing together what had happened. She remembered a man coming up to her in the parking lot, asking for a recommendation to a breakfast place. She'd had the sense of someone suddenly behind her and had started to turn, but not before she felt a jolt like a hundred bees stinging her all at once between the shoulder blades—then oblivion.

She didn't have any experience with these things, but Liz was pretty sure that she had been hit with a stun gun.

As she regained consciousness, she realized that her face was pressed into the leather upholstery of the back seat of a large SUV. The vehicle smelled new and expensive. She looked up and saw that the windows were tinted to the point of being nearly blacked out.

She tried to sit up, and realized that her hands were bound behind her. She could feel the restraints cutting into the skin of her wrists and shifted to take the weight off them. That felt better.

Then she lay still, deciding that it might be better to pretend that she was still out of it.

Liz took stock. What had happened? What was this all about? Where was she going? She did not feel any sense of panic, but something closer to anger. She wanted some answers, goddammit.

Her earlier movements must have given her away, because she heard a man's voice say, "That's it, honey. Rise and shine. We know you're awake."

Giving up the ruse, Liz struggled to a sitting position. Her head ached and her mouth felt like a bucket of sand. She didn't seem to have any saliva left.

Two men sat in the front seats and she studied the backs of their heads. Both had short haircuts and thick necks. The man in the passenger seat looked really big; the top of his head nearly brushed the ceiling of the large vehicle. On the dash, she noticed a Cadillac symbol and also a map displayed on the dashboard screen. The field of the map was too tight for her to recognize the network of roads, but she saw a lot of blue water coming up. That must mean they were headed east.

The man in the passenger seat shifted so that he could see her, and she could see him. He looked vaguely familiar. Liz's addled brain struggled to place him.

"My name's Blister," he said. "You must be Liz."

"What's going on?" she demanded. Liz had intended to sound calm, in charge, but she heard the angry tone of her voice. "Where are you taking me?

"Oh, I think you know," Blister said. "You and your friend Franklin Scott Keane have something that my boss wants. The lost star. If you tell us about it now, we can cut this ride real short."

Then it clicked. Liz knew where she had seen this man before. They had passed him in the hallway at Tailwinds. This was the guy who had spooked Franklin into driving out of there like a bat out of hell.

"You work for Charles Montgomery, don't you?"

"Smart girl. Are you smart enough to tell me what I want to know?"

"I'm not telling you anything," Liz snapped.

"That's what I thought you'd say," Blister said. He sneered in a way that made Liz's blood run cold. "They all do at first."

"If you let me out now, I can pay you. Montgomery doesn't need to know you found me."

Blister barked out a laugh. "It's not about money. All we want is information. I'll find out what you know. Don't you worry your pretty little head about that. And if you don't have the information we want, we'll use you to get your boyfriend to tell us."

"My boyfriend?"

"Keane." Blister stared at the blank look on her face, then laughed. "You mean you didn't know that he was your boyfriend? Well, there you go! We're supposed to get information from you, not the other way around, but you can consider that a freebie. Anyhow, once he knows we've got you, he'll tell us what we want to know."

"Are we going to Tailwinds?"

"That's the plan, honey. Unless you'd rather go to my place?"

Liz didn't bother to answer. God, her mouth felt parched. It must have been a side effect of the stun gun. "Can I have some water?"

"Maybe later, if you're good."

Blister turned back around in his seat, signaling that their conversation was over. Liz tried to get comfortable, but the wrist restraints were tight, and it was hard not to put more pressure on them. She wasn't wearing a seatbelt, but she was pretty sure that not being belted in was the least of her worries.

It was not a comforting thought that no one knew where she was. If she'd been lucky, someone in the parking lot could have witnessed what happened and called the police. But the parking lot had mostly been deserted at that time of the morning. Besides, these guys seemed like professionals who would make sure that no one saw anything that they didn't want them to see. For all intents and purposes, she had disappeared.

They were going to tell Franklin that they had her, and he would probably try to rescue her or negotiate with Colonel Montgomery, but Liz knew it was just a trap for him. While she liked to hold out hope that Montgomery and his thugs would let them go once they had what they wanted, deep down she knew better. Once Montgomery had them both, they were as good as dead.

The dashboard map had shown water, and now through the tinted glass, she could see that the SUV was about to go over the Chesapeake Bay Bridge. This made sense if they were headed toward Tailwinds on the Eastern Shore; otherwise, they would have taken I-95 out of Baltimore. Blister seemed to be telling the truth about their destination.

Where was Franklin, anyway? Still at Fort McHenry, she supposed. She had no idea yet what he had found there.

She thought about the strange experience that she'd had yesterday when Franklin had glimpsed one of her childhood memories. She still wasn't sure how she felt about that, or about Franklin's ... abilities. The whole idea of what he called retrocognition was a little out there for her. It certainly wasn't normal. She never would have believed it if Franklin hadn't gone through with his demonstration. The thought of it raised new goosebumps up and down her arms.

What Franklin couldn't have known was that her father had died—not that day at the swimming hole, but a couple of years later. He had suffered a massive heart attack while mowing the lawn. Paramedics had arrived and worked over him, their gear spread out on the grass near her tire swing, and an ambulance had rushed him to the hospital, but he had died on the way. She suddenly felt an overwhelming rush of sadness. In a sense, everything that she had accomplished in her life so far had been done to please her father, even though he wasn't there to see it. Being kidnapped—and probably killed at the hands of these thugs—meant that she would never achieve all the things that she had imagined doing to make her father proud.

Suddenly furious, Liz reacted. She didn't have any particular plan. She knew that she just wanted out. Never mind the fact that they were in the middle of the four-mile-long bridge and a couple of hundred feet in the air.

Ignoring the fresh pain it caused her wrists, she forced herself back in the seat until she could bring her legs up between the front seats of the Cadillac. She drew back her knee and kicked the driver, catching his arm at the elbow. Her second kick was even higher, hitting him in the head. He took one hand off the wheel to bat at her legs as she continued to kick him.

The SUV swerved. The guardrail loomed closer, and beyond it was the long fall to the water. From this height, it would be like hitting concrete. They wouldn't have a prayer of survival. Liz didn't give a damn, as long as it meant these two were going over with her.

The driver struggled to regain control of the vehicle. Liz didn't want to give him that chance. She kicked him again.

"Goddammit!" he cried as the SUV headed for the side of the bridge. She heard the tires screech as he hit the brakes, but at this speed, it wasn't going to be enough. Horns blared around them.

Liz tried to kick him again, but Blister caught her right foot and then pinned her legs down with his powerful left arm. She couldn't get in another shot at the driver, who was still wrestling with the wheel. The SUV swayed like it might tip over, and then they were back in their lane.

"That was close," the driver said. He was supposed to be a tough guy, she supposed, but he was shaking all over and his eyes when he glanced at her in the rearview mirror had gone wide in fear. "You bitch!"

Liz struggled to get her legs free, but Blister held them down effortlessly with his left arm. He leaned into the space between the seats and she could see that in his right hand he held a gun. Pointed at her head. The black hole of the muzzle looked as big as a cannon. Blister brought the gun so close to the bridge of her nose that she could smell the metal and gun oil. The muzzled yawned wide like a hole she was about to fall into. Liz froze.

"You know what my dad used to say? He used to say, 'Don't make me pull this car over,' " Blister said. "Believe me, you don't want to make me pull the car over. Don't do that again, honey."

43

Once they were out on the open water, Beau steered a course up the bay.

"We're headed north," Keane observed. He had a mug of coffee in one hand, and a ham sandwich in the other. "The last time I checked, the Choptank River was to the south."

"We need to pick up a few things," Beau explained. "It sounds as if Colonel Montgomery's compound is going to have some serious security."

"You don't have to do this," Keane said.

"Don't go talking shit," Beau said with a laugh.

Keane nodded and smiled grimly. It went without saying that Beau would walk barefoot through broken glass if Keane needed him to, and Keane would do the same for Beau. Besides, Beau wouldn't miss it for the world if there was a remote chance that guns and violence were involved. Beau lived for this kind of thing.

Soon, the bluffs that marked the entrance to the Sassafras River hove into sight. Erosion had caused the shoreline cliffs to slide down into the water, giving the cliff faces a naked or bald appearance that contrasted with the thick green forests that marched to the river's edge. World's End was just a few miles upriver, beyond Ordinary Point.

Fortunately, this was one of the rare charters that originated from the dock at World's End, so there was no need for Beau to drop anyone in Rock Hall.

There were just three men in the charter. Two left with curt farewells, obviously unhappy that their fishing trip had been cut short by the run to Baltimore. The third man—the one who had broken Keane's leap onto the deck of *Rascal*—wasn't so eager to leave.

"You need a hand?" he asked.

"We got this, bro," Beau said.

"It might not be any of my business, but whatever you two are up against, it seems to me like two guys aren't going to be enough."

Beau seemed to reconsider. "Why the hell would you want to help us?"

"Hey, I've been divorced for two years. There's nothing waiting for me at home but a microwaved burrito and ESPN. This sounds a whole lot better."

"All right, but you'll have to sign a waiver."

"Really?"

Beau gave him a look. "Seriously? There's no goddamn waiver. Come over here and keep an eye on the fuel pump while I get my shit together. What's your name again?"

"Joe."

"Welcome aboard, Joe."

"Awesome! Listen, though, I've got one question for you guys. Just to be clear. We're not doing anything illegal, right?"

Keane and Beau exchanged a glance.

Keane shrugged. "Don't ask me. I'm a historian, not a lawyer."

"But technically speaking, we're not committing any felonies?" Joe asked.

"Not unless somebody gets shot," Beau said.

"Thank you for clarifying that."

They left Joe at the boat and got in Beau's old pickup truck at the dock. Beau dropped Keane at the house, where he collected the pizza box containing the lost star from the Star-Spangled Banner. If that's what it took to get Elizabeth back, it was well worth the price. He left behind the rucksack containing the letter from James Madison. He stepped back outside, and a few minutes later Beau picked him up on the way back to the dock.

When Beau had mentioned gathering supplies, he hadn't been talking about water bottles and power bars. In the bed of the pickup were several gearboxes. Inside the boxes were tactical vests, ammunition, and guns. Ominously, another package contained medical supplies.

"Take your pick, fellas," Beau said. "I brought a variety."

"Cool," said Joe, selecting an AR-15.

"You know how to work that thing?" Beau asked skeptically.

"Hey, I was in the National Guard for six years." Joe grinned, then worked the action. "Just like riding a bicycle."

Keane wasn't eager to be armed. "As much as I want to get Elizabeth back safely, I am not interested in shooting anyone."

"The problem is that they might be interested in shooting *you*, so it's best to be prepared if you need to shoot back." Beau pressed a Mossberg 500 Mariner shotgun on him. With its short barrel, and with a magazine loaded with double-ought, it was an excellent close-range tactical weapon.

The final weapon that Beau carried aboard was a Thompson M1A1 submachine gun with a thirty-round box magazine firing .45 caliber rounds. The thing was practically an antique, but Keane had fired it a few times at World's End, and knew that it was a formidable weapon. The Thompson also made an impressive racket. Beau had plenty of extra magazines.

"You brought your machine gun?" Keane said.

"If push comes to shove, this will make sure they keep their heads down. Nobody wants to be a hero with big fat .45 rounds buzzing through the air."

Beau wasn't the only one who had returned to the boat prepared. Keane opened up the pizza box and looked down at the tattered cloth star, its once-brilliant white linen now stained by age.

"That's what all this is about?" Beau asked, looking over his shoulder. "That looks like one of those things that old ladies put over the backs of chairs in their parlors. A what do you call it?"

"An antimacassar," Keane said. "I can see the resemblance, but it's just a little more valuable than that."

"I thought you found something in the fort."

"I did. A letter. But that's not what Montgomery wants. He doesn't even know about it. He was after this star long before I ever visited Fort McHenry. I'm fairly certain that he killed two men over it."

"Huh," Beau said. "I can see why he wants it to go along with the rest of the Star-Spangled Banner that he stole. Greedy bastard, isn't he? Are you going to give it to him?"

"Not if I don't have to," Keane said. "But giving him the lost star may be the only way to get Elizabeth back safely. Of course, I don't trust that he's going to hold up his end of the bargain. Do you have a Ziploc bag?"

Beau found one—he kept boxes of them on hand for rockfish fillets—and Keane slipped the star inside to keep it dry. Then he folded it over and stuffed it into a pocket of his dark cargo pants. Any conservator would be horrified. He was even a little horrified himself. Too much was at stake to be concerned about the niceties of historic conservation. This star might very well be worth Elizabeth's life.

Less than an hour after arriving at the dock, they were refueled and ready to go.

From the dock at World's End, it was seventy-five nautical

miles or about three hours to Charles Montgomery's Tailwinds compound on the Choptank River. Conditions were in their favor in that the bay was calm. *Rascal* cut through the smooth water like a tomahawk, powered by her 485 horsepower Cummins diesel motor. They passed Kent Island and swept beneath the Chesapeake Bay bridge. To the west, the sun began to sink lower and the breeze cooled. Keane was glad that he had brought along his Craghoppers windbreaker. Joe rooted around in the cabin and found a bright pink sweatshirt with the words *Eye Candy* in bright blue letters across the front.

"Please tell me that's not yours," Keane said to Beau.

"One of my fishing trip clients left it behind. I thought I was doing her a favor by keeping it buried in a footlocker." Beau shrugged at Joe. "Looks good on you, though. Makes an ironic statement, you know?"

At dusk, the Choptank came into sight. Much of James Michener's novel, *Chesapeake*, had taken place on the Choptank, making the river famous around the world. This was a fine river for sailing and normally the Choptank would be dotted with sails, but in the autumn twilight, they mostly had the water to themselves.

They cruised under the Route 50 bridge at Cambridge and then passed the lights of the Hyatt resort on the southern shore. It was shaping up to be a fine, crisp early autumn evening. Guests had gathered around the resort's outdoor fireplace to sip wine and hot cider, and to toast marshmallows. A few waved at the passing vessel. Keane would gladly have traded places with them rather than confront the evil and the danger before them tonight. But for all his calm demeanor, Keane had never backed down from physical danger. Beau hadn't, either. It was a lesson imparted to them by their grandfather. Perhaps there had been a method to the old man's madness, after all.

The river narrowed. They passed the lights of houses and

docks, but the farther up the reaches of the river that they went, the land tended toward marsh so that the shore was dark over these vast empty places. Beau kept a careful eye on the depth finder. The last thing they needed now was to run *Rascal* aground.

Tailwinds was located in the upper reaches of the river. In colonial times, the idea had been to locate the plantation in such a way as to take advantage of the river but also to have access to the overland routes across the Delmarva Peninsula. Even now, the area was largely undeveloped.

"That's it," Keane said, his eyes on the screen of his smartphone, where he had Google maps pulled up.

The house was located several hundred feet from the water. In colonial times, plantation owners hadn't been overly concerned about enjoying the water view.

From the water, the house hardly looked formidable. A few lights glowed in the windows. He wondered which room held Elizabeth.

Beau killed the engine, letting the boat slowly drift past the dock and shoreline. Aboard *Rascal* was a two-person rubber raft with oars. They put the raft into the water at the stern, and Keane carefully lowered himself into it. Beau handed down the shotgun after him.

"Maybe I should be the one to go ashore," Beau said.

"No, you look after the boat," Keane replied. "I've been in the house, so I know the layout."

"If you're not back here in thirty minutes, I'll take that as a sign that I need to start shooting," Beau said. "Meanwhile, try not to get killed."

Keane rowed away from the boat. The lightweight oars were made of aluminum and high-grade plastic, enabling him to propel the rubber dinghy through the water almost soundlessly. The Navy SEALs couldn't have asked for a better landing craft. He rowed with his back to the shore, watching the dark

hulk of the deadrise grow smaller. He couldn't help but wonder
if he would be seeing Beau and the boat again. Remembering
Charles Montgomery's well-armed compound from his
previous visit, he was heading into the lion's den.

Tailwinds had its own beach on the Choptank and once he
reached shallow water Keane let the dinghy's momentum carry
him onto the sand. Moving as quietly as possible, he dragged
the dinghy away from the waterline and hid it behind a clump
of reeds. Beau had insisted that he bring the shotgun, but
Keane left it behind in the dinghy. He didn't plan on shooting
his way into or out of the compound. Instead, he would rely on
stealth.

Crouching there, he looked around to get his bearings. The
manor house itself was well-lighted, but the manicured and
landscaped lawn leading down to the waterfront was dark,
which was just fine with Keane. The compound itself was
extremely isolated. Not only did Montgomery own this historic
house, but he owned a substantial amount of property
surrounding it. No neighboring lights were visible. Just to the
east of the tillable land began a vast tidal marsh. Earlier resi-
dents had made use of the marsh for trapping and hunting, but
for Montgomery it would create a buffer zone that added to his
privacy. The marsh appeared even darker than the rest of the
land, and the singing of night insects was strongest there.

Keane listened for any sign that his arrival had already been
discovered. He strained his ears into the darkness. He heard the
river lapping at the shore, the symphony of late-season crickets,
and even the distant hoot of an owl across the marshes to the
east.

Slowly, he rose from a crouch and started across the expan-
sive lawn, making a direct line for the house. His dark clothes
hid him perfectly.

Keane had no good plan for what to do once he reached the
house itself. He would simply have to slip inside, then locate

where Elizabeth was being held. There seemed to be enough people at Tailwinds, mostly likely coming and going at all hours, that getting into the house itself shouldn't be too much of a problem. He could slip inside right behind them.

Where would be the most natural place to hold someone against their will at a place like Tailwinds? He doubted that Elizabeth had been taken to a conference room or even to a bedroom. No, Montgomery would be holding her somewhere in the cellar. Once Keane got inside, that's where he would look for her.

He was already more than halfway toward the house. He had been ashore for perhaps five minutes, which still gave him plenty of time. Beau had not been kidding about shooting once thirty minutes had elapsed and Keane had not returned. Beau liked any excuse to start shooting.

Keane had no idea what sort of security measures to expect on the grounds. There might be motion detectors or even dogs —although he hadn't heard any patrols so far. It was just a chance he would have to take. He moved silently across the grass, zigzagging between shrubs and trees to keep out of the open and break up his silhouette.

In the darkness ahead, a tree trunk seemed to split into two. He halted, taken by surprise. Then a powerful flashlight beam hit him full in the face, blinding him. Off to his right, he sensed movement as another sentry approached from that direction.

"That's far enough, Doctor Keane," said a business-like voice. "Hands on your head, please. Slowly."

Keane had no choice but to do as he was told. The second sentry materialized beside him, took his hands off his head, and quickly Zip-tied his wrists together. He was patted down.

"He's clean," the second sentry said. He had been looking for concealed weapons, so he hadn't bothered with the Ziploc bag in his pocket that contained the lost star.

"Follow me, Doctor Keane," said the man with the flashlight, taking the beam off his face and using it to illuminate their path instead.

"How do you know my name?" he asked.

"Colonel Montgomery has been expecting you," the sentry with the flashlight said. "Now this way, please."

It had all happened to fast. Instead of rescuing Elizabeth, Keane realized that he was now a prisoner himself.

44

T he guards took him through a side door into the house. This time, there would be no congenial tour of the old mansion. Keane was brought down a set of steps to the cellar, just as he had predicted. They went along a hallway and past several doors, one of which was labeled "Shooting Range" while another bore a sign identifying at as the theater. There must have been as much of Tailwinds underground as aboveground. Keane took careful note of the route, glancing back over his shoulder from time to time to get his bearings, in case he had the opportunity to make a getaway.

"Can you tell me where we're going?"

"Just keep moving, please."

The fact that his captors were coldly polite and business-like was all the more unnerving. He had the impression that they had done this sort of thing before, probably in places like Afghanistan and Iraq.

Finally, they stopped at an unmarked door, which made it seem all the more ominous. "In here," the man who had wielded the flashlight said.

He paused in front of the door and knocked. It was opened

by a big man whom Keane recognized instantly as Montgomery's henchman. This was the same man he had encountered at Lindermann's condo in Baltimore and who had spotted Keane on his earlier visit to Tailwinds—thus upsetting the apple cart and setting in motion everything that had led up to this point. Keane noted the smirk on the man's face.

"Well, look who it is," the man said. He took Keane by the shoulder and roughly half-shoved, half-dragged him inside.

The room was utilitarian with a single door, no windows or decor, but only harsh florescent lights overhead that illuminated the dismal gray concrete floors and walls. The room was perhaps twenty-five feet wide and slightly longer than it was wide, although the space at the back was taken up by some sort of mechanical systems. Keane thought that it appeared to be a propane-fired instant water heater.

In the center of the concrete floor was a folding utility table about three feet wide and six feet long, surrounded by folding metal chairs. In the chair closest to the door he saw Elizabeth, stooped slightly forward. He realized that her hands were bound like his own. Charles Montgomery sat across from her. On the table between them sat two unopened water bottles, a notepad and pen, and more ominously, a stun gun.

The big man picked up the stun gun, but Montgomery raised a hand to stop him. "That won't be necessary just yet, Blister."

Blister set down the stun gun, slightly farther away from Keane. He smiled at Keane in a way that let him know the stun gun was very much still an option.

Keane glanced at Elizabeth. His heart ached at the sight of Elizabeth tied up like that. She looked exhausted, but unharmed. To his surprise, the expression in her eyes was not fear, but anger. If her eyes had been lasers, they would have bored holes right through Blister and Montgomery.

"Elizabeth!" he exclaimed. "Are you all right?"

"I've been better," she said.

"Keane," Montgomery said. The expression on his face made it clear that he was very pleased with himself. "We were expecting you. But you never came to the property gate."

"I came by boat," he said.

Montgomery raised an eyebrow. "You're full of surprises, aren't you?"

"You have no idea."

The ex-Army officer laughed. "You know what Sun Tzu said. Never underestimate your enemy. However, that's probably not fair. I don't know that we would characterize ourselves as enemies, not when we both want the same thing."

Now it was Keane's turn to appear surprised. "What might that be?"

"We want Americans to appreciate our history."

"By stealing it? We both know you were the one who took the Star-Spangled Banner from the Smithsonian."

Montgomery laughed. "I'm not stealing history, Keane. I'm saving it. I should clarify that. You see, I am saving our *heritage*. You still haven't quite figured out what I'm up to, have you?"

Keane could only stare. He'd had the impression before that there was something off about Montgomery. Previously, he had suspected that Montgomery was just one of those men driven by a need to be in the limelight that Keane himself could neither understand nor appreciate. Add to the mix was a healthy dose of the narcissism typical of any television personality. But now, he looked more closely into the colonel's eyes and thought he saw the dancing light of madness.

"What *are* you up to?" Keane asked.

"Do you know what else Sun Tzu said? He said, *Let your plans be dark and impenetrable as night, and when you move, fall like a thunderbolt.* My thunderbolt is about to fall, Keane."

"Sun Tzu was writing about war. What are you referring to?"

"There is a cultural war going on, Keane. My thunderbolt is

about to fall. I am going to destroy the Star-Spangled Banner
live, online, for all of these United States to see."

"What! Why would you do that?" Keane stared at him in
shock.

Montgomery smiled, then said, "Allow me to show you
something, Keane."

Montgomery prodded him out of the room at gunpoint,
leaving Liz alone with Blister. They didn't go far. Just down the
hall behind an unmarked door leading to a darkened room.

"What's this?"

"You'll see. After you, Doctor Keane."

Keane had no choice but to step inside. Lights came on, and
he was surprised to see several video cameras set up on tripods,
along with studio lighting. Keane realized that this was exactly
what this was—a studio. He blinked at the red, white, and blue
fabric heaped in a cavernous colonial-era fireplace.

"The flag!"

Montgomery nodded. "For a long time now I have watched
our country circling the drain. It's more a matter of indifference
than anything. People are just too busy to care. Meanwhile,
they have left the business of governing up to professional
politicians who are only interested in in-fighting or getting
their sound bite in the media. We need a unifying event. Wars
and acts of terrorism tend to do that, but I've been a soldier, and
believe me, I'm not interested in an actual war, or in seeing
innocent people die—at least, not a large number of innocent
people. In any struggle, there will be casualties."

Keane still didn't like the sound of that. "Go on."

"What if I could galvanize Americans with a more bloodless
statement? So, on September fourteenth, the anniversary of the
battle of Baltimore, I am going to burn the Star-Spangled
Banner flag live on the internet."

"How can you do that? You will be vilified."

"Oh, it won't be *me* doing the burning. The flag will be

burned by an organization known as the Islamic Mosaic. It's a cultural organization, but it will make a perfect scapegoat. They are wholly innocent of that particular crime, and perhaps of any crimes, but I have some very talented young cy-ops people who have hacked into their website and at the appropriate time will stream the flag burning live online using this group's social media accounts. I think Americans are going to be a little upset. In our outrage, we shall find unity, as we often do. It will be an opportunity for my organization—for me—to be at the forefront of change."

All that Keane could do was stare at Montgomery. "You're a madman," he finally said.

"Do you really think so? Americans always want to return to our core values in a crisis, and when the time comes, I will be leading that discussion. We've been doing some polling ... it's even possible that I may run for office if things look favorable. Come now, let's return. It would be rude to keep the others waiting."

A few steps later, they were back in the room with Liz and Blister. Montgomery gestured to a chair, and Keane sat, his arms still bound behind him.

"I still don't understand why you're doing this," Keane said.

"What's going on?" Liz asked.

"He's got the flag in some sort of studio next door. He's going to burn it."

"What?"

Montgomery grinned at them. "Don't be so alarmed. When we destroy or lose one symbol, there is an opportunity to replace it with another. Of course, we'll be talking about it in detail on my news program. My organization, Anacreon, will be one of the leaders of this movement. It's all about positioning, you see. The destruction of the flag will jumpstart a fresh new conversation about where we are going as Americans."

"This is crazy."

"Speaking of jumpstarting, we need to have a conversation about the missing piece of the flag that you found. You see, for my little demonstration to be effective, I need to make certain that I destroy *all* of the flag. I need that star, Keane."

"I don't know what you're talking about."

"Oh, I think you do." Montgomery nodded significantly at the bucket on the floor, and the jumper cables leading to a car battery. Keane felt his belly quiver nervously. "Once the Smithsonian asked you to look into the theft of the Star-Spangled Banner, it didn't take you long to determine that Galarza and Lindermann had somehow tracked down the lost star that was cut from the Star-Spangled Banner so many years ago."

"How did Esteban ever get involved with you?"

"Esteban shared many of our concerns," Montgomery said. By *our*, Keane took that to mean the like-minded army that the former colonel had assembled at Tailwinds. "When you interviewed me before, I was being disingenuous about my acquaintance with Esteban. He did have me autograph his copy of my book. He was, in fact, a member of Anacreon. You might think that someone named Esteban Galarza was an unlikely member of Anacreon, but he was a true American. He became my contact at the Smithsonian as I planned the heist. Oh, he was unaware of what I planned to do. Esteban never would have agreed to the destruction of the flag. He was fettered by convention. However, he was unwittingly helpful in furthering my understanding of all the details involved."

"But you killed him?"

"Sadly, he might have put two and two together very quickly once the flag was stolen, so Blister here arranged for him to have a mishap in Rock Creek Park. He had told me that he and Lindermann were looking for the lost star. Esteban was quite excited about it. I asked Lindermann about the star, but he wasn't very cooperative. You know how that ended for him. I hope that you won't make the same mistake."

"You've gone mad."

"I'm sure that's just what people warned Sam Adams or Paul Revere or James Madison. Do their bold actions and ideas seem like madness now?"

Keane had no response to that. It was clear that Montgomery did not know about the existence of the letter from James Madison. He exchanged a look with Elizabeth. She looked both incredulous and angry.

"Surely you can achieve your ends in another way," Keane said.

"Bold actions, Keane. To make my point, I can't have a piece of the flag surviving. It's too much of a symbol. So let me ask you again, where is the star?"

"I'm afraid I don't know." Keane kept his face perfectly blank.

Montgomery sighed. "Miss Graham said much the same, which is why I had Blister bring out some, uh, tools to help you change your mind."

Blister smiled. "I've been looking forward to this."

All of their eyes went to the bucket of water, the jumper cables, and the car battery.

"That's how Blister got his nickname, you see. He was always very good at this sort of thing. Raising blisters. This car battery trick of his does that and more. It can make the flesh bubble."

"This is monstrous," Keane said, struggling to control his voice. "Killing people, burning the flag, threatening to torture us."

"I'm afraid that you are the one forcing us to take these measures," Montgomery said. "All that I need to know is the location of this lost star."

"I'm going to make you work for it, Montgomery. Go ahead and hook me up to that thing."

"You'll get your turn, Keane. But I think that you'll be more willing to talk if we take the ladies first approach. Blister, start with Miss Graham."

Blister slid the bucket of water closer to Elizabeth. "Please," she stammered. "Don't."

"We've got a new battery here, fully charged," he said. "It's rated for eight hundred cold-cranking amps, which is impressive. I added salt to the water to make it a better conductor. It's a little trick I learned in the sandbox."

Elizabeth tried to move her chair away, sliding it a few inches across the concrete floor. Blister reached out and dragged her back.

"That's enough," Keane said.

"Do you have something to say, Keane?" Montgomery asked with interest.

"I can give you the star," he said.

"Franklin, don't!" Elizabeth said.

"This has gone far enough," Keane said. "I have the star in my pocket."

Montgomery looked at Blister. "I thought you said he was searched!"

Blister shrugged. "For weapons."

"Give us the star, if you please."

"Why don't you free my hands, so that I can get into my pocket?"

Blister reached into his back pocket and took out a switch-blade, and flicked the blade open.

"Wait," Montgomery said. "Don't be so eager to cut him loose."

"This geek?" Blister waved the knife. "He's no threat to me, tied up or not."

"What about me?" Elizabeth demanded. "These damn plastic ties are killing my wrists."

Montgomery nodded, and Blister cut their plastic bonds

with a single stroke of the razor-sharp blade. However, he bound Elizabeth's wrists again, this time in front of her.

"Hey!"

"You, I don't trust. Remember that little episode on the bridge?"

Elizabeth started to say more, but Montgomery cut her off with a wave of his hand. He turned his attention to Keane. "Now, give me the star. Do it slowly."

Keane stood so that he could reach—slowly—into his cargo pocket. Montgomery and Blister were both on their feet, watching him like hawks. Once again, he was surprised that Montgomery was rather short. Maybe this whole crazed scheme of his was the result of some Napoleon complex. Blister, however, was taller and much heavier than Keane. Muscles bulged everywhere under his polo shirt. Up close, he was a formidable man.

Keane extracted the Ziploc bag that held the star, and placed it on the table. Folded up, the old fabric with its tea-stained patina was less than impressive.

"That's it?" Blister asked.

Montgomery picked up the bag. His voice took on a reverent tone. "Incredible. Just imagine, this is part of the flag that flew over Fort McHenry. It's the flag that Francis Scott Key watched as he wrote what would become *The Star-Spangled Banner*."

"And you're going to burn it!" Elizabeth said.

"Yes, I am, along with the rest of the flag," Montgomery said. "To make a point. Blister, please continue."

"Wait!" Keane shouted. "I gave you what you wanted."

"Yes, you did, and you saved us a lot of trouble," Montgomery said. "But have you told us everything you know? For example, what were you up to at Fort McHenry?"

"Research."

"You took an awful risk to spend the night there. Yes, I know all about that. What piece of this puzzle are you not sharing with me?"

"I'm telling you again, Montgomery. It was research, but nothing pertinent to the Star-Spangled Banner."

"Maybe. We'll find out." He nodded at Blister, who turned toward Elizabeth again, that unpleasant smirk on his face. He picked up one end of the jumper cables, which were made more horrible by the fact that they were old and rusty. "Like the colonel said, ladies first."

That's when the shooting started. Even down in the basement they could hear the rattle of what sounded like a machine gun, punctuated with a few deep booms that might have been a shotgun.

Right on schedule, Beau had opened fire.

Montgomery spun around and glared at Keane. "I said no police!"

"That's not the police," Keane said. "That's the cavalry."

Montgomery tossed the star on the table, still in its plastic bag. "Watch them, Blister, while I deal with this. I'll be right back."

Montgomery went out, leaving them alone in the room with the colonel's henchman.

"Don't worry," Blister said. "The colonel won't be gone for long. As soon as he gets back, the real fun can begin."

Still in the chair, Kane looked around frantically, desperate for some means of escape. The drab concrete walls stared back at him.

Elizabeth sneezed. At least, it was *supposed* to be a sneeze. It was probably the worst fake sneeze that Keane had ever heard. "Dusty down here," she said. "It makes my allergies flare up."

"That's the least of your worries," Blister said.

"*Achoo!*" Elizabeth fake-sneezed again. And this time, as if jolted by the sneeze, her foot lashed out and kicked over the bucket of saltwater. The water spread out in a pool across the concrete floor, puddling around Blister's feet.

"Are you serious?" The big man sounded annoyed. "I don't know what you're trying to accomplish. I can just get more water. Believe me when I say that only making this harder on yourself. And that has to be the worst phony sneeze I've ever heard."

While Blister was distracted, Keane reached across the table and picked up the stun gun. He had never used one before, but how hard could it be? The operation looked fairly simple. He pushed a red trigger button on the stun gun, and an angry spark of electric shot between the two connections.

Blister just smirked at him. "You do know that you actually have to touch me with that thing? I'll break both your arms before you can do that. As a matter of fact, now I might just break your arms for fun."

"That won't be necessary," Keane said. He leaned forward in the chair and touched the stun gun to the puddle of water in which Blister was still standing. A glimmer of realization appeared in Blister's eyes just as Keane hit the trigger again.

Blister went down as if not only the rug, but the entire floor, had been yanked out from under him. He hadn't been exaggerating about saltwater amplifying the effects of electricity. He flew up in the air and landed in the puddle. Keane hit him with another jolt. Blister cried out and his whole body quivered, but he was still managing to move. Keane hit the trigger again, but Blister was already rolling free of the water. Shaking his head groggily, he was trying to get back on his feet.

He never had the chance. Even with her hands tied together, Elizabeth was able to hit him over the head with one of the metal folding chairs. He went down again and lay on the floor, groaning.

"Should I hit him another time?" Elizabeth wondered. "I'd kind of like to."

"That's enough for now. Hold on." Keane snagged the switchblade out of Blister's back pocket and popped the blade. He waved the knife at Elizabeth. "Hold out your hands."

Once he had cut through the plastic tie, Keane put the knife in his pocket and grabbed the star off the table.

"Now, let's get the hell out of here."

45

They fled the way that Keane had come in. As before, these basement hallways seemed to be deserted. Outside, the chatter of the Thompson submachine gun was even louder. Beau's diversion had been very effective. Keane just hoped he wasn't shooting toward the house. He had no desire to be caught by one of those fat .45 slugs gone astray. It wasn't for nothing that a .45 round was sometimes called a flying ashtray.

Down at the beach, there was enough ambient light for him to see that some of Montgomery's minions were taking shelter behind overturned picnic tables and trees, starting to fire back at the boat. That avenue of escape was now closed. Keane just hoped that Beau had the good sense to pull back before someone on Montgomery's team brought in the heavy artillery. *Rascal* was a fishing boat, not a dreadnought. With any luck, one of the neighbors on the far shore of the Choptank had called the state police.

"Which way?" Elizabeth asked.

"Good question." Quickly, Keane considered their escape route. With the firefight taking place at the beach, their best option seemed to be making a run for the road. But Keane recalled that the entire perimeter of the property was securely fenced off. Ostensibly, the tall fence was intended to keep deer out, but it was just as effective at keeping two-legged intruders out—or in, in this case.

He turned his attention to the dark gloom of the marsh to the east. A Stygian atmosphere hung over the vast marshland. Keane knew from experience that an Eastern Shore marsh was virtually impassable on foot. It was no wonder that Montgomery had not bothered to fence off the marsh because the landscape in that direction cut off Tailwinds from the rest of the world as effectively as a moat.

"Do you trust me?" he asked.

"We've made it this far," she said. "Why stop now?"

Keane took Elizabeth by the hand, and together they ran across the lawn in the direction of the marsh. The lawn ended abruptly at a ditch that had had been cut to separate the boggy marshland. They leaped across and landed in a patch of cattails, reeds with distinctive brown tops that reminded Keane of miniature versions of the bearskin helmets worn by the guards at Buckingham Palace. Keane waded into the chest-high reeds, with Elizabeth right behind him. His only thought was to get away from Tailwinds. Once they had made some headway into the marsh, they could angle to the north. Surely there would be a road in that direction.

He began to have the nagging feeling that they had leaped out of the frying pan—and into the swamp.

* * *

DOWN AT THE BEACH, the press of gunfire from Montgomery's team had forced the boat to move farther out into the Choptank, where it turned off its running lights and effectively disappeared from view.

"Keep your eyes peeled!" he ordered. "If they come back in, light 'em up!"

Montgomery was headed back to the mansion when Blister came running toward him. He noticed that Blister had one hand pressed to the back of his head.

"What the hell are you doing out here?" the colonel demanded. "What about Keane and that woman?"

"They got away, sir."

"What? What are you talking about?"

"Keane got me with the stun gun, and that bitch hit me over the head with a chair." He touched his head ahead. "I'm going to need stitches, goddammit."

"Never mind that. We've got to find them."

"What about the boat?"

"Keane's so-called cavalry pulled back once we made things a little hot for them. But it won't be long before the police or DNR shows up to see what all the shooting was about. We need to find Keane and that woman before that. Any idea which way they went?"

"Beats the hell out of me."

"Goddammit, Blister! I *will* beat the hell out of you, if we don't find them! Now think!"

"If Keane went out the same way he came in, it means he wouldn't come out the door around back. Let's go check."

The two men ran around to the back of the house. Both had powerful Maglites, and both carried handguns. They saw no sign of Keane at the back door.

Montgomery played his light over the dewy grass. He noticed that he could see their own tracks through the wet grass where they had come around from the front of the house. This particular door was not used very much, so there was not an abundance of tracks coming and going to it. He searched in widening circles until he found two side by side paths leading away from the house.

"Found them," he said. "Looks like they headed toward the marsh."

Montgomery was surprised. He would have thought that Keane would have made a run straight up the driveway, toward the county road leading toward Tailwinds. Of course, the gate and the perimeter fence would have stopped them and they would soon have been back in Montgomery's basement interrogation room. They sure as hell wouldn't be leaving that room again once he caught them—not alive, anyhow.

However, escaping through the marsh seemed like a desperate alternative. Keane was either braver, or more foolish, then Montgomery had thought.

"Over here!" Blister shouted. He was pointing across the ditch at the edge of the lawn, to where the cattails had been flattened and mashed by someone passing through them.

"Come on. They can't have gotten far."

"Shouldn't I get a team together?"

"There's no need for that. We'll find them a few feet into the marsh. Besides, those two are unarmed—unless the girl brought her folding chair along."

Blister scowled. "Yes, sir."

"Come on."

Montgomery jumped across the ditch, and Blister followed.

* * *

WHAT KEANE HAD NOT COUNTED ON WAS how quickly the marsh swallowed them up. They began to encounter patches of phragmites, an invasive species of reed that grew much taller than the native cattails and that had sharp edges to slash at their exposed hands and faces. It was hard to see where they were going beyond the wall of green facing them. One good thing was that this late in the year, hardly any mosquitoes pestered them.

"Ugh!" said Elizabeth. "I wish I had a machete."

"At this rate, we may need a compass too," Keane said. "It's almost impossible to get our bearings." It did not help that a foggy miasma had risen out of the marshy ground, shrouding the sky from view.

"Maybe this wasn't the best idea," Elizabeth said. "Although it's a whole lot better than being locked up in the basement with a car battery and some jumper cables, and a demented mercenary."

"I hope you're right about that. Let's stop here a minute just to see if we can figure out any clue about where we are."

They paused. The thick marsh grass around them seemed to have blotted out any sound. Even the late-season crickets had stopped chirping. They certainly could not hear the shooting anymore from the direction of the river. Maybe Beau had wisened up and retreated farther out into the Choptank.

Keane listened for some clue as to where they might be, hoping for the sound of a passing car on a far-away road or even the barking of a dog in some distant waterfront estate. Nothing. It was as if the marsh grass and the boggy ground had absorbed all sound. He was about to give up when he heard a splash, and a muttered curse, from behind them— no more than a couple hundred feet away.

"Did you hear that?" Elizabeth whispered.

"They came after us and they're close," he said. "We've got to hurry!"

Keane pressed ahead through the marsh. Solid ground was becoming hard to find, the deeper through the marsh that they went. They came to a shallow tidal creek and splashed across, but Keane stopped short of the opposite bank.

"Hold on, I have an idea. Stay here."

He clambered up the bank on the opposite side of the creek, mashing down as many reeds as he could. Once he had gone several feet into the reeds, he turned around and waded

into the creek once more. Then he led Elizabeth about thirty
feet downstream, and they slipped up the bank, being careful
not to disturb the reeds.

"Maybe that will buy us some time."

"Where did you learn to do that?" Elizabeth asked.

"Beau and I used to spend all day hiking and just exploring
when we were kids," Keane explained. "One of the things we
used to do was play war, or foxes and hounds. Leaving a false
trail was one of our favorite tricks."

"Let's just hope Montgomery and his pals fall for it."

46

For Montgomery and Blister, following the trail through the reeds was easy enough. The trail could not have been clearer if Keane and the woman had put up a road sign.

They splashed across a tidal creek and followed the trail where it picked up on the other side. The reeds began to thin out and they entered a vast fen over which hung a kind of fog that was drifting in off the Choptank. One thing for sure, the going was easier. Soon, however, the trail petered out. It became clear that Keane had laid a false trail, and tricked them.

"That son of a bitch!" Montgomery was livid. "He's supposed to be a fucking historian, not a Green Beret!"

Montgomery looked the part of a fit military man thanks to time spent in a carpeted and climate-controlled gym. It had been years since he taken part in anything resembling field maneuvers. He realized that Keane evidently knew a good bit more about field tactics than he himself did.

"Got any bright ideas, Blister?"

"We'll just have to backtrack, sir, and try to figure out where he came out of that water. It can't be too hard to find."

"Goddammit."

Montgomery was turning to go, when he noticed the lights.

At first, he thought that his eyes were playing tricks on him. Two glowing orbs drifted above the ground, maybe one hundred feet away. The orbs were about waist-high above the marsh. The more that he thought about it, the more it made sense that what he was seeing were flashlights being carried by Keane and Graham. Funny that he hadn't seen those before.

He pointed. "What the hell is that?"

"Must be Keane. That son of a bitch is gonna be sorry when I catch up to him. I'm gonna—"

"All right, all right. Let's just catch them first."

They hurried after the lights. The marsh here was boggy, but solid enough that they could cover ground at a trot. But as fast as they moved, the lights managed to move faster, staying just ahead of them. Try as they might, they just couldn't catch up.

Then the orbs suddenly winked out.

"Where did they go?"

"To hell if I know. Turn off your flashlight a minute."

They both clicked off their Maglites and found themselves enveloped in a darkness that stuck to them like duct tape. They strained to see or hear their quarry, but there was no sound or light.

"Huh," Blister remarked, breaking the silence. "Which way do you think it is back to the house?"

"I've got to admit, I have no idea where we are."

Then the lights reappeared, hanging in the air no more than a few yards away.

"There they are!" Blister shouted. "I've got them!"

He snapped on his flashlight and took off running at the spheres.

Montgomery stood rooted to the spot. There was something spooky about those lights. By now, he was fairly certain it was not Keane and the woman, but something else altogether.

What, though, he wasn't sure. He watched Blister's flashlight bob up and down as he ran after the glowing blobs. No matter how fast Blister ran, he couldn't seem to catch up.

"Come back here!" Montgomery shouted. "It's not them, you idiot!"

But Blister and the lights kept getting farther away. Finally, he heard a startled cry, then a loud splash, and Blister's flashlight winked out.

Montgomery started running in that direction. He had his gun out, although he wasn't sure what good it would do him. His heart was hammering in his chest far beyond the exertion required to cover the distance. He struggled through the reeds for several minutes.

Up ahead, the lights had stopped, as if waiting for him. These radiant orbs were just plain weird.

Montgomery stopped, too. He found himself standing at the edge of a deep tidal pool. A glow was visible at the bottom, several feet down, barely filtering up through water that was tea-colored from the vegetation and silt. But this was no spooky marsh light. It was Blister's flashlight, at the bottom of the pool.

"Blister?" he called.

No answer. The man was somewhere at the bottom of that pool. Montgomery didn't dive in after him. Too much time had passed to save him. As Montgomery stared into the water, the beam of the Maglite faded and went out.

Oddly, the orbs hovered nearby. Then they slowly started to drift off. Not sure what else to do, and with no idea anymore where the hell he was, Montgomery followed. He realized that a part of him was simply mesmerized by the lights. He was being drawn to them like a moth to a flame.

The lights kept going, with Montgomery stumbling along after them. He began to worry less about where he was putting his feet and more about keeping up with the lights. He was lost;

maybe the radiant spheres would lead him out of this godfor-saken marsh.

The boggy surface of the marsh gave way to muck and mire, but Montgomery pressed on after the lights. They seemed to be his best hope of getting out of this place. He found himself up to his knees in mud, and then his thighs. Soon, he was strug-gling in mud that was waist-high.

That's when he stopped.

He went no farther into the mud, but he was still sinking. He tried to wade out, but found that the mud had reached his chest, and then his armpits.

Still, he was sinking into the mud.

Panicked now, Montgomery called for help. "Keane! I know you're out here! Help me! Please!"

No one responded. He flailed at the mud. Now it was up to his chin. He fired the pistol, hoping to attract attention. Then he lost his grip on the gun, and the flashlight, which both sank into the mud. The pool of mud around him remained illumi-nated by the marsh lights, which had drifted back and floated to one side, as if the two pale-green orbs, lit by some invisible cold fire, were watching him.

"Help me!" he called to the lights.

Now mud and foul water filled his mouth and got into his nostrils, then his ears. He sank deeper. The last sight that Charles Montgomery saw was the two pale orbs against the mists of the marsh, and then the mire covered his head and claimed him forever.

* * *

KEANE AND ELIZABETH emerged from the thickets of reeds into a vast tidal flat. The grass was shorter, probably because the area was prone to tidal flooding. The ground, what there was of it, was so wet that they could hear the water percolating through it, almost like drops of rain falling around their feet. The day had been warm, but the enveloping mist felt cold. This thick, drifting mist seemed to cover the entire area, obscuring the distance and blotting out the stars.

Keane hated to admit it, but they were utterly lost out here.

They heard shouting behind them, and Keane recognized Colonel Montgomery's voice. Then came a gunshot.

"Hurry, Franklin," Elizabeth said. "It sounds as if they aren't far behind us."

The problem was that it was almost impossible to hurry. The night was too dark to see much ahead, so that they had to grope their way.

That's when he saw the lights. Two pale blue spheres drifting through the mist just ahead of them.

Keane gasped. He knew those lights. He had seen lights just like these the night that Amanda had disappeared. That night, the orbs had drifted out from the marsh and across the river itself. The strange radiance had seemed harmless then, and even playful, but Keane suspected otherwise. There had been something otherworldly about those lights, and he had always believed that they had somehow played a role in what had befallen Amanda. It didn't make sense, not even to him, and no one had believed him.

"Look at that," Elizabeth said. She gripped his arm. "They somehow got ahead of us and cut us off. Those must the flashlights of whoever is chasing us."

"Those aren't flashlights," he said quietly. "Those are will o' wisps."

"Will o' wisps? I don't understand."

The lights hovered, then moved away and drifted back again, just the way that a dog indicates that it wants you to follow him.

"My God, what *are* those?" Elizabeth's question had more of a tone of wonder, than of fear. "It's like they are trying to communicate with us."

"Don't follow them."

"Do we have any better options? We are being chased by some crazy people, we're lost, and we don't even have a flash-light. I say we follow the lights."

Elizabeth started after them

"Elizabeth, please don't!"

When she kept going, Keane felt he had no choice but to follow.

The way through the marsh grew more treacherous. Deep pools of water loomed out of the darkness, and mires of tidal quicksand. At any moment, Keane felt sure that they would step into a bottomless tidal pool, never to be seen again. But the spheres led the way through, seeming to follow a narrow deer path through the fen.

The orbs burned with a pale fire from within, throbbing green and blue with tinges of yellow. Keane half expected to hear a crackle of flame, but the lights blazed with an eerie silence.

Maybe it was Keane's imagination, but the ground slowly began to grow more solid. However, the reeds grew thick again. The narrow deer path vanished. Still, they followed the lights, pushing their way through the reeds.

"Come on," Elizabeth cried. "They're going faster."

And the lights were. Keane crashed through the reeds just ahead of Elizabeth, hoping that if he fell into a pool, she might have enough warning to save herself. Soon, he was panting with the effort of trying to keep up with the will o' wisps. At the same time, the reeds seemed to close over their heads, blotting out what few stars they could see through the mists.

And then Keane shoved aside a final veil of reeds and found himself standing on a paved road. Elizabeth crashed through just behind him and they stood side by side on the deserted road. The marsh continued, on and on, judging by the vast darkness ahead, but there was no need for Keane and Elizabeth to go any further. They could follow this road to safety, wherever it led. It was a miracle that they had made it through the marsh. They were covered in mud, soaked through, and slashed in dozens of places by tiny cuts from the sharp edges of the reeds, but they had made it.

The lights had paused on the other side of the road. Side by side, the lights floated at waist height above the ground. Keane stared, mesmerized, and as he did so, a strange phenomenon occurred.

The lights began to change shape, and he saw that they were not orbs at all, but glowing lanterns. The mist around them shifted and it became clear that the lanterns were not floating, but each one was being held aloft by a hand, that was attached to an arm. Ephemeral bodies began to take shape, and then faces. Keane saw the face of a boy, perhaps twelve years old, wearing an old-fashioned linsey-woolsey shirt and breeches with hose. It was the same boy whom he had glimpsed at the Cannonball House in St. Michaels.

Awestruck, all that Keane could do was stand rooted to the spot. He thought that he was losing his mind.

Beside him, he heard Elizabeth gasp. She was seeing this, too.

Then the second figure began to take shape. This form was taller—an adult. The features of the face formed into familiar planes. Keane realized that he was looking upon Amanda.

The inhuman sound that came from his throat was one of loss and longing. Amanda's gaze, however, filled him with peace. He felt love and contentment pouring into him the way that cool water fills an empty cup in the desert. He realized now that the details of what had happened to her that night might always be a mystery to him. But whatever Amanda had become, wherever she had gone, he sensed that she was at peace.

She wished him the same peace, urging him to go his own way at last, but it was too much. He started across the road. He had to go to her.

"Amanda!"

But just as they had emerged from nothing, now the figures of his lost wife and the boy who had given his life for St. Michaels faded away. The lights were lanterns no more, but only orbs again, glowing and pulsing with an intangible energy. The lights hovered for another moment, and then began to drift out across the reeds beyond the road, slowly at first, then faster and faster, until they disappeared into the vast emptiness of the dark marsh.

EPILOGUE

A few days later, Keane drove down to the Smithsonian and presented Director Biesty with the lost star from the Star-Spangled Banner flag. The flag itself had already been rescued from the madman's basement studio and quietly returned to the Smithsonian. Keane transported the star in the same pizza box, now even more battered and stained, although Keane had made a concession to conservation by lining the box with acid-free tissue paper.

Biesty was looking much more relaxed than he had the last time Keane had seen him. The former astronaut appeared more like a man who had just successfully splashed down after a mission than someone who had been forced to intone, "Houston, we have a problem."

However, Biesty appeared puzzled at first by the sight of the pizza box.

"I'd be happy to take you to lunch, Franklin," he said. "It's the least I could do. There was no need to bring a pizza!"

"Please, just take a look inside."

Biesty opened the box and stared inside for a long time at the star. Slowly, the realization of what he was seeing settled over his features and he looked up at Keane in amazement. "Is this what I think it is? My God! Where did you find it?"

"The credit belongs to Bob Lindermann and Esteban Galarza," Keane explained. "They were the ones who found it. Of course, it will have to be studied and verified, which I'm sure that your chief textiles curator will be happy to do."

Biesty shook his head. "Amazing. At least something good came out of all of this. The Star-Spangled Banner is finally whole again."

Next, Keane reached inside his jacket for an accounting of his expenses, and passed it across.

Biesty glanced at it and frowned. "That's it? One night at the Willard Hotel and a couple of meals? I'd call that a bargain price for what you did. But what's this here about repairing bullet holes in a boat?"

Keane grinned. "That's a story best left for another day."

Keane knew that he could never share the entire story with the Smithsonian director. Biesty never would have understood about the lights in the marsh. And then there was the matter of the letter that Keane had found at Fort McHenry.

* * *

THE DAY before his trip to D.C., he had climbed the steps to the attic of the old house at World's End, carrying the glass cylinder that contained President James Madison's letter to Rear Admiral Cockburn. The attic was dusty, hot even in autumn, and smelled of mice. His grandfather had not been diligent about cleaning out the attic, and Keane hadn't been, either. There were crates and boxes going back two hundred years up here, with the more recent ones added by the Keane family, including boxes and boxes of Keane silver.

Carefully, picking his way through the jumble by the beam of a flashlight, he made his way to the northern end of the attic.

He dragged an old trunk with dry-rotted leather straps into position exactly three paces from the end wall with its enormous brick chimney. He opened the trunk to reveal that it was half-filled with ladies' hats long out of fashion, and what appeared to be a fox stole, its glass eyes glinting at him in the flashlight beam.

Perfect, Keane thought.

Francis Scott Key had not wanted to destroy the letter of surrender from James Madison, but he had wanted to keep it hidden. Keane had to hand it to his famous ancestor; Francis Scott Key had not only been a fine lawyer and poet, but he had also been a very wise man. In protecting American morale during the War of 1812 by keeping the letter secret, he had been far more of a patriot that someone like Charles Montgomery could have ever hoped to be.

Keane tucked the glass cylinder among the fur, and shut the lid of the trunk. The letter still existed, but there was a very good chance that it would never be found again.

The flag itself had been quietly returned and was once again on display to the public. The FBI had paid a visit to Montgomery's compound and shut it down. His army of followers had dispersed—at least for now. Colonel Montgomery and his henchman, Blister, were still missing and presumed drowned in the marsh that bordered the Tailwinds plantation.

* * *

AFTER MEETING WITH THE DIRECTOR, Keane went downstairs to the actual museum to visit the flag. No one was the wiser that it had been missing, except for a few key museum staff members. The flag was already back on display.

Keane entered the Star-Spangled Banner exhibit hall. The dim lighting and hushed atmosphere made it seem as if he were visiting some cathedral to democracy. He saw the flag, once again safely behind its glass partition, an American icon returned safe and sound.

A few people stood beside Keane, quietly admiring the flag. To his right was a young family, the mother and father holding hands with a boy and girl. Spontaneously, the little girl began to sing in her sweet, high voice, *O, say does that Star-spangled Banner yet wave ... o'er the land of the free and the home of the brave?*

Keane felt a crush of emotion. Almost simultaneously, his eyes well up and he felt himself smile. You couldn't be an American and not have some visceral reaction to that song.

* * *

LEAVING the Smithsonian and Washington behind, he drove the Corvette up Route 50 and across the Chesapeake Bay bridge, and then south toward St. Michaels.

Elizabeth was working at the Cannonball House, which had finally reopened to visitors. The police had not yet returned the cannonball, so a replica had been found to replace it. Keane followed Elizabeth into the house, noticing that she still moved a stiffly after their ordeal in the marshes.

"I have something for you," he said.

He presented her with another pizza box, just like the one that had held the tattered lost star.

"Oh no," she said. "I hope that's not what I think it is."

She opened the box, to reveal a beautiful new United States flag. Elizabeth breathed a sigh of relief and lifted out the flag. The flag reflected the War of 1812 era, with fifteen stars and fifteen stripes. A flag holder was already mounted by the front door, so Keane helped her fit it to the pole and hang it. The red, white, and blue colors popped vividly in the autumn sunlight.

"I love it," she said, and hugged him.

They seemed reluctant to let go of one another and found themselves face to face. Keane leaned in to kiss her, and Elizabeth closed her eyes.

Before their lips could touch, they were interrupted by the sound of someone clearing his throat, then asking, "Are you open for tours today?"

They both turned to see two families on the brick walk leading to the house. Keane and Elizabeth had been so caught up that they hadn't noticed the group approaching.

The father who had asked the question added, "I hope we aren't interrupting something, but we understand that this house was hit by a cannonball during the War of 1812. And we hear that you have a ghost."

Elizabeth smiled. "Not a ghost. More like a guardian. Please, come in and I'll tell you all about it." She turned to Keane. "Rain check?"

He nodded. "History calls," Keane said.

ABOUT THE AUTHOR

David Healey lives in Maryland, where he worked as a jour-
nalist for more than 20 years. He is a member of the
International Thriller Writers and a frequent contributor to
The Big Thrill magazine. Visit him online at www.
davidhealeyauthor.com or www.facebook.com/david.healey.
books

Thank you for reading! If you enjoyed the story, please consider
leaving a review on Amazon.com.

Printed in Dunstable, United Kingdom

65374064R00173